Leslie Charteris

Leslie Charteris was born in Singapore on 12 May 1907. In 1919 he moved to England with his mother and brother and attended Rossall School in Lancashire before moving on to Cambridge University. His studies there came to a halt when a publisher accepted his first novel. His third book, entitled *Meet – The Tiger!*, was written when he was twenty years old and published in 1928. It introduced the world to Simon Templar, a.k.a. the Saint.

He continued to write about the Saint up until 1983, when the last book, *Salvage for the Saint*, was published by Hodder & Stoughton. The books, which have been translated into over twenty languages, have sold over 40 million copies around the world. They've inspired fifteen feature films, three TV series, ten radio series and a comic strip that was written by Charteris and syndicated around the world for over a decade.

Leslie Charteris enjoyed travelling, but settled for long periods in Hollywood, Florida, and finally in Surrey, England. In 1992 he was awarded the Cartier Diamond Dagger in recognit⁣⁣⁣ ⁣⁣⁣⁣⁣⁣⁣⁣⁣⁣ ⁣⁣⁣ife⁣time of achievement. He died the following

Leslie Charteris

Leslie Charteris was born in Singapore on 12 May 1907. In 1919 he moved to England with his mother and brother and attended Rossall School in Lancashire before winning a place at Cambridge University to study law. His studies there came to an end when a publisher accepted his first novel. His third book introduced the world to Simon Templar, alias The Saint.

He continued to write about the Saint until 1983, when the last book, Salvage for the Saint, was published by Hodder & Stoughton. The books, which have been translated into over twenty languages, have sold over 40 million copies around the world. They have inspired fifteen feature films, three TV series, ten radio series and a comic strip that was published by Columbia and syndicated around the world for over a decade.

Leslie Charteris enjoyed travelling, but settled for long periods in Hollywood, Ireland and finally Surrey, England. In 1992 he was awarded the Cartier Diamond Dagger in recognition of a lifetime of achievement. He died the following year.

LESLIE CHARTERIS

The Happy Highwayman

Series Editor: Ian Dickerson

MULHOLLAND
BOOKS
HODDER

First published in Great Britain in 1939 by Hodder & Stoughton

This paperback edition first published in 2013 by Mulholland Books
An imprint of Hodder & Stoughton
An Hachette UK company

1

A CIP catalogue record for this title is available from the British Library

Paperback ISBN 978 1 444 76626 4
eBook ISBN 978 1 444 76627 1

Printed and bound by Clays Ltd, St Ives plc

Hodder & Stoughton policy is to use papers that are natural, renewable
and recyclable products and made from wood grown in sustainable
forests. The logging and manufacturing processes are expected to
conform to the environmental regulations of the country of origin.

Hodder & Stoughton Ltd
338 Euston Road
London NW1 3BH

www.hodder.co.uk

To Stuart Walker
To whom time and changes make no difference
But always leave him just the same grand guy

CONTENTS

INTRODUCTION

With over fifty books featuring the Saint's adventures, most of them containing a number of short tales about the charming and buccaneering Simon Templar, there is certainly no shortage of Saint stories.

But *The Happy Highwayman* is an important and notable collection on a number of counts.

Simon Templar is something of a timeless hero. He made his debut in 1928 and took his final bow in print either in 1963 (the last of the true Leslie Charteris titles) or 1983 (the last of the books attributed to Charteris and various collaborators). In all those years of legal and illegal activity, mayhem, mischief and amorous adventures, Templar remains essentially ageless and unchanging.

The world around him, however, changed considerably. With the result that some of the Saint's earlier adventures could seem like slightly creaky period pieces when they were still being reprinted in much later years. This particularly became an issue as the time span began to stretch between the earliest editions and later reprints. Perhaps the most dramatic example of this was *Featuring the Saint*, with nearly 40 years between its first appearance (1931) and its revamped reissue (1969).

By that time Charteris had decided to deal with the dated aspects of some of the stories by the simple expedient of including an apology in the foreword to the volume.

But before this he'd actually taken pains to try and update

the early stories, so they could 'pass' among contemporary readers. And *The Happy Highwayman* (first published 1939, reissued 1963) is an example of such a revised volume.

You can see the effects of these revisions most clearly in 'The Star Producers' where luminaries of the 1930s have been replaced by more modern movie stars – although the fees quoted remain the same. So we have Marlon Brando, and William Holden, where the earlier equivalents were John Barrymore and William Powell. Interestingly, Charles Laughton features in both versions, a tribute to his longevity as a star.

This updating can also be discerned, more subtly, in 'The Man Who Liked Ants', which was first published in 1937 in the magazine *Double Detective*. Any devotee of comics will instantly spot the reference in the story to the art of Walt Kelly, famous for his satirical funny-animal newspaper strip *Pogo* – and know that this couldn't have dated from 1937, when Kelly was still labouring as an anonymous animator at the Walt Disney studios.

Indeed, the original 1937 text contains instead a reference to the art of Otto Soglow, who created the comic strip *The Little King*, which ran in magazines and newspapers from 1931 until 1975. But by the 1960s Soglow and his creation had become sufficiently obscure for Charteris to make the Walt Kelly alteration.

But 'The Man Who Liked Ants' is notable for much more than this subtle adjustment. It stands as one of the Saint's few forays into pure horror and science fiction – and probably the most notable one, serving as it did for the basis of an unforgettable episode of the television series, evocatively retitled 'The House on Dragon's Rock'. If the reader wants to avoid spoilers they should go no further here before reading the story itself.

'The Man Who Liked Ants' deals with a classic mad

scientist who has hit on a method (refreshingly, not radiation but simply the application of red light – this was 1937, after all) of breeding ants of an extraordinary size.

No prizes for guessing what goes wrong.

The mad scientist is also possessed of the obligatory beautiful niece (although in some cases it's a daughter) whom Simon Templar rescues, before despatching the scientist himself, Dr Sardon, with astonishing casual ruthlessness: 'the door had started to move when he shot him twice through the heart.'

Of course, the madman has been pointing a gun at Templar – having only momentarily swung it carelessly away from his target – and he is about to unleash a plague of massive ants on humanity . . .

Moral considerations aside, 'The Man Who Liked Ants' is a very striking piece of fiction. The dryly low-key title adds considerably to the power of the tale, as does the painstaking care taken to build up a convincing background for Sardon's research. Real scientists and real technical terms are skilfully blended with pure fantasy.

And the sparing, elliptical descriptions of the monstrous ants also add to their impact.

'The Man Who Liked Ants' is a highly influential story. It was not only the basis for a memorable episode of the television series; it may also have served as inspiration for the classic giant ant movie *Them!* (1954). Saint scholar Jonathan Rigby has pointed out that the story was reprinted in *Fantasy and Science Fiction* magazine in June 1953, and *Them!* began production in October of the same year at Warner Bros. Hmm . . .

The fact that 'The Man Who Liked Ants' is such an unusual story in the Simon Templar canon has led to speculation that it was ghostwritten. This is entirely possible. It's well known that Leslie Charteris did employ ghostwriters at

various times, and to varying degrees. And what some regard
as the uncharacteristic prose style of this story, along with its
wildly unusual subject matter, argue strongly that it may well
be one of those which Charteris farmed out.

To many Saint aficionados the question is not so much
whether the story was ghostwritten, as who the ghostwriter
might have been.

A number of science fiction, horror and fantasy writers
have been named as collaborating with Charteris on Saint
stories. It's quite a distinguished roll-call, including Henry
Kuttner, Theodore Sturgeon and Harry Harrison.

But the name that most persistently attaches itself to 'The
Man Who Liked Ants' is Cleve Cartmill. One of the more
obscure science fiction writers of the period, Cartmill also
has the distinction of being identified as the author of that
other great Saint horror tale 'The Convenient Monster',
which features a well-known watery beast from Loch Ness . . .

Balanced against this is a conversation in the 1990s with
Charteris that Ian Dickerson recounts, where the author
happily admitted Cartmill's extensive involvement with the
Saint story 'The Darker Drink' (aka 'Dawn') but seemed
quite certain, even these many years – and stories – later, that
'The Man Who Liked Ants' was entirely his own work.

The story is also a little early for such ghostwriting or
collaborations (appearing in print ten years before 'The
Darker Drink').

In any case, Cleve Cartmill remains one of Leslie
Charteris's most intriguing collaborators. And he certainly
had the science fiction – and science – credentials for involvement with one of the Saint's most fantastical adventures.

Under his own name Cartmill was responsible for a
genuine, 24-carat science fiction classic, and a milestone of
the genre. This was his short story 'Deadline'. Published in
1944 in *Astounding* magazine, it gave such an eerily

prescient account of a nuclear fission weapon – of exactly the kind being secretly developed by the Manhattan Project – that it resulted in the magazine's editor being questioned by the FBI.

Such a writer could surely have taken giant ants in his stride.

But, personally, I like the theory that Cartmill wrote 'The Man Who Liked Ants' for a much simpler reason – because he may well be a distant relative of mine.

Andrew Cartmel

The Man Who Was Lucky

Somewhat optimistically, the editorial writer of the *News-Chronicle* spoke one morning to a million breakfasting Britons, as follows:

The rebel of yesterday is the hero of tomorrow.

Simon Templar, known as the Saint, whose arrest was the ambition of every policeman in London a few years ago because of his efforts to enforce his own brand of extra-legal justice, is photographed beside film stars at first nights, and has to be rescued by the police from a mob of admirers clamouring for his autograph.

The converse is also true.

Lucky Joe Luckner, the idol of Soho, leader of a race-gang which came close to being an English equivalent of the racketeers of America, is committed for trial on a charge of attempted murder.

We see no need for the Saint to go back to his old games. Our criminals are taken care of as they should be, by the men who are employed to do so, with the whole strength of public opinion behind them.

Simon Templar kept the cutting. He had a weakness for collecting the miscellaneous items of publicity with which the press punctuated his career from time to time.

He had been publicly called a great many names in his life, and they all interested him. To those who found themselves sadder or poorer or even deader by reason of his interference in their nefarious activities, he was an unprintable illegitimate. To those whose melancholy duty it was to discourage his blithe propensity for taking the law into his own hands, he was a perpetually disturbing problem. To a few people he was a hero; to himself he was only an adventurer, finding the best romance he could in a dull atomic age, fighting crime because he had to fight something, and not caring too much whether he himself transgressed the law in doing so. A quite simple code, really.

Sometimes his adventures left him poorer, more often they left him richer; but always they were exciting. Which was all that the Saint asked of life.

He showed the cutting to Chief Inspector Claud Eustace Teal at Scotland Yard the next day, and the detective rubbed his round chin and gazed at him with sleepy china-blue eyes.

'There's something in it,' he said.

Simon detected the faintly hesitant inflection in the other's voice, and raised his eyebrows gently.

'Why only something?'

'You've seen the papers?'

The Saint shrugged.

'Well, they've passed him on to the Old Bailey, and that's further than you ever got him before.'

'Oh, yes.' The detective's tone was blunt and sardonic. 'He'll be tried at the next sessions – if there's any case left by that time. And meanwhile one of the principal witnesses has already been coshed so badly that it's about ten chances to one he'll die of it, and the other's disappeared.'

The Saint nodded thoughtfully. 'There's no doubt that he's guilty?'

'You know as much as I do about juries,' said Teal with caustic restraint. 'You think it out for yourself. That fellow that the attempted murder charge is about is a little bookie who'd only just started in business. The Luckner Boys told him he'd got to pay protection for his pitch. You know – the usual race-gang procedure. He said he didn't see why he should pay for their protection, so they bashed him. I got that straight from his assistant, Romaro, after it happened.

'It was just our luck that Luckner was at Epsom himself and the scene of the bashing, and this fellow Romaro recognized him. But you saw how they coshed Romaro after he picked out Luckner at the identification parade, so whether Romaro will tell the same story at the Old Bailey is another matter.'

Teal unwrapped a wafer of chewing gum and bit on it with concentrated viciousness. 'You know your way round as well as I do, Saint – or you used to. And you ask me if Luckner's guilty!'

Simon swung a long leg over the arm of his chair and gazed at the detective through the drifting smoke of his cigarette with a glimpse of idle mockery twinkling deep down in his blue eyes.

'One gathers that Lucky Joe wouldn't be so lucky if you were allowed to use the third degree over here,' he remarked.

Mr Teal blinked; but he nodded. 'If Luckner could be hanged on this charge, he would not get more than he deserves. He's the kind of thug we can do without in this country—'

He stopped rather abruptly, as though he had only just realized the trend of his argument. Perhaps the quietly speculative smile on the Saint's lips, and the rakish lines of the dark fighting face, brought back too many memories to let him continue with an easy conscience.

For there had been days, before that tacit armistice to which the leader writer of the *News-Chronicle* had referred when that lean, debonair outlaw lounging in his armchair had been disconcertingly prone to put such unlawful ideas into sensational effect.

'I don't mean what you're thinking,' Teal said heavily. 'Luckner is going to be taken care of. That's the sort of job

I'm here for. And don't you forget the rest of that article. You stick to taking Marlene Dietrich to first nights and signing autograph albums, and we shan't have any trouble.'

The Saint grinned lazily.

'You know me, Claud,' he murmured. 'I never want to make you overtax your brain.'

His tone was so innocent and docile that Teal glared at him for a moment suspiciously. But the Saint laughed at him and took him out to lunch and talked to him so engagingly about the most harmless topics that that momentary flash of uneasiness had faded from the plump detective's mind by the time they parted. Which was exactly what the Saint had meant it to do.

Simon Templar never asked for superfluous trouble – quite enough of it came his way in the normal course of events without encouraging him to invite extra donations without good reason.

As a matter of fact, the luck of Lucky Joe Luckner might well have slipped away into the background of his memory and remained there permanently, for it seemed to be one of those cases where it was hardly necessary for him to intervene.

He had thought no more about it a couple of days later when he saw a face that he remembered coming out of a travel agency in Piccadilly. The girl was so intent on hurrying through the crowd that she might not have noticed him, but he caught her arm as she went by and turned her round.

'Hullo, Cora,' he drawled. 'Are you going to see the world?'

She looked at him with a queer mixture of fear and defiance that surprised him. The look had vanished a moment after she recognized him, but it remained in his memory with the beginning of a question mark after it. He kept his hand on her arm.

'Why – hullo, Saint!'

He smiled. 'Hush,' he said. 'Not so loud. I may be an honest citizen to all intents and purposes, but I haven't got used to it. Come and have a drink and tell me the story of your life.'

'I'm sorry—' Did he imagine that she still seemed a trifle breathless, just as he might have imagined that swift glimmer of fright in her eyes when he caught hold of her? 'Not just now. Can't we have lunch or something tomorrow? I – I've got an appointment.'

'With Marty?' Simon asked.

He was sure now. There was a perceptible hesitation before she answered, exactly as if she had paused to consider whether to tell him the truth or invent a story.

'Yes. Please – I'm in a hurry.'

'So am I.' The Saint's voice was innocently persuasive. 'Can I give you a lift? I'd like to see Marty again.'

'I'm afraid he's ill—'

This was a lie. The Saint knew it, but the genial persuasion of his smile didn't alter. Those who knew him best had learned that that peculiarly lazy and aimless smile was the index of a crystallizing determination which was harder to resist than most men's square-jawed aggression.

A taxi came conveniently crawling by. He stopped it and opened the door; and he still held her arm.

'Where to?' he asked as they settled down.

She leaned her head back and closed her eyes. After a moment she gave him an address. He relayed it to the driver and took out a packet of cigarettes. They rode on for a while in silence, and he studied her thoughtfully without seeming to stare. She had always been pretty in a fair-haired and rather fluffy way, but now for the first time he was aware of a background of character which he hadn't noticed particularly when he had known her before. Perhaps it had always been there, but he hadn't observed her closely enough to see it.

He cast his mind back over the time when they had first
met. She was going about with Marty O'Connor then, and
apparently they were still together. That indicated some kind
of character at least – he wasn't quite sure what kind. After
they had driven a few blocks he reached forward and closed
the glass partition to shut them off from the driver.

'Well darling, do you tell me about it or do I drag it out of
you? Is Marty in trouble again?'

She nodded hesitantly.

The Saint drew at his cigarette without any visible indi-
cations of surprise. When one is a race-course tout, and
expert at the three-card trick, and a reputed fixer of horses
like Marty O'Connor, one is liable to be in trouble pretty
frequently.

Simon concentrated for a moment on trying to blow a
couple of smoke-rings. The draught from the open window
broke them up, and he said: 'Who started it?'

'Why do you want to know?'

'Marty did something for me once. If he's in trouble I'd
like to do something for him. I suppose it's immoral, but I
always had a soft spot for that old blackguard. On the level,
Cora.'

She looked at him for some seconds before she answered,
and then her answer was only made indirectly. She leaned
forward and opened the partition again for long enough to
change the address he had given the driver to another in the
same district.

'You know the game,' said the Saint appreciatively, and for
the first time she looked him full in the eyes.

'I have to,' she said. 'The Luckner Boys have been comb-
ing the town for Marty for the last three weeks. And so have
the splits.'

Simon raised his eyebrows without emotion.

'What did he do? Has he been driving at thirty-one miles

an hour in a built-up area, or did he buy a packet of cigarettes after eight o'clock?'

She looked at him queerly for a moment, then when she laughed there was a sharp note of strain in the sound.

'The trouble is he knows too much about that bookie who was bashed at Epsom. He'd be the star witness against Luckner if they could get his evidence.'

'And he doesn't want to give it?'

'He doesn't want to die,' said the girl brutally.

Simon put his feet up on the spare seat opposite him and smoked placidly. Coincidence was a queer thing, but he had ceased to marvel at its complexities. Once again, through that chance encounter, he found the subject of Lucky Joe Luckner thrust into his mind; and the repetition gave it enough weight to make it stay there. But he was wise enough not to press the girl for any more details during the drive. In the fullness of time he would know all that he wanted to know, and he was prepared to wait. He would see Marty himself.

The cab stopped outside a dingy house in a squalid street near Paddington Station. Half a dozen grimy guttersnipes were playing raucous football in the road. The windows in the front of the house were clouded with the accumulated dirt of ages.

Inside the front door, the dark hall was paved with a strip of threadbare linoleum; and Simon felt the slithery gloss of thick dust under his fingertips when he put his hand on the banister as they climbed the stairs to the first floor. His nose wrinkled in response to a faint pervasive odour of ancient cooking.

A slight frown creased itself into his forehead. To find Marty O'Connor in a place like that, even as a hideout, was a mystery in itself – Marty who had always been such a snappy dresser with a highly developed taste for spring mattresses and Turkey carpets and flash decoration.

The girl opened a door and they went into the living-room of the flat. The furniture there was in keeping with what anyone would have expected from a preliminary survey of the building – cheap, shoddy and shabby – but Simon noticed that unlike the rest of the place, it appeared to be clean.

Cora pulled off her hat. 'Hullo, Marty,' she called. 'I brought a friend to see you.'

Marty O'Connor appeared in the doorway of the bedroom. He was in his shirt sleeves, a shirt open at the neck, and he kept one hand behind him. He stared at the Saint blankly, and then his comely face broke into a slow grin.

'Well, for—Where did you come from, guv'nor?'

The Saint chuckled. Marty brought his right hand from behind him and pocketed his life-preserver, and they shook hands.

'I wouldn't have believed you could get any uglier, Marty, but you made it.'

Marty hauled him towards a chair and sat him down. He looked a little less well-fed than he had been when the Saint saw him last, and there seemed to be a trace of hollowness in his unshaven cheeks. The feckless twinkle in his faded eyes was the same as that by which Simon had first been beguiled from his antipathy to the ordinary run of race-course sharps.

'It's good to see you again, Mr Templar. It's a long time since we had a drop o' beer together.' O'Connor dusted the table with his handkerchief and sat on it. He turned round. 'Cora! See if there's any o' that wallop left . . . Well, I'm blowed!' He looked at the Saint again, beaming with a simple pleasure that had temporarily wiped away the furtive defensiveness with which he had emerged from the bedroom.

'Where've you been all this time?'

'Here and there,' said the Saint vaguely. 'I cover a good deal of ground. Have you been looking after yourself?'

'Not so badly.'

The girl came back into the room, bearing a bottle and three cheap glasses.

'It's all right, Marty,' she said. 'I told him.'

O'Connor scratched his head, and for a moment his heavy face sank into its mask of dour suspicion. And then he grinned rather ruefully, like an unrepentant urchin.

'Well, you know how it is, Saint,' he said apologetically.

Simon shook his head. 'That's just what I don't quite know.'

Marty tipped beer into the three glasses, and passed one of them over. He sat down again.

'Well . . .' He picked a half-smoked cigarette out of the ashtray and relighted it. 'You know how Cora always used to go on at me about how she would never go out with me without wondering when some busybody would tap me on the shoulder an' say, "MrO'Connor, would you mind taking a walk with me down to the station?" '

'Well, she nagged me so much I thought it was better to go honest, than be nagged to death. I expect she always was right, anyhow. So I got a job with a fellow who was starting up as a bookie on his own, and made up my mind to go straight an' keep out of trouble from then on. An' then he goes an' gets himself bashed by the Luckner Boys. Did you read about it in the papers?'

'I've heard of it.'

'I did one or two jobs for Luckner once, helping the wrong horses to lose – you know when. I never liked him, but it was just business. You know I nearly poked him in the eye lotsa times when he'd try to make Cora go out with him.'

'He never did any harm,' said the girl lightly.

'And that wasn't for want of tryin',' growled O'Connor. 'I never saw anyone make such a rush for a girl as he did for Cora. Why, he told her once he'd have my brains bashed out an' marry her himself if she'd say the word.'

Marty laughed in his throat, but the sound was without humour. 'You can trust Luckner as far as you'd trust a snake. I told this bloke I was workin' for that he couldn't fight the Luckner Boys an' he'd better pay up an' put it down to expenses, but he wouldn't listen. 'I'm not payin' any blackmail to those hooligans,' he says.

'So they gave him all they had – coshes an' razors and everything. I saw 'em do it. If I talked to those busies who're looking for me, I bet they'd touch their hats to me every time they saw me for the rest o' my life.'

'That might be useful if you were making a fresh start, Marty,' said the Saint speculatively.

The other grinned slowly. 'I'd be makin' my fresh start under a slab of marble. I would not lift a finger for Lucky if they were going to string him up tomorrow, but I think a lot o' my own health. You saw what happened to Romaro after he identified Luckner?

'I know Lucky, an' I know the Boys have orders what to do about anyone who turns up as a witness against him. So Cora an' me move in here where we hope nobody'll ever look for us, an' I haven't been outside the door since. It's not been easy, with no money coming in – but we're still alive.'

The Saint's blue eyes travelled slowly over the room again; took in the dingy carpet worn down almost to its backing, the wobble of the rickety table on which Marty was perched, the hideous upholstery of the gimcrack chairs.

'I suppose it would be difficult,' he said.

Marty nodded. 'Still we've had a bit o' luck,' he said. 'I got a job the other day. We were just wonderin' what we were goin' to do next, and I remembered a pal o' mine back in Ireland who used to have a small stable with four or five leppers in training. He hasn't got so much money either, but he wrote back he could give me a job to see me through for a bit if I could get there.

'Cora went round an' borrowed the money – she had to be pretty careful 'cause they're lookin' for her, too, knowin' she'd probably lead 'em back to me. She went out to buy our tickets today – I suppose that's when you met her. So if I can get clear without bein' stopped we ought to get along all right.'

Simon didn't laugh, although for a moment the idea of Marty O'Connor, who had done well for himself in his time and spent his money as liberally as anyone else of his kind, currying horses for fifteen shillings a week was humorous enough. But he looked round the apartment again, and his gaze came to rest on the face of the girl Cora with a certain understanding.

He knew now what subconscious intuition had made him revise his casual opinion of her, even in those brief minutes in the taxi. Stranger things had happened in that unpredictable substratum of civilization in which he had spent half his life.

'It's a pity you can't take some cash with you and buy a share in this stable,' he said. He knew before he started to elaborate the suggestion into an offer that it would be refused.

Later on in the evening he had an even better idea, and he talked for half an hour before he was able to induce Marty to accept it. What argument it was that finally turned the scale he would have found it hard to remember, but once the Saint was on the trail of an inspiration he had a gift of persuasiveness that would have sold a line of rubber boots to a colony of boa-constrictors.

Lucky Joe Luckner, a free man on bail recuperating from the ordeal of the police court proceedings in his luxurious house in Hampstead, was still satisfied with his good luck in spite of the quiet and inconspicuous man who loafed on the opposite side of the street all day and followed him at a discreet distance whenever he went out.

Luckner had no intention of jumping his bail. He had never been a fugitive – he couldn't imagine himself in the part. Quite confidently, he was waiting for an acquittal at his trial which would leave him a free man without a single legal stain on his character; and if his lawyer did not quite share this sublime confidence he had to admit that Luckner's previous brushes with the law lent some support to it.

'Bet they can't even send me down for seven days,' he declared boastfully, to his personal bodyguard.

The saturnine Mr Toscelli agreed encouragingly, which was one of his lighter duties. Lucky Joe rewarded him with a slap on the back and a cigar. Few men are offended by hearing their boasts enthusiastically echoed, and Luckner was known to be more than ordinarily vulnerable.

He was a short thickset man with a dark and fleshy kind of good looks. His extravagances were of a type that ran to loud check shirts, yellow spats, strangely hued hats, and large diamonds. He imagined that these outward evidences of good taste and prosperity were the secret of his hypnotic power over women. This hypnotic power was one of his more whimsical fantasies, but his associates had found it healthier to accept it with tactful solemnity.

He boasted that he had never failed to conquer any woman whom he desired to possess, and he had a convenient faculty for forgetting the many exceptions which tended to disprove the rule. But apart from this one playful weakness he was about as sentimental as a scorpion; and the Saint estimated the probabilities with some care before he approached Lucky Joe in person.

If he had been cautious he would never have gone at all; but Simon Templar was a confirmed believer in direct action, and he knew exactly the strength of his hand.

He drove out to Hampstead on a pleasant sunny day and sauntered up the steps of Luckner's house under the critical eyes of one or two disapproving neighbours who observed him from their windows. The Saint could see no good reason why they should be disapproving, for he felt very contented with himself that morning and considered that he was more than ordinarily beautiful and definitely an ornament to the scenery. He realized that the knowledge that Lucky Joe Luckner was at home must have cast a certain amount of cloud over the tranquillity of the other residents of that respectable neighbourhood.

Perhaps they had some good reason to fear that a man with that loose and rather buccaneering stride and that rather reckless cut of face was only another manifestation of the underworld invasion which had disturbed the amenities of their peaceful purlieus; and in a way they were right, but the Saint didn't care. With his hands in his pockets and his spotless white panama tilted jauntily over one eye, he stood at the top of the steps and leaned his elbow patiently against the bell.

Presently the door opened to exhibit a blue chin and a flat fish-like stare which Simon easily identified as being more deserving of the neighbourhood's disapproval than himself. The door stayed open just far enough for that; and the stare absorbed him with the expressionlessness of a dead cod.

'Hullo, body,' murmured the Saint affably. 'When did they dig you up?'

The stare darkened, without taking on any more expression.

'Wotcher want?' it asked flatly.

'I want to see Lucky Joe.'

'He ain't here.'

'Tell him it's about Marty O'Connor,' said the Saint gently. 'And tell Joe he doesn't know how lucky he is.'

The man looked at him for a moment longer and then closed the door suddenly. Simon lighted, a cigarette and waited imperturbably. The door opened again.

'Come in.'

Simon went in. The man who had let him in stayed behind him, with his back to the door. Another blue-chinned individual in the hall looked at him with the same flat fish-like stare and indicated a door on the right.

The Saint wandered on into the room. Another man of similarly taciturn habits and lack of facial expression sat on the arm of a chair by the window, thoughtfully picking his teeth. Luckner sat on the settee, in his shirt sleeves, with his feet on a low table. He took the cigar out of his mouth and looked at the Saint reflectively.

Simon came to a halt in front of him and touched two fingers to the brim of his hat in a lazy and ironical salute. He smiled, with a faint twinkle in his blue eyes.

Luckner glowered at him uncertainly. 'Well – what is it?'

The Saint put his cigarette to his lips. 'I just dropped in,' he said. 'I wondered if you were as handsome in the flesh as the stories I've read about you made you out to be. I'm afraid they exaggerated, Joe ... However, I also heard you'd be interested in any news about Marty O'Connor.'

'Where is he?'

Simon's smile widened by a vague seraphic fraction.

'That's my secret.'

Luckner took his feet off the table and got up slowly until he faced the Saint. He was six inches shorter than Simon, but he thrust his face up as close as he could under the Saint's nose.

'Where is he?'

'It's just possible,' said the Saint, in his slow soft voice, without a shift of his eyes, 'that you've got some mistaken ideas about what I am and what I've come here for. If you had an idea, for instance, that your face was so dazzlingly lovely that I'd swoon into your arms as soon as I saw it, or that I'd tell you anything before I was ready to tell it – well, we'd better go back to the beginning and start again.'

Luckner glared at him silently for a second; and then he said in a very level tone: 'Who the hell are you?'

'I am the Saint.'

The man on the arm of the chair took the toothpick out of his mouth and forgot to close his mouth behind it. The man by the door sucked in his breath with a sharp hiss like a squirt of escaping steam. Only Luckner displayed no active expression of emotion; but his face went a shade lighter in colour and froze into wooden restraint.

Simon allowed the announcement to sink into the brains of his audience at its own good leisure, while he let the smoke of his cigarette trickle through his lips to curl in a faintly mocking feather before Luckner's stony eyes. There was something so serene, something so strong and quietly dangerous about him which, coupled with his almost apologetic self-introduction, was like the revelation of an unsheathed sword, that none of the men made any move towards him. He looked at Luckner unruffledly, with those very clear and faintly bantering blue eyes.

'I am the Saint,' he said. 'You should know the name. I know where to find Marty O'Connor. The only question you have to answer is – how much is he worth to you?'

Luckner's knees bent until he reached the level of the settee. He put the cigar back in his mouth.

'Sit down,' he said. 'Let's talk this over.'

The Saint shook his head. 'Why waste the time, Joe? You ought to know how much Marty's worth. He knows you and your precious gang, and he ought to be able to make a great squeal if they get him in the witness box. Not that I'd lose any sleep if you were going to be topped, but I suppose we can't put everything right at once. You'll get what's coming to you. Sooner or later. But just for the moment, this is more important.'

Simon studied his fingernails. 'I owe Marty something,

but I can't give it to him myself. That's one of the disadvantages of the wave of virtue which seems to have come over everybody. But I don't see why you shouldn't do it for me.'

The Saint's eyes lifted again suddenly to Luckner's face with a cold and laconic directness. 'I don't care what you do about Marty so long as you pay what I think he's worth.'

'And what's that?'

'That is just five thousand pounds.'

Luckner stiffened as if a spear had been rammed up his backbone from his sacrum to his scalp.

'How much?'

'Five thousand per-luscious Peppiatts,' said the Saint calmly. 'And cheap at the price. After all, that only works out at about five hundred a year on the sentence you'll get if you don't pay. I'll take it in fivers, and I shall want it by ten o'clock tonight.'

The dilated incredulity of Luckner's eyes remained set for a moment. Then they narrowed back to their normal size and remained fixed on the Saint's face like glittering beads. It was symptomatic of Luckner's psychology that he made no further attempt to argue.

The Saint didn't have the air of a man who was prepared to devote any time to bargaining, and Luckner was shrewd enough to know it. It didn't even occur to him to question the fundamental fact of whether Simon Templar was really in a position to carry out his share of the transaction.

The Saint's name, and the reputation which Luckner still remembered, was sufficient guarantee of that. There was only one flimsy quibble that Luckner could see at all, and he had a premonition that even this was hopeless before he tried it.

'Suppose we kept you here without any five thousand quid and just saw what we could do about persuading you to tell us where Marty is?'

The Saint smiled rather wearily. 'Of course I'd never have thought of that. It wouldn't have occurred to me to have somebody waiting outside here who'd start heading south if I didn't come out of this house safe and sound in' – he looked at his watch – 'just under another three minutes.

'And I wouldn't have thought of telling this guy that if he had to beat it without me he was to get Marty and take him straight along to see dear old Claud Eustace Teal at Scotland Yard . . . You're taking an awful lot for granted, Joe; but if you think you can make me talk in two and a half minutes I can't stop you trying.'

Luckner chewed his cigar across from one side of his mouth to the other. He was in a corner, and he was capable of facing the fact.

'Where do we do this deal?'

'You can send a couple of the Boys with the money down to Thames Ditton tonight. I'll be waiting in a car a little way short of the level crossing. If the dough is okay I'll tell them where to find Marty, and they can have him in five minutes. What they do when they see him is none of my business.'

The Saint's blue eyes rested on Luckner again with the same quiet and deadly implication. 'Is that all quite clear?'

Luckner's head remained poised for a moment before it jerked briefly downwards.

'The dough will be okay,' he said.

The Saint smiled again. 'They didn't know how lucky you were going to be when they gave you your name, Joe,' he said.

For some time after Templar had gone, Luckner sat in the same position, with his hands on his spread knees, chewing his cigar and staring impassively in front of him. The man with the toothpick continued his endless foraging. The man who had guarded the front door, and the man who had stood in the hall, lighted cigarettes and gazed vacantly out of the window.

The situation was perfectly clear, and Luckner had enough cold-blooded detachment to review it with his eyes open. After a while he spoke.

'You better go, Luigi,' he said. 'You and Karlatta. Better take guns this time – I don't want any more half jobs like you did on Romaro.'

Toscelli nodded phlegmatically and garaged his toothpick in his waistcoat pocket.

'Do we take the dough?'

'You're damn right you take the dough. You heard what he said? You give him the dough and he'll tell you where to find Marty. I'll write a cheque and you can go to the bank this afternoon and collect it. And don't kid yourselves. If there are any tricks, that bucker has thought of them all. You remember what he did to Ganning and Baldy Mossiter?'

'It's a lot of money, Lucky,' said MrToscelli gloomily.

Joe Luckner's jaw hardened. 'Ten years is a lot of hard labour,' he said stolidly. 'Never mind the dough. Just see that Marty keeps his mouth shut. Perhaps we can do something about the money afterwards.'

Even then he kept his belief in his lucky star, although the benefit it had conferred on him was somewhat ambiguous. A more captious man might have quibbled that a price ticket of five thousand pounds was an expensive present, but to Luckner it represented fair value. Nor did he feel any compunction about the use to which he proposed to put the gift.

In this respect at least, MrLuigi Toscelli was able to agree with him. The chief strain on MrToscelli's nerves was the responsibility of the cargo of crisp five pound notes which he had collected during the afternoon. He felt a certain relief when he arrived at the rendezvous and found a closed car parked by the roadside and waiting for him exactly as the Saint had promised that it would be. Even so, he kept one hand on his gun while the Saint received the parcel of currency through the window.

Simon examined its contents carefully under the dashboard light and satisfied himself that there was no deception.

'A very nice little nest-egg,' he murmured. 'You must be sorry to see it go, Luigi. By the way you needn't clutch that gun so desperately – I've got you covered from here, and you're a much better target than I am.'

Toscelli wavered, peering at him sombrely out of the dark. It was true that it grieved him to see so much hard cash taken out of his hands. But he remembered Luckner's warning, and he had heard of the Saint's reputation himself.

'Where do we go?' he growled.

The shiny barrel of the Saint's automatic, resting on the edge of the window, moved in a briefly indicative arc.

'Over the crossroads and straight on past Hurst Park racecourse. Park your car beside the waterworks and wait for results. He'll be travelling towards Walton, looking for a car parked exactly where you're going to be – but he won't expect you to be in it. You won't make any mistake, because I've marked his car; the near-side headlight has a cross of adhesive tape on the lens, and I hope it will give you pious ideas. On your way, brother.'

Simon drove slowly down the Portsmouth road. About a mile beyond Esher he pulled into the side of the road again and stopped there. He flicked his headlights two or three times before he finally switched them out. He had hardly done so when a subdued voice hailed him cautiously from the shadows at the roadside.

The Saint grinned, and opened the door. 'Hullo, there, Marty,' he said. He buttoned his coat and slipped out. 'Are you ready to travel?

'If there's nothing to stop us.'

'There isn't.' Simon punched him gently in the stomach, and their hands met. 'The world is yours between here and Holyhead, and you can leave the car at Fairfield's and I'll pick it up later. You'll find five thousand quid in one of the pockets. And any time I'm in Cork I'll drop by your stable and take one of your nags over the jumps. This'll just even up what you did for me one time.' He gripped Marty's shoulder for a moment, and then turned to the other slighter figure who stood beside them. 'Take care of him, Cora – and yourself, too.'

'I'll do that.'

A match flared in the Saint's hand for an instant; but his eyes were intent on the cigarette he was lighting.

'You called Lucky Joe as I told you to?' he asked casually. 'Told him you were through with Marty and couldn't bear to wait another day to take up with the new love?'

'Yes – an hour ago.'

'I bet he fell for it.'

'He said he'd be there.' She hesitated. 'I don't know why you've done all this for us, Saint, and I don't know how you did it – but why did you want me to do that?'

The Saint smiled invisibly in the dark.

'Because I made a date for him by those Hurst Park water-works and I wanted to be sure he'd keep it. Some friends of his will be there to meet him. I have to work in these devious ways these days, because Claud Eustace warned me to keep out of trouble. Don't lose any sleep over it, kid. Be good.'

He kissed her, and held the door while they got into the car. By about that time, he estimated, Mr Toscelli should be obeying Lucky Joe's last orders.

The Smart Detective

Inspector Corrio was on the carpet. This was a unique experience for him, for he had a rather distinguished record in the Criminal Investigation Department. While he had made comparatively few sensational arrests, he had acquired an outstanding reputation in the field of tracing stolen property, and incidentally in pursuit of this specialty had earned a large number of insurance company rewards which might have encouraged the kind-hearted observer to list a very human jealousy among the chief causes of his unpopularity. He was a very smug man about his successes, and he had other vanities which were even less calculated to endear him to the other detectives whom his inspired brilliance had more than once put in the shade.

None of these things, however, were sufficient to justify his immediate superiors in administering the official flattening which they had long been yearning to bestow. It was with some pardonable glow of satisfaction that Chief Inspector Claud Eustace Teal, who was as human as anyone else if not more so, had at last found the adequate excuse for which his soul had been pining wistfully for many moons.

For at last Inspector Corrio's smug zeal had overreached itself. He had made an entirely gratuitous, uncalled for, and unauthorized statement to a writer on the *Bulldog* which had been featured under two-column headlines and decorated with Inspector Corrio's favourite photograph of himself on the first inside sheet of that enterprising but sensation-loving weekly.

This copy of the paper lay on MrTeal's desk while he spoke his mind to his subordinate, and he referred to it several times for the best quotations which he had marked off in blue pencil in preparation for the interview.

One of these read: 'If you ask me why this man Simon Templar was ever allowed to come back to England, I can't tell you. I don't believe in idealistic crooks any more than I believe in reformed crooks, and the Department has got enough work to do without having any more troubles of that kind on its hands. But I can tell you this. There have been a lot of changes in the system since Templar was last here, and he won't find it so easy to get away with his tricks as he did before.'

Teal read out this and other extracts in his most scorching voice, which was a very scorching voice when he put his heart into it, and let his temper rise a bit.

'I hadn't heard the news about your being appointed Police Commissioner,' Teal said heavily. 'But I'd like to be the first to congratulate you. Of course a gentleman with your education will find it a pretty soft job.'

Inspector Corrio shrugged his shoulders sullenly. He was a dark and rather flashily good-looking man who obviously had no illusions about the latter quality, with a wispy moustache and the slimmest figure consistent with the physical requirements of the Force.

'I was just having a chat with a friend,' he said. 'How was I to know he was going to print what I said? I didn't know anything about it until I saw it in the paper myself.'

Teal turned to page sixteen and read out from another of his blue-pencilled panels: 'Inspector Corrio is the exact reverse of the popular conception of a detective. He is a slender well-dressed man who looks rather like Clark Gable and might easily be mistaken for an idol of the silver screen.

'You didn't know that he'd say that either, did you?' Teal

inquired in tones of acid that would have seared the skin of a rhinoceros.

Inspector Corrio's face reddened. He was particularly proud of his secretaryship of the Ponders End Amateur Players, and he had never been able to see anything humorous in his confirmed conviction that his destined home was in Hollywood and that his true vocation was that of the dashing hero of a box-office-shattering series of romantic melodramas.

Having dealt comprehensively with these lighter points, Mr Teal opened his shoulders and proceeded to the meatier business of the conference. In a series of well-chosen sentences, he went on to summarize his opinion of Inspector Corrio's ancestry, past life, present value, future prospects, looks, clothes, morals, intelligence, and assorted shortcomings, taking a point of view which made up in positiveness and vigour for anything which it may have lacked in absolute impartiality.

'And understand this,' he concluded. 'The Saint hasn't come home to get into any trouble. I know him and he knows me, and he knows me too well to try anything like that. And what's more, if anybody's got to take care of him I can do it. He's a grown-up proposition, and it takes a grown-up detective to look after him. And if any statements have to be made to the papers about it I'll make them.'

Corrio waited for the storm to pass its height, which took some time longer.

'I'm sure you know best, sir – especially after the way he's often been able to help you,' he said humbly, while Teal glared at him speechlessly. 'But I have a theory about the Saint.'

'You have a what?' repeated Mr Teal, as if Corrio had uttered an indecent word.

'A theory, sir. I think the mistake that's been made all along is in trying to get something on the Saint *after* he's done a job. What we ought to do is pick out a job that he looks likely to do, watch it, and catch him red-handed. After all, his character is so well known that any real detective ought to be able to pick out the things that would interest him with his eyes shut. There's one in that paper on your desk – I noticed it this morning.'

'Are you still talking about yourself?' Teal demanded unsympathetically. 'Because if so—'

Corrio shook his head.

'I mean that man Oppenheim who owns the sweat shops. It says in the paper that he's just bought the Vanderwoude emerald collection for a quarter of a million pounds to give to his daughter for a wedding present. Knowing how Oppenheim got his money and knowing the Saint's line, it's my idea that the Saint will try to do something about those jewels.'

'And try something so feeble that even a fairy like you could catch him at it,' snarled MrTeal discouragingly. 'Go back and do your detecting at Ponders End, Corrio. I hear there's a bad ham out there that they've been trying to find for some time.'

If he had been less incensed with his subordinate, MrTeal might have perceived a germ of sound logic in Corrio's theory, but he was in no mood to appreciate it. Two days later he did not even remember that the suggestion had been made; which was an oversight on his part, for it was at that time that Simon Templar did indeed develop a serious interest in the unpleasant MrOppenheim.

This was because Janice Dixon stumbled against him late one night as he was walking home in the general direction of Park Lane through one of the dark and practically deserted streets of Soho. He had to catch her to save her from falling.

'I'm sorry,' she muttered.

He murmured some absent-minded commonplace and

straightened her up, but her weight was still heavy on his hand. When he let her go she swayed towards him and clung on to his arm.

'I'm sorry,' she repeated stupidly.

His first thought was that she was drunk, but her breath was innocent of the smell of liquor. Then he thought the accident might be only the excuse for a more mercenary kind of introduction; but he saw her face was not made up as he would have expected it to be in that case. It was a pretty face, but so pale that it looked ghostly in the semi-darkness between the far-spaced street lamps; and he saw that she had dark circles under her eyes and that her mouth was without lipstick.

'Is anything the matter?' he asked.

'No – it's nothing. I'll be all right in a minute. I just want to rest.'

'Let's go inside somewhere and sit down.'

There was an all-night snack bar on the corner, and he took her into it. It seemed to be a great effort for her to walk, and another explanation of her unsteadiness flashed into his mind. He sat down at the counter and ordered two cups of coffee.

'Would you like something to eat with it?'

Her eyes lighted up, and she bit her lip. 'Yes. I would. But – I haven't any money.'

'I shouldn't worry about that. We can always hold up a bank.'

The Saint watched her while she devoured a sandwich, a double order of bacon and eggs, and a slice of pie. She ate intently, quickly, without speaking. Without seeming to stare at her, his keen blue eyes took in the shadows under her cheek bones, the neat patch on one elbow of the cheap dark coat, the cracks in the leather of shoes which had long since lost their shape.

'I wish I had your appetite,' he said gently, when at last she had finished.

She smiled for the first time, rather faintly. 'I haven't had anything to eat for two days,' she said. 'And I haven't had as much to eat as this all at once for a long time.'

Simon ordered more coffee, and offered her a cigarette. He put his heels up on the top rung of his stool and leaned his elbows on his knees. She told him her name, but for the moment he didn't answer with his own.

'Out of a job?' he asked quietly.

She shook her head. 'Not yet.'

'You aren't on a diet by any chance, are you?'

'Yes. A nice rich diet of doughnuts and coffee, mostly.' She smiled rather wearily at his puzzlement. 'I work for Oppenheim.'

'Doesn't he pay you?'

'Oh, yes. But maybe you haven't heard of him. I'm a dressmaker. I work with fifty other girls in an attic in the East End, making handmade underwear. We work ten hours a day, six days a week, sewing. If you're clever and fast you can make four pieces in a day. They pay you two shillings apiece. You can buy them in Brompton Road for a pound or more, but that doesn't do us any good. I made two pounds twelve shillings last week, but I had to pay the rent for my room.'

It was Simon Templar's first introduction to the economics of the sweat shop; and hardened as he was to the ways of chisellers and profiteers, the cold facts as she stated them made him feel slightly sick at his stomach. He realized that he had been too long in ignorance of the existence of such people as MrOppenheim.

'Do you mean to say he gets people to work for him on those terms?' he said incredulously. 'And how is it possible to live on two pounds twelve shillings a week?'

'Oh, there are always girls who'll do it if they can't get anything else. I used to get six pounds a week doing the same work in Kensington, but I was ill for a couple of weeks and they used it as an excuse to let me go. I didn't have any job at all for three months, and two pounds twelve a week is better than nothing. You learn how to live on it. After a while you get used to being hungry; but when you have to buy shoes or pay bills, and the rent piles up for a few weeks, it doesn't do you any good.'

'I seem to have heard of your MrOppenheim,' said the Saint thoughtfully. 'Didn't he just pay a quarter of a million pounds for a collection of emeralds?'

Her lips flickered cynically. 'That's the man. I've seen them, too. I've been working on his daughter's trousseau because I've got more experience of better class work than the other girls, and I've been going to the house to fit it. It's just one of those things that makes you feel like shooting people sometimes.'

'You've been in the house, have you?' he said, even more thoughtfully. 'And you've seen these emeralds?' He stopped himself, and drew smoke from his cigarette to trickle it thoughtfully back across the counter. When he turned to her again, his dark reckless face held only the same expression of friendly interest that it had held before.

'Where are you going to sleep tonight?'

She shrugged.

'I don't know. You see, I owe three weeks' rent now, and they won't let me in until I pay it. I expect I'll take a stroll down to the Embankment.'

'It's healthy enough, but a bit draughty.' He smiled at her suddenly, with disarming frankness. 'Look here, what would you say if I suggested that we wander around to a little place by here where I can get you a room? It's quiet and clean, and I don't live there. But I'd like to do something for you. Stay there tonight and meet me for dinner tomorrow, and let's talk it over.'

She met him the following evening; and he had to do very little more than keep his ears open to learn everything that he wanted to know.

'They're in Oppenheim's study – on the first floor. His daughter's room is next door to it, and the walls aren't very thick. He was showing them to her yesterday afternoon when I was there. He has a big safe in the study, but he doesn't keep the emeralds in it. I heard him boasting about how clever he was.

'He said, "Anybody who came in looking for the emeralds would naturally think they'd be in the safe, and they'd get to work on it at once. It'd take them a long time to open it, which would give us plenty of chances to catch them; but anyhow they'd be disappointed. They'd never believe that I had a quarter of a million pounds' worth of emeralds just tucked away behind a row of books on a shelf. Even the man from the detective agency doesn't know it – he thinks the safe is what he's got to look after." '

'So they have a private detective on the job, have they?' said the Saint.

'Yes. A man from Ingerbeck's goes in at seven every evening and stays till the servants are up in the morning. The butler's a pretty tough-looking customer himself, so I suppose Oppenheim thinks the house is safe enough in his hands in the day time . . . Why do you want to know all this?'

She looked at him with an unexpected clearness of understanding.

'Is that what you meant when you said you'd like to do something about me? Did you think you could do it if you got hold of those emeralds?'

The Saint lighted a cigarette with a steady and unhurried hand, and then his blue eyes came back to her face for a moment before he answered with a very quiet and calculating directness.

'That was more or less my idea,' he said calmly.

She was neither shocked nor frightened. She studied him with a sober and matter-of-fact attention as if they were discussing where she might find another job, but a restrained intenseness with which he thought he could sympathize came into her voice.

'I couldn't call anybody a criminal who did that,' she said. 'He really deserves to lose them. I believe I'd be capable of robbing him myself if I knew how to go about it. Have you ever done anything like that before?'

'I have had a certain amount of experience,' Simon admitted mildly. 'You may have read about me. I'm called the Saint.'

'You? You're pulling my leg.' She stared at him, and the amused disbelief in her face changed slowly into a weakening incredulity. 'But you might be. I saw a photograph once . . . Oh, if you only were! I'd help you to do it – I wouldn't care what it cost.'

'You can help me by telling me everything you can remember about Oppenheim's household and how it works.'

She had been there several times; and there were many useful things she'd remembered, which his skilful questioning helped to bring out. They went down into the back of his mind and stayed there while he talked about other things. The supremely simple, obvious, and impeccable solution came to him a full two hours later, when they were dancing on a small packed floor off Shaftesbury Avenue.

He took her back to their table as the three-piece orchestra expired, lighted a cigarette, and announced serenely:

'It's easy. I know just how MrOppenheim is going to lose his emeralds.'

'How?'

'They have a man in from Ingerbeck's at night, don't they? And he has the run of the place while everybody else is asleep.

They give him breakfast in the morning when the servants get up, and then he takes a cigar and goes home. Well, the same thing can happen just once more. The guy from Ingerbeck's comes in, stays the night, and goes home. Not the usual guy, because he's sick or been run over by a truck or something. Some other guy. And when this other guy goes home, he can pull emeralds out of every pocket.'

Her mouth opened a little. 'You mean you'd do that?'

'Sure. Apart from the fact that I don't like your MrOppenheim, it seems to me that with a quarter of a million's worth of emeralds, one could do a whole lot of amusing things which Oppenheim would never dream of. To a bloke with my imagination—'

'But when would you do it?'

He looked at his watch mechanically.

'Eventually – why not now? Or at least this evening.' He was almost mad enough to consider it; but he restrained himself. 'But I'm afraid it might be asking for trouble. It'll probably take me a day or two to find out a few more things to get organized to keep him out of the way on the night I want to go in. I should think you could call it a date for Friday.'

She nodded with a queer childish gravity.

'I believe you'd do it. You sound very sure of everything. But what would you do with the emeralds after you got them?'

'I expect we could trade them in for a couple of hot dogs – maybe more.'

'You couldn't sell them.'

'There are ways and means.'

'You couldn't sell stones like that. I'm sure you couldn't. Everything in a famous collection like that would be much too well known. If you took them in to a dealer he'd recognize them at once, and then you'd be arrested.'

The Saint smiled. It has never been concealed from the lynx-eyed student of these chronicles that Simon Templar had his own very human weaknesses; and one of these was a deplorable lack of resistance to the temptation to display his unique knowledge of the devious ways of crime, like a peddler spreading his wares in the marketplace, before a suitably impressed and admiring audience.

'Not very far from here, in Bond Street,' he said, 'there's a little bar where you can find the biggest fence in England any evening between six and eight o'clock. He'll take anything you like to offer him across the table, and pay top prices for it. You could sell him the Crown Jewels if you had them. If I borrow Oppenheim's emeralds on Friday night I'll be rid of them by dinner time Saturday. And then we'll meet for a celebration and see where you'd like to go for a holiday.'

He was in high spirits when he took her home much later to the lodging house where he had found her a room the night before. There was one virtue in the indulgence of his favourite vice; talking over the details of a coup which he was freshly planning in his mind helped him to crystallize and elaborate his own ideas, gave him a charge of confidence, and optimistic energy from which the final strokes of action sprung as swiftly and accurately as bullets out of a gun.

When he said good night to her he felt as serene and exhilarated in spirit as if the Vanderwoude emeralds were already his own. He was in such good spirits that he had walked a block from the lodging house before he remembered that he had left her without trying to induce her to take some money for her immediate needs, and without making any arrangement to meet her again.

He turned and walked back. Coincidence, an accident of time involving only a matter of seconds, had made incredible differences to his life before. This, he realized later, was only another of those occasions when an overworked guardian angel seemed to play with the clock to save him from disaster.

The dimly lighted desert of the hall was surrounded by dense oases of potted palms, and one of these obstructions was in a direct line from the front door, so that anyone who entered quietly might easily remain unnoticed until he had circumnavigated this clump of shrubbery.

The Saint, who from the ingrained habit of years of dangerous living moved silently without conscious effort, was just preparing to step around this divinely inspired decoration when he heard someone speaking in the hall and caught the sound of a name which stopped him dead in his tracks. The name was Corrio.

Simon stood securely hidden behind the fronds of imported vegetation, and listened for as long as he dared to some of the most interesting lines of dialogue which he had ever overheard.

When he had heard enough, he slipped out again as quietly as he had come in, and went home without disturbing Janice Dixon. He would get in touch with her the next day: for the moment he had something much more urgent to occupy his mind.

It is possible that even Inspector Corrio's smugness might have been shaken if he had known about this episode of unpremeditated eavesdropping, but this unpleasant knowledge was hidden from him. His elastic self-esteem had taken no time at all to recover from the effects of Teal's reprimand. And when Mr Teal happened to meet him on a certain Friday afternoon he looked as offensively sleek and self- satisfied as he had always been. It was beyond Teal's limits of self-denial to let the occasion go by without making the use of it to which he felt he was entitled.

'I believe Oppenheim has still got his emeralds,' he remarked, with a certain feline joviality.

Inspector Corrio's glossy surface was unscratched.

'Don't be surprised if he doesn't keep them much longer,' he said. 'And don't blame me if the Saint gets away with it. I gave you the tip once, and you wouldn't listen.'

'Yes, you gave me the tip,' Teal agreed benevolently. 'When are you going out to Hollywood to play Sherlock Holmes?'

'Maybe it won't be so long now,' Corrio said darkly. 'Paragon Pictures are pretty interested in me – apparently one of their executives happened to see me playing the lead in our last show at the Ponders End Playhouse, and they want me to take a screen test.'

MrTeal grinned evilly.

'You're too late,' he said. 'They've already made a picture of *Little Women*.'

He had reason to regret some of his jibes the next morning, when news came in that every single one of MrOppenheim's emeralds had been removed from its hiding place and taken out of the house, quietly and without any fuss, in the pockets of a detective of whom the Ingerbeck agency had never heard.

They had, they said, been instructed by telephone that afternoon to discontinue the service, and the required written confirmation had arrived a few hours later, written on MrOppenheim's own flowery letterhead and signed with what they firmly believed to be his signature. Nobody had been more surprised and indignant than they were when MrOppenheim, on the verge of an apoplectic fit, had rung up MrIngerbeck himself and demanded to know how many more crooks they had on their payroll and what the *blank blank* they proposed to do about it.

The impostor had arrived at the house at the usual hour in the evening, explained that the regular man had been taken ill, and presented the necessary papers to accredit himself. He had been left all night in the study, and let out at breakfast time according to the usual custom. When he went out he was worth a quarter of a million pounds as he stood up. He was, according to the butler's rather hazy description, a tallish man with horn-rimmed glasses and a thick crop of red hair.

'That red hair and glasses is all nonsense,' said Corrio, who was in Chief Inspector Teal's office when the news came in. 'Just an ordinary wig and a pair of frames from any optician's. It was the Saint all right – you can see his style right through it. What did I tell you?'

'What the devil do you think you can tell *me*?' Teal roared back at him. Then he subdued himself. 'Anyway, you're crazy. The Saint's out of business.'

Corrio shrugged.

'Would you like me to take the case, sir?'

'What, you?' Mr Teal disrobed a wafer of chewing gum with the same distaste with which he might have undressed Inspector Corrio. 'I'll take the case myself.' He glowered at Corrio thoughtfully for a moment. 'Well, if you know so much about it you can come along with me. And we'll see how clever you are.'

It was a silent journey, for Teal was too full of a vague sort of wrath to speak, and Corrio seemed quite content to sit in a corner and finger his silky moustache with an infuriatingly tranquil air of being quite well satisfied with the forthcoming opportunity of demonstrating his own brilliance.

In the house they found a scene of magnificent confusion. There was the butler, who seemed to be getting blamed for having admitted the thief. There was a representative of Ingerbeck's whose temper appeared to be fraying rapidly under the flood of wild accusations which Oppenheim was flinging at him. There was a very suave and imperturbable official of the insurance company which had covered the jewels.

And there was MrOppenheim himself, a short, fat, yellow-faced man, dancing about like an agitated marionette, shaking his fists in an ecstasy of rage, screaming at the top of his voice, and accusing everybody in sight of crimes and perversions which would have been worth at least five hundred years at Dartmoor if they could have been proved.

Teal and Corrio had to listen while he unburdened his soul again from the beginning.

'And now what you think?' he wound up, 'these dirty crooks, this insurance company, they say they don't pay anything. They say they repudiate the policy. Just because I tried to keep the emeralds where they couldn't be found, instead of leaving them in a safe that anyone can open.'

'The thing is,' explained the official of the insurance company, with his own professional brand of unruffled unctuousness, 'that MrOppenheim has failed to observe the conditions of the policy. It was issued on the express understanding that if the emeralds were to be kept in the house, they were to be kept in this safe and guarded by a detective from some recognized agency. Neither of these stipulations have been complied with, and in the circumstances—'

'It's a dirty swindle!' shrieked Oppenheim. 'What do I care about your insurance company? I will cancel all my policies. I'll buy up your insurance company and throw you out in the street to starve. I'll offer my own reward for the emeralds. I will pay a hundred – I mean five thousand pounds to the man who brings back my jewels!'

'Have you put that in writing yet?' asked Inspector Corrio quickly.

'No. But I'll do so at once. Bah! I will show these dirty, double-crossing crooks.'

He whipped out his fountain pen and scurried over to the desk.

'Here, wait a minute,' said Teal, but Oppenheim paid no

attention to him. Teal turned to Corrio. 'I suppose you have to be sure of the reward before you start showing us how clever you are,' he said nastily.

'No, sir. But we have to consider the theory that the robbery might have been committed with that in mind. Emeralds like those would be difficult to dispose of profitably. I can only think of one fence in London who'd handle a package of stuff like that.'

'Then why don't you pull him in?' snapped Teal unanswerably.

'Because I've never had enough evidence. But I'll take up that angle this afternoon.'

Corrio took no further part in the routine examinations and questionings which Teal conducted with dogged efficiency, but on the way back to Scotland Yard he pressed his theory again with unusual humility.

'After all, sir, even if this isn't one of the Saint's jobs, whoever did it, they're quite likely to deal with this chap I've got in mind, and we aren't justified in overlooking it. I know you don't think much of me, sir,' said Corrio with unwonted candour, 'but you must admit that I was right a few days ago when you wouldn't listen to me, and now I think it'd be only fair to give me another chance.'

Almost against his will, Teal forced himself to be just.

'All right,' he said grudgingly. 'Where do we find this fence?'

'If you can be free about a quarter to five this afternoon,' said Corrio, 'I'd like you to come along.'

Simon Templar walked north along Bond Street. He felt at peace with the world. At such times as this he was capable of glowing with a vast and luxurious contentment, the same deep and satisfying tranquillity that might follow a perfect meal eaten in hunger or the drinking of a cool drink at the end of a hot day.

As usually happened with him, this mood had made its mark on his clothes; and he was a very beautiful and resplendent sight as he sauntered along the sidewalk with the brim of his hat tilted piratically over his eyes, looking like some swashbuckling medieval brigand who had been miraculously transported into the twentieth century and put into modern dress without losing the swagger of a less inhibited age.

In one hand he carried a brown paper parcel.

Chief Inspector Teal's pudgy hand closed on his arm near the corner of Burlington Gardens; and the Saint looked around and recognized him with a delighted and completely innocent smile.

'Why, hullo there, Claud Eustace,' he murmured. 'The very man I've been looking for.' He discovered Corrio coming up out of the background, and smiled again. 'Hi, Gladys,' he said politely.

Corrio seized his other arm and worked him swiftly and scientifically into a doorway. There was a gleam of excitement in his dark eyes.

'It looks as if my theory was right again,' he said to Teal.

Mr Teal kept his grip of the Saint's arm. His rather froglike eyes glared at the Saint angrily, but not with the sort of anger that most people would have expected.

'You damn fool,' Teal said, rather damn-foolishly. 'What did you have to do it for? I told you when you came home that you couldn't get away with that stuff any more.'

'What stuff?' asked the Saint innocently.

Corrio had grabbed the parcel out of his hand, and he was tearing it open with impatient haste.

'I think that this is what we're looking for,' he said.

The broken string and torn brown paper fluttered to the ground as Corrio ripped them off. When the outer wrappings were gone he was left with a cardboard box. Inside the box there was a layer of crumpled tissue paper.

Corrio jerked it out and remained staring frozenly at what was finally exposed. There was a fully dressed and very life-like doll with features that were definitely familiar. Tied around its neck on a piece of ribbon was a ticket on which was printed: 'Film Star Series, No. 12: *clark gable.* 2/11.'

An expression of delirious and incredulous relief began to creep over the chubby curves of Teal's pink face – much the same expression as might have come into the face of a man who, standing close by the crater of a rumbling volcano, had seen it suddenly explode only to throw off a shower of fairy lights and coloured balloons. The corners of his mouth began to twitch, and a deep vibration like the tremor of an approaching earthquake began to quiver over his chest.

Corrio's face was black with fury. He tore out the rest of the packing paper and squeezed out every scrap of it between his fingers, snatched the doll out of the box and twisted and shook it to see if anything could have been concealed inside it. Then he flung that down also among the mounting fragments of litter on the ground. He thrust his face forward until it was within six inches of the Saint's.

'Where are they?' he snarled savagely.

'Where are who?' asked the Saint densely.

'You know damn well what I'm talking about,' Corrio said through his teeth. 'What have you done with the stuff you stole from Oppenheim's last night? Where are the Vanderwoude emeralds?'

'Oh, them,' said the Saint mildly. 'That's a funny question for *you* to ask.' He leaned lazily on the wall against which Corrio had forced him, took out his cigarette case, and looked at Teal.

'As a matter of fact,' he said calmly, 'that's what I wanted to see you about. If you're particularly interested I think I could show you where they went to.'

The laugh died away on Teal's lips, to be replaced by the

startled and hurt look of a dog that has been given an unexpected bone and then kicked almost as soon as it has picked it up.

'So you know something about that job,' he said slowly.

'I know plenty,' said the Saint. 'Let's take a cab.'

Templar straightened up off the wall. For a moment Corrio looked as if he would pin him back there, but Teal's intent interest countermanded the movement without speaking or even looking at him.

Teal was puzzled and disturbed, but somehow the Saint's quiet voice and unsmiling eyes told him that there was something there to be taken seriously. He stepped back, and Simon walked past him unhindered and opened the door of a taxi standing by the kerb.

'Where are we going to?' asked Teal, as they turned in to Piccadilly.

The Saint grinned gently, and settled back in his corner with his cigarette. He ignored the question.

'Once upon a time,' he said presently, 'there was a smart detective. He was very smart because after some years of ordinary detecting he discovered that the main difficulty about the whole business was that you often have to find out who committed a crime, and this is liable to mean a lot of hard work and a good many disappointments.

'So this guy, being a smart fellow, thought of a much simpler method, which was more or less to persuade the criminals to tell him about it themselves. For instance, suppose a crook got away with a tidy cargo of loot and didn't want to put it away in the refrigerator for icicles to grow on. He could bring his problem to our smart detective, and our smart detective could think it over and say, "Well, Featherstonehaugh, that's pretty easy. All you do is just go and hide this loot in a dustbin on Greek Street or hang it on a tree in Hyde Park, or something like that, and I'll do a very smart piece of detecting and find it. Then I'll collect the reward and we'll go shares in it.'

'Usually this was pretty good business for the crook, the regular fences being as miserly as they are; and the detective didn't starve on it either. But somehow it never seemed to occur to the other detectives to wonder how he did it.'

He finished speaking as the taxi drew up at a small and dingy hotel near Charing Cross.

MrTeal was sitting forward, with his round moon-face looking like a surprised plum-pudding and his eyes fixed sleepily on the Saint's face.

'Go on,' he said gruffly.

Simon shook his head and indicated the door. 'We'll change the scene again. Just be patient.'

He got out and paid off the driver, and the other two followed him into the hotel. Corrio's face seeemd to have gone paler under its olive tan.

Simon paused in the lobby and glanced at him.

'Will you ask for the key, or shall I? It might be better if you asked for it,' he said softly, 'because the porter will recognize you. Even if he doesn't know you by your right name.'

'I don't quite know what you're talking about,' Corrio said coldly, 'but if you think you can wriggle out of this with any of your wild stories, you're wasting your time.' He turned to Teal. 'I haven't got a room here, sir. I just use it sometimes when I'm kept in town late and I can't get home. It isn't in my own name, because – well, sir, you understand – I don't always want everybody to know who I am. This man has got to know about it somehow, and he's just using it to try to put up some crazy story to save his own skin.'

'All the same,' said Teal, with surprising gentleness, 'I'd like to go up. I want to hear some more of this crazy story.'

Corrio turned on his heel and went to the desk. The room

was on the third floor – an ordinary cheap hotel room with the usual revolting furniture to be found in such places.

Teal glanced briefly over its salient features as they entered, and looked at the Saint again. 'Go on,' he said. 'I'm listening.'

The Saint sat down on the edge of the bed and blew smoke-rings.

'It would probably have gone on a lot longer,' he said, 'if this smart detective hadn't thought one day what a supremely brilliant idea it would be to combine business with profit. And have the honour of convicting a most notorious and elusive bandit known as the Saint – not forgetting, of course, to collect the usual cash reward in the process.

'So he used a very good-looking young damsel – you ought to meet her sometime, Claud, she really is a peach – having some idea that the Saint would never run away very fast from a pretty face. In which he was damn right . . . She had a very well-planned hard-luck story, too, and the whole act was most professionally staged. It had all the ingredients that a good psychologist would bet on to make the Saint feel that stealing Oppenheim's emeralds was the one thing he had left glaringly undone in an otherwise complete life.

'Even the spade-work of the job had already been put in, so that she could practically tell the Saint how to pinch the jewels. So that our smart detective must have thought he was sitting pretty, with a sucker all primed to do the dirty work for him and take the rap if anything went wrong – besides being still there to take the rap when the smart detective made his arrest and earned the reward if everything went right.'

Simon smiled dreamily at a particularly repulsive print on the wall for a moment.

'Unfortunately I happened to drop in on this girl one time when she wasn't expecting me, and I heard her phoning a guy named Corrio to tell him I was well and truly hooked,' he

said. 'On account of having read in the *Bulldog* some talk by
a guy of the same name about what he was going to do to me,
I was naturally interested.'

Corrio started forward. 'Look here, you—'

'Wait a minute.' Mr Teal held him back with an unexpectedly powerful arm. 'I want the rest of it. Did you do the job,
Saint?'

Simon shook his head sadly. It was at that point that his
narrative departed, for the very first time, from the channels
of pure veracity in which it had begun its course – but Mr Teal
was not to know this.

'Would I be such a sap, Claud?' he asked reproachfully. 'I
knew I could probably get away with the actual robbery,
because Corrio would want me to. But as soon as it was over,
knowing in advance who'd done it, he'd be chasing round to
catch me and recover the emeralds. So I told the girl I'd
thought it all over and decided I was too busy.'

The Saint sighed, as if he was still regretting a painful
sacrifice. 'The rest is pure theory. But this girl gave me a
cloak room ticket from Victoria Station this morning and
asked me if I'd collect a package this afternoon and take it
along to an address on Bond Street. I didn't do it because I
had an idea what would happen; but my guess would be that
if somebody went along and claimed the parcel they'd find
the emeralds in it.

'Not all the emeralds, probably because that'd be too risky
if I got curious and opened it; but some of them. The rest are
probably here – I've been looking around since we've been
here, and I think there's some new and rather amateurish
stitching in the upholstery of that chair. I could do something
with that reward myself.'

Corrio barred his way as he got off the table.

'You stay where you are,' he grated. 'If you're trying to get
away with some smart frame-up—'

'Just to make sure,' said the Saint, 'I fixed a dictagraph under the table yesterday. Let's see if it has anything to say.'

Teal watched him soberly as he prepared to play back the record. In Chief Inspector Teal's mind was the memory of a number of things which he had heard Corrio say, which fitted into the picture which the Saint offered him much too vividly to be easily denied. Then the dictagraph began to play. And Teal felt a faint shiver run up his spine at the uncannily accurate reproduction of Corrio's voice.

'*Smart work, Leo ... I bet these must be worth every penny of the price on them.*'

The other voice was unfamiliar.

'*Hell, it was easy. The layout was just like you said. But how're you gain' to fix it on the other chap?*'

'*That's simple. The girl gets him to fetch a parcel from Victoria and take it where I tell her to tell him. When he gets there, I'm waiting for him.*'

'*You're not goin' to risk givin' him all that stuff?*'

'*Oh, don't be so wet. There'll only be just enough to frame him. Once he's caught, it'll be easy enough to plant the rest somewhere and find it.*'

Corrio's eyes were wide and staring.

'It's a plant!' he screamed hysterically. 'That's a record of the scene I played in the film test I made yesterday.'

Simon smiled politely, cutting open the upholstery of the armchair and fishing about for a leather pouch containing about two hundred thousand pounds' worth of emeralds which should certainly be there unless somebody else had found them since he chose that ideal hiding place for his loot.

'I only hope you'll be able to prove it, Gladys,' he murmured; and watched Teal grasp Corrio's arm with purposeful efficiency.

The Wicked Cousin

INTRODUCTION BY LESLIE CHARTERIS[1]

In recent times, the common courtesy of trying to avoid wantonly stepping on people's toes has developed into an editorial phobia of almost psychotic intensity.

This exaggerated concern for the tender toe has of course been vociferously encouraged by every sort of hypersensitive minority. The most frantic form of it is displayed by movie producers, who are more sensitive to the tinkle of the cash register than any other species of artistic entrepreneur, and who also know that they are catering to a more infantile audience than that of any other medium except television.

It is a fact that many of our most distinguished gangsters have been of Italian descent; but to portray a gangster with an Italian name of the screen is not only an automatic way to discover more pro-Italian clubs, societies, and protective associations than you would otherwise have known existed, but not so long ago would have seen the fist of Mussolini shaken at State Department level. A Latin-American heavy in a picture might strain the whole structure of Pan-American amity. Even on the domestic scene, Negroes, Chinese, Jews, Catholics, Baptists or Holy Rollers can only be depicted as lovable paragons. It has reached the point where the only villain who can be safely used today is a white American or British agnostic, preferably named Smith.

Only one step is lacking to achieve the final reductio ad

[1] From *The Second Saint Omnibus* (1952)

absurdum, and that will be when a few more firebrands found the Society for the Preservation of the Caucasian Race, the International Association of Agnostics, and the League Against Libelling People Named Smith. After which the only villains at our disposal will be men from Mars – until the Committee for the Protection of Martians takes over. Then all the writers whose stories depend on the conflict between goodness and villainy can fold up their typewriters and silently steal away. Except that the Authors' League would certainly object to the mere suggestion that writers would steal anything.

To a lesser degree, there has grown up a similar taboo against combining moral turpitude with physical defects. If Robert Louis Stevenson had been writing *Treasure Island* today, he would probably be told that his picture of Long John Silver might give offense to a large body of unfortunate amputees. Sir James Barrie would probably have been urged to reconsider the anatomy of Captain Hook. And Victor Hugo would have been warned that the Hunchback of Notre Dame might be construed as an attack on all hunchbacks.

An extension of this thinking (or lack of it) has even begun to make it seem in bad taste to make even kindly fun of an infirmity. As soon as this movement has really taken hold, I expect clowns to be banned from circuses, on the ground that their make-up is a direct affront to any man who is naturally afflicted with a bulbous nose, and that their oversized splay-footed shoes might wound the feelings of anyone suffering from fallen arches.

Well, it should be known by now that the Saint, and therefore presumably his creator, is not in the business of persecuting or deriding the underprivileged or the unfortunate. But I promise you here that any time a good story reason calls for me to produce a villain or a comic who is a

Negro, an Eskimo, a Jew, a Catholic, a Christian Scientist, a diabetic, or a dwarf – I am going to do it, and let the squawks rise to heaven.

This story contains a character with an impediment in his speech, perhaps even a cleft palate. His misfortune is essential to the story. So if any of you readers are stutterers or honkers, I just hope you have a sense of humour.

There was a girl called Jacqueline Laine whom Simon Templar remembered suddenly, as one does sometimes remember people, with a sense of startling familiarity and a kind of guilty amazement that he should have allowed her to slip out of his mind for so long.

This was on one of the rare occasions when he was not thinking about business. Simon Templar's business had an unfortunate habit of falling into categories which gave many people good reason to wonder what right he had to the nickname of the Saint by which he was far more widely known than he was by his baptismal titles; but 'business' was the polite name he gave it.

It is true that these buccaneering raids of his which had earned him the sub-title of 'The Robin Hood of Modern Crime' were invariably undertaken against the property, and occasionally the persons, of citizens who by no stretch of imagination could have been called desirable; but the Law took no official cognizance of such small details. The Law, in the Saint's opinion, was a stodgy and elephantine institution which was chiefly justified in its existence by the pleasantly musical explosive noises which it made when he broke it.

He picked up the telephone. 'Hullo, Jacqueline,' he said when she answered. 'Do you know who this is?'

'I know,' she said. 'It's Julius Caesar.'

'You have a marvellous memory. Do you still eat?'

'Whenever I'm thirsty. Do you?'

'I nibble a crumb now and then. Come out with me tonight and see if we can still take it.'

'Simon, I'd love to; but I'm in the most frantic muddle—'

'So is the rest of the world, darling. But it's two years since I've seen you, and that's about seven hundred and thirty days too long. Don't you realize that I've been all the way around the world, surviving all manner of perils and slaying large numbers of ferocious dragons, just to get back in time to take you out to dinner tonight?'

'I know, but – Oh, well. It would be so thrilling to see you. Come around about seven, and I'll try to get a bit straightened out before then.'

'I'll be there,' said the Saint.

Half an hour later he drove his great cream and red car westwards out of London. Somewhere beyond Bagshot he turned off to the right and began to wander through narrow winding lanes in which the feverish main-road traffic which he had just left was very quickly forgotten. He found his way with the certainty of vivid remembrance; and he was fully ten minutes early when he pulled the car into the roadside before the gate of Jacqueline Laine's house.

He climbed out and started towards the gate, lighting a cigarette as he went; and as he approached it he perceived that somebody else was approaching the same gate from the opposite side. Changing his course a little to the left so that the departing guest would have room to pass him, the Saint observed that he was a small and elderly gent arrayed in clothes so shapeless and ill-fitting that they gave his figure a comical air of having been loosely and inaccurately strung together from a selection of stuffed bags of cloth. He wore a discoloured Panama hat of weird and wonderful architecture, and carried an incongruous green umbrella, furled, but still flapping in a bedraggled and forlorn sort of way, under his left arm; his face was rubicund and bulbous like his body, looking as if it had been carelessly slapped together out of a few odd lumps of pink modelling clay.

As Simon moved to the left, the elderly gent duplicated the manoeuvre. Simon turned his feet and swerved politely to the right. The elderly gent did exactly the same, as if he were Simon's own reflection in a distorting mirror. Simon stopped altogether, and decided to economize energy by letting the elderly gent make the next move in the ballet.

Whereupon he discovered that the game of undignified dodging in which he had just prepared to surrender his part was caused by some dimly discernible ambition of the elderly gent's to hold converse with him. Standing in front of him and blinking shortsightedly upwards from his lower altitude to the Saint's six foot two, with his mouth hanging vacantly open like an inverted U and three long yellow teeth hanging down like stalactites from the top, the elderly gent tapped him on the chest and said, very earnestly and distinctly: 'Hig fwmgn glugl phnihkln hgrm skheglgl?'

'I beg your pardon?' said the Saint vaguely.

'Hig fwmgn,' repeated the elderly gent, 'glugl phnihkln hgrm skhlglgl?'

Simon considered the point. 'If you ask me,' he replied at length, 'I should say sixteen.'

The elderly gent's knobbly face seemed to take on a brighter shade of pink. He clutched the lapels of the Saint's coat, shaking him slightly in a positive passion of anguish.

'Flogh ghoglusk,' he pleaded, 'klngnt hu ughlgstghnd?'

Simon shook his head. 'No,' he said judiciously, 'you're thinking of weevils.'

The little man bounced about like a rubber doll. His eyes squinted with a kind of frantic despair.

'Ogmighogho,' he almost screamed, 'klngt hu ughglstghnd? Ik ghln ngmnpp sktlghko! Klugt hu hgr? *Ik wgnt hlg phnihkln hgrm skhlglgl!*'

The Saint sighed. He was by nature a kindly man to those whom the gods had afflicted, but time was passing and he was thinking of Jacqueline Laine.

'I'm afraid not, dear old bird,' he murmured regretfully. 'There used to be one, but it died. Sorry, I'm sure.'

He patted the elderly gent apologetically upon the shoulder, steered his way around him, and passed on out of earshot of the frenzied sputtering noises that continued to honk despairingly through the dusk behind him. Two minutes later he was with Jacqueline.

Jacqueline Laine was twenty-three; she was tall and slender; she had grey eyes that twinkled and a demoralizing mouth. Both of these temptations were in play as she came towards him; but he was still slightly shaken by his recent encounter.

'Have you got any more village idiots hidden around?' he asked warily, as he took her hands; and she was puzzled.

'We used to have several, but they've all gone into Parliament. Did you want one to take home?'

'My God, no,' said the Saint fervently. 'The one I met at the gate was bad enough. Is he your latest boy friend?'

Her brow cleared. 'Oh, you mean the old boy with the cleft palate? Isn't he marvellous? I think he's got a screw loose or something. He's been hanging around all day – he keeps ringing the bell and bleating at me. I'd just sent him away for the third time. Did he try to talk to you?'

'He did sort of wag his adenoids at me,' Simon admitted, 'but I don't think we actually got on to common ground. I felt quite jealous of him for a bit, until I realized that he couldn't possibly kiss you nearly as well as I can, with that set of teeth.'

He proceeded to demonstrate this.

'I'm still in a hopeless muddle,' she said presently. 'But I'll be ready in five minutes. You can be fixing a cocktail while I make myself presentable.'

In the living-room there was an open trunk in one corner and a half-filled packing case in the middle of the floor. There were scattered heaps of paper around it, and a few partially wrapped and unidentifiable objects on the table. The room had that curiously naked and inhospitable look which a room has when it has been stripped of all those intimately personal odds and ends of junk which make it a home, and only the bare furniture is left.

The Saint raised his eyebrows. 'Hullo,' he said. 'Are you moving?'

'Sort of.' She shrugged. 'Moving out, anyway.'

'Where to?'

'I don't know.'

He realized then that there should have been someone else there, in that room.

'Isn't your grandmother here any more?'

'She died four weeks ago.'

'I'm sorry.'

'She was a good soul. But she was terribly old. Do you know she was just ninety-seven?' She held his hand for a moment. 'I'll tell you all about it when I come down. Do you remember where to find the bottles?'

'Templars and elephants never forget.'

He blended gin, curaçao, vermouth and bitters skilfully and with the zeal of an artist, while he waited for her, remembering the old lady whom he had seen so often in that room. Also he remembered the affectionate service Jacqueline had always lavished on her, cheerfully limiting her own enjoyment of life to meet the demands of an unconscious tyrant who would allow no one else to look after her, and wondered if there was any realistic reason to regret the ending of such a long life. She had, he knew, looked after Jacqueline herself in her time, and had brought her up as her own child since she was left an orphan at the age of three; but life must always belong to the young ... He thought that for Jacqueline it must be a supreme escape. But he knew that she would never say so.

She came down punctually in the five minutes which she had promised. She had changed her dress and put a comb through her hair, and with that seemed to have achieved more than any other woman could have shown for an hour's fiddling in front of a mirror.

'You should have been in pictures,' said the Saint; and he meant it.

'Maybe I shall,' she said. 'I'll have to do something to earn a living now.'

'Is it as bad as that?'

She nodded. 'But I can't complain. I never had to work for anything before. Why shouldn't I start? Other people have to.'

'Is that why you're moving out?'

'The house isn't mine.'

'But didn't the old girl leave you anything?'

'She left me some letters.'

The Saint almost spilt his drink. She sat down heavily on the edge of the table.

'She left you some *letters*? After you'd practically been a slave to her since you got out of school? What did she do with the rest of the property – leave it to a home for stray cats?'

'No, she left it to Harry.'

'Who?'

'Her grandson.'

'I didn't know you had any brothers.'

'I haven't. Harry Westler is my cousin. He's – well, as a matter of fact he's a sort of black sheep. He's a gambler, and he was in prison for forging a cheque. Nobody else in the family would have anything to do with him, and if you believe what they used to say about him they were probably quite right; but Granny always had a soft spot for him. She never believed he could do anything wrong – he was just a mischievous boy to her. Well, you know how old she was . . .'

'And she left everything to him?'

'Practically everything. I'll show you.'

She went to a drawer of the writing table and brought him a typewritten sheet. He saw that it was a copy of a will, and turned to the details of the bequests.

To my dear grand-daughter Jacqueline Laine, who has taken care of me so thoughtfully and unselfishly for four years, One Hundred Pounds and my letters from Sidney Farlance, knowing that she will find them of more value than anything else I could leave her.

To my cook, Eliza Jefferson, and my chauffeur, Albert Gordon, One Hundred Pounds each, for their loyal service.

The remainder of my estate, after these deductions, including my house and other personal belongings, to my dear grandson Harry Westler, hoping that it will help him to make the success of life of which I have always believed him capable.

Simon folded the sheet and dropped it on the table from his fingertips as if it were infected.

'Suffering Judas,' he said helplessly. 'After all you did for her – to pension you off on the same scale as the cook and the chauffeur! And what about Harry – doesn't he propose to do anything about it?'

'Why should he? The will's perfectly clear.'

'Why shouldn't he? Just because the old crow went off her trolley in the last few days of senile decay is no reason why he shouldn't do something to put it right. There must have been enough for both of you.'

'Not so much. They found that Granny had been living on her capital for years. There was only about four thousand pounds – and the house.'

'What of it? He could spare half.'

Jacqueline smiled – a rather tired little smile.

'You haven't met Harry. He's – difficult . . . He's been here, of course. The agents already have his instructions to sell the house and the furniture. He gave me a week to get out, and the week is up the day after tomorrow. I couldn't possibly ask him for anything.'

Simon lighted a cigarette as if it tasted of bad eggs, and scowled malevolently about the room.

'The skunk! And so you get chucked out into the wide world with nothing but a hundred quid.'

'And the letters,' she said ruefully.

'What the hell are these letters?'

'They're love letters,' she said; and the Saint looked as if he would explode.

'Love letters?' he repeated in an awful voice.

'Yes. Granny had a great romance when she was a girl. Her parents wouldn't let her get any further with it, because the boy hadn't any money and his family wasn't good enough. He went abroad with one of those heroic young ideas of making a fortune in South America and coming back in a gold-plated carriage to claim her. He died of fever somewhere in Brazil very soon after, but he wrote her three letters – two from British Guiana and one from Colombia.

'Oh, I know them by heart – I used to have to read them aloud to Granny almost every night, after her eyes got too bad for her to be able to read them herself. They're just the ordinary simple sort of thing that you'd expect in the circumstances but to Granny they were the most precious thing she had. I suppose she had some funny old idea in her head that they'd be just as precious to me.'

'She must have been screwy,' said the Saint.

Jacqueline came up and put a hand over his mouth. 'She was very good to me when I was a kid,' she said.

'I know, but—' Simon flung up his arms hopelessly. And then, almost reluctantly, he began to laugh. 'But it does mean that I've just come back in time. And we'll have so much fun tonight that you won't even think about it for a minute. We'll just be old friends on a lark.'

Probably he made good his boast, for Simon Templar brought to the solemn business of enjoying himself the same gay zest and inspired impetuosity which he brought to his battles with the technicalities of the Law. But if he followed her into the living-room of the house again much later, for a nightcap, the desolate scene of interrupted packing, and the copy of the will still lying on the table where he had put it down, brought the thoughts with which he had been subconsciously playing throughout the evening back into the forefront of his mind.

'Are you going to let Harry get away with it?' he asked her, with a sudden characteristic directness.

The girl shrugged. 'What else can I do?'

'I have an idea,' said the Saint; and his blue eyes danced with an unholy delight which she had never seen in them before . . .

Mr Westler was not a man whose contacts with the Law had conspired to make him particularly happy about any of its workings; and therefore when he saw that the card which was brought to him in his hotel bore in its bottom left-hand corner the name of a firm with the word 'Solicitors' underneath it, he suffered an immediate hollow twinge in the base of his stomach for which he could scarcely be blamed. A moment's reflection, however, reminded him that another card with a similar inscription had recently been the forerunner of an extremely welcome windfall, and with this reassuring thought he told the page boy to bring the visitor into his presence.

Mr Tombs, of Tombs, Tombs and Tombs, as the card introduced him, was a tall lean man with neatly brushed white hair, bushy white eyebrows, a pair of gold-rimmed and drooping pince-nez on the end of a broad black ribbon, and an engagingly avuncular manner which rapidly completed the task of restoring Harry Westler's momentarily shaken confidence. He came to the point with professional efficiency combined with professional pomposity.

'I have come to see you in connection with the estate of the – ah – late Mr. Laine. I understand that you are her heir.'

'That's right,' said Mr Westler.

He was a dark, flashily dressed man with small greedy eyes and a face rather reminiscent of that of a sick horse.

'Splendid.' The lawyer placed his fingertips on his knees and leaned forward, peering benevolently over the rims of his glasses. 'Now I for my part am representing the Sesame Mining Development Corporation.'

He said this more or less as if he were announcing himself as the personal herald of Jehovah, but Mr Westler's mind ran in practical channels.

'Did my grandmother have shares in the company?' he asked quickly.

'Ah – ah – no. That is – ah – no. Not exactly. But I under-stand that she was in possession of a letter or document which my clients regard as extremely valuable.'

'A letter?'

'Exactly. But perhaps I had better give you an outline of the situation. Your grandmother was, in her youth, greatly – ah – enamoured of a certain Sidney Farlance. Perhaps at some time or other you have heard her speak of him.'

'Yes.'

'For various reasons her parents refused to give their

consent to the alliance; but the young people for their part refused to take no for an answer, and Farlance went abroad with the intention of making his fortune in foreign parts and returning in due course to claim his bride. In this ambition he was unhappily frustrated by his – ah – premature decease in Brazil. But it appears that during his travels in British Guiana he did become the owner of a mining concession in a certain inaccessible area of territory. British Guiana, as you are doubtless aware,' continued Mr Tombs in his dry pedagogic voice, 'is traditionally reputed to be the source of the legend of El Dorado, the Gilded King, who was said to cover himself with pure gold and to wash it from him in the waters of a sacred lake called Manoa—'

'Never mind all that baloney,' said Harry Westler, who was not interested in history or mythology. 'Tell me about his concession.'

Mr Tombs pressed his lips with a pained expression, but he went on.

'At the time it did not appear that gold could be profitably obtained from this district, and the claim was abandoned and forgotten. Modern engineering methods, however, have recently revealed deposits of almost fabulous value in the district, and my clients have obtained a concession to work it over a very large area of ground. Subsequent investigations into their title, meanwhile, have brought out the existence of this small – uh – prior concession granted to Sidney Farlance, which is situated almost in the centre of my client's territory and in a position which – ah – exploratory drillings have shown to be one of the richest areas in the district.'

Mr Westler digested the information; and in place of the first sinking vacuum which had afflicted his stomach when he saw the word 'solicitor' on his visitor's card, a sudden and ecstatic awe localized itself in the same place and began to cramp his lungs as if he had accidentally swallowed a rubber balloon with his breakfast and it was being rapidly inflated by some supernatural agency.

'You mean my grandmother owned this concession?'

'That is what – ah – my clients are endeavouring to discover. Farlance himself, of course, left no heirs, and we have been unable to trace any surviving members of his family. In the course of inquiries, however, we did learn of his – ah – romantic interest in your grandmother, and we have every reason to believe that in the circumstances he would naturally have made her the beneficiary of any such asset, however problematical its value may have seemed at the time.'

'And you want to buy it out – is that it?'

'Ah – yes. That is – ah – provided that our deductions are correct and the title can be established. I may say that my clients would be prepared to pay very liberally—'

'They'd have to,' said Mr Westler briskly. 'How much are they good for?'

The lawyer raised his hands deprecatingly.

'You need have no alarm, my dear Mr Westler. The actual figure, would, of course, be a matter for negotiation, but it would doubtless run close to a million pounds. But first of all, you understand we must trace the actual concession papers which will be sufficient to establish your right to negotiate. Now it seems that in view of the relationship between Farlance and your grandmother, she would probably have treasured his letters as most women do, even though she later married someone else, particularly if there was a document of that sort among them. People don't usually throw things like that away. In that case you will doubtless have inherited these letters along with her other personal property. Possibly you have not yet had an occasion to peruse them, but if you would do so as soon as possible—'

One of Harry Westler's few Napoleonic qualities was a remarkable capacity for quick and constructive thinking.

'Certainly I have the letters,' he said, 'but I haven't gone through them yet. My lawyer has them at present, and he's in Edinburgh today. He'll be back tomorrow morning, and I'll get hold of them at once. Come and see me again tomorrow afternoon and I expect I'll have some news for you.'

'Tomorrow afternoon, Mr Westler? Certainly. I think that will be convenient. Ah – certainly.' The lawyer stood up, took off his pince-nez, polished them, and revolved them like a windmill on the end of their ribbon. 'This has indeed been a most happy meeting, my dear sir. And may I say that I hope that tomorrow afternoon it will be even happier?'

'You can go on saying that right up till the time we start talking prices,' said Harry.

The door had scarcely closed behind Mr Tombs when Mr Westler was on the telephone to his cousin. He suppressed a sigh of relief when he heard her voice, and announced as casually as he could his intention of coming down to see her.

'I think we ought to have another talk – I was terribly upset by the shock of Granny's death when I saw you the other day, and I'm afraid I wasn't quite myself, but I'll make all the apologies you like when I get there,' he said in an unfamiliarly gentle voice which cost him a great effort to achieve, and was grabbing his hat before the telephone was properly back on its bracket.

He made a call at the bank on his way, and sat in the hired car which carried him out into the country as if its cushions had been upholstered with hot spikes. The exact words of that portion of the Will which referred to the letters drummed through his memory with a staggering significance. '*My letters from Sidney Farlance, knowing that she will find them of more value than anything else I could leave her.*' The visit of Mr Tombs had made him understand them perfectly. His grandmother had known what was in them; but did Jacqueline know? His heart almost stopped beating with anxiety.

As he leapt out of the car and dashed towards the house he cannoned into a small and weirdly apparelled elderly gent who was apparently emerging from the gate at the same time. Mr Westler checked himself involuntarily; and the elderly gent, sent flying by the impact, bounced off a gatepost and tottered back at him. He clutched Harry by the sleeve and peered up at him pathetically.

'Glhwf hngwglgl,' he said pleadingly, 'kngnduk glu bwtl-hjp mnyihgli?'

'Oh, go choke yourself,' snarled Mr Westler impatiently.

He pushed the little man roughly aside and went on.

Jacqueline opened the door to him, and Mr Westler steeled himself to kiss her on the forehead with cousinly affection.

'I was an awful swine the other day, Jackie. I don't know what could have been the matter with me. I've always been terribly selfish,' he said with an effort, 'and at the time I didn't really see how badly Granny had treated you. She didn't leave you anything except those letters, did she?'

'She left me a hundred pounds,' said Jacqueline calmly.

'A hundred pounds!' said Harry indignantly. 'After you'd given up everything else to take care of her. And she left me more than four thousand pounds and the house and everything in it. It's disgusting! But I don't have to take advantage of it, do I? I've been thinking a lot about it lately—'

Jacqueline lighted a cigarette and regarded him stonily. 'Thanks,' she said briefly. 'But I haven't asked you for any charity.'

'It isn't charity,' protested Mr Westler virtuously. 'It's just a matter of doing the decent thing. The lawyers have done their share – handed everything over to me and seen that the will was carried out. Now we can start again. We could pool everything again and divide it the way we think it ought to be divided.'

'As far as I'm concerned, that's been done already.'

'But I'm not happy about it. I've got all the money, and you know what I'm like. I'll probably gamble it all away in a few months.'

'That's your affair.'

'Oh, don't be like that, Jackie. I've apologized, haven't I? Besides, what Granny left you is worth a lot more than money. I mean those letters of hers. I'd willingly give up a thousand pounds of my share if I could have had those. They're the one thing of the old lady's which really mean a great deal to me.'

'You're becoming very sentimental all of a sudden, aren't you?' asked the girl curiously.

'Maybe I am. I suppose you can't really believe that a rotter like me could feel that way about anything, but Granny was the only person in the world who ever really believed any good of me and liked me in spite of everything. If I gave you a thousand pounds for those letters, it wouldn't be charity – I'd be paying less than I think they're worth. Let's put it that way if you'd rather, Jackie. An ordinary business deal. If I had them,' said Mr Westler, with something like a sob in his voice, 'they'd always be a reminder to me of the old lady and how good she was. They might help me to go straight—'

His emotion was so touching that even Jacqueline's cynical incredulity lost some of its assurance. Harry Westler was playing his part with every technical trick that he knew, and he had a mastery of these emotional devices which victims far more hard-boiled than Jacqueline had experienced to their cost.

'I'm thoroughly ashamed of myself, and I want to put things right in any way I can. Don't make me feel any worse than I do already. Look here, I'll give you two thousand pounds for the letters and I won't regret a penny of it. You won't regret it either, will you, if they help me to keep out of trouble in future?'

Jacqueline smiled in spite of herself. It was not in her nature to bear malice, and it was very hard for her to resist an appeal that was made in those terms. Also, with the practical side of her mind, she was honest enough to realize that her grandmother's letters had no sentimental value for her whatever, and that two thousand pounds was a sum of money which she could not afford to refuse Unless her pride was compelled to forbid it; her night out with the Saint had helped her to forget her problems for the moment, but she had awakened that morning with a very sober realization of the position in which she was going to find herself within the next forty-eight hours.

'If you put it like that I can't very well refuse, can I?' she said, and Harry jumped up and clasped her fervently by the hand.

'You'll really do it, Jackie? You don't know how much I appreciate it.'

She disengaged herself quietly. 'It doesn't do me any harm,' she told him truthfully. 'Would you like to have the letters now?'

'If they're anywhere handy. I brought some money along with me, so we can fix it all up right away.'

She went upstairs and fetched the letters from the dressing table in her grandmother's room. Mr Westler took them and tore off the faded ribbon with which they were tied together with slightly trembling fingers which she attributed to an unexpected depth of emotion. One by one he took them out of their envelopes and read rapidly through them. The last sheet of the third letter was a different kind of paper from the rest. The paper was discoloured and cracked in the folds, and the ink had the rusty brown hue of great age; but he saw the heavy official seal in one corner and strained his eyes to decipher the stiff old-fashioned script.

We, Philip Edmond Wodehouse, Commander of the Most Noble Order of the Bath, Governor in the name of Her Britannic Majesty of the Colony of British Guiana, by virtue of the powers conferred upon us by Her Majesty's Privy Council, do hereby proclaim and declare to all whom it may concern that we have this day granted to Sidney Farlance, a subject of Her Majesty the Queen, and to his heirs and assigns being determined by the possession of this authority, the sole right to prospect and mine for minerals of any kind whatsoever in the territory indicated and described in the sketch map at the foot of this authority, for the term of nine hundred and ninety-nine years from the date of these presents.

Given under our hand and seal this third day of January Eighteen Hundred and Fifty-six.

At the bottom of the sheet, below the map and description, was scrawled in a different hand: '*This is all for you S. F.*'

Harry Westler stuffed the letters into his pocket and took out his wallet. His heart was beating in a delirious rhythm of ecstasy and sending the blood roaring through his ears like the crashing crescendo of a symphony. The Gates of Paradise seemed to have opened up and deluged him with all their reservoirs of bliss. The whole world was his sweetheart. If the elderly gent whose strange nasal gargling he had dismissed so discourteously a short time ago had cannoned into him again at that moment, it is almost certain that Mr Westler would not have told him to go choke himself. He would probably have kissed him on both cheeks and given him a shilling.

For the first time in his life, Harry Westler counted out twenty hundred-pound notes as cheerfully as he would have counted them in.

'There you are, Jackie. And I'm not foolish – it takes a load off my mind. If you think of anything else I can do for you, just let me know.'

'I think you've done more than anyone could have asked,' she said generously. 'Won't you stay and have a drink?'

Mr Westler declined the offer firmly. He had no moral prejudice against drinking, and in fact he wanted a drink very badly, but more particularly he wanted to have it in a place where he would not have to place any more restraint on the shouting rhapsodies that were seething through his system like bubbles through champagne.

Some two hours later, when Simon Templar drifted into the house, he found Jacqueline still looking slightly dazed. She flung her arms around his neck and kissed him.

'Simon!' she gasped. 'You must be a mascot or something. You'll never guess what's happened.'

'I'll tell you exactly what's happened,' said the Saint calmly. 'Cousin Harry has been here, told you that he'd rather have dear old Granny's love letters than all the money in the world, and paid you the hell of a good price for them. At least I hope he paid you the hell of a good price.'

Jacqueline gaped at him weakly. 'He paid me two thousand pounds. But how on earth did you know? Why did he do it?'

'He did it because a lawyer called on him this morning and told him that Sidney Farlance had collared an absolutely priceless mining concession when he was in British Guiana, and that there was probably something about it in the letters which would be worth a million to whoever had them to prove his claim.'

She looked at him aghast. 'A mining concession? I don't remember anything about it—'

'You wouldn't,' said the Saint kindly. 'It wasn't there until I slipped it in when I got you to show me the letters at breakfast time this morning. I sat up for the other half of the night faking the best imitation I could of what I thought a concession ought to look like, and apparently it was good enough for Harry. Of course I was the lawyer who told him all about it, and I think I fed him the oil pretty smoothly, so perhaps there was some excuse for him. I take it that he was quite excited about it – I see he didn't even bother to take the envelopes—'

Jacqueline opened her mouth again, but what she was going to say with it remained a permanently unsolved question, for at that moment the unnecessarily vigorous ringing of a bell stopped her short. The Saint cocked his ears speculatively at the sound, and a rather pleased and seraphic smile worked itself into his face.

'I expect this is Harry coming back,' he said. 'He wasn't supposed to see me again until tomorrow, but I suppose he couldn't wait. He's probably tried to ring up at the address I had printed on my card, and discovered that there ain't no such lawyers as I was supposed to represent. It will be rather interesting to hear what he has to say.'

For once, however, Simon's guess was wrong. Instead of the indignant equine features of Harry Westler, he confronted the pink imploring features of the small and shapeless elderly gent with whom he had danced prettily around the gateposts the day before. The little man's face lighted up, and he bounced over the doorstep and seized the Saint joyfully by both lapels of his coat.

'Mnyng hlfwgl!' he crowed triumphantly. 'Ahkgap glglgl hndiuphwmp!'

Simon recoiled slightly. 'Yes. I know,' he said soothingly. 'But it's five o'clock on Fridays. Two bob every other yard.'

'Ogh hmbals!' said the little man.

He let go the Saint's coat, ducked under his arms, and scuttled on into the living-room.

'Hey!' said the Saint feebly.

'May I explain, sir?'

Another voice spoke from the doorway, and Simon perceived that the little man had not come alone. Someone else had taken his place on the threshold – a thin and mournful-looking individual whom the Saint somewhat pardonably took to be the little man's keeper.

'Are you looking after that?' he inquired resignedly. 'And why don't you keep it on a lead?'

The mournful-looking individual shook his head.

'That is Mr Horatio Ive, sir. He is a very rich man, but he suffers from an unfortunate impediment in his speech. Very few people can understand him. I go about with him as his interpreter, but I have been in bed for the last three days with a chill—'

A shrill war-whoop from the other room interrupted the explanation.

'We'd better go and see how he's getting on,' said the Saint.

'Mr Ive is very impulsive, sir,' went on the sad-looking interpreter. 'He was most anxious to see somebody here, and even though I was unable to accompany him he has called here several times alone. I understand that he found it impossible to make himself understood. He practically dragged me out of bed to come with him now.'

'What's he so excited about?' asked the Saint, as they walked towards the living-room.

'He's interested in some letters, sir, belonging to the late Mr. Laine. She happened to show them to him when they met once several years ago, and he wanted to buy them. She refused to sell them for sentimental reasons, but as soon as he read of her death he decided to approach her heirs.'

'Are you talking about her love letters from a bird called Sidney Farlance?' Simon asked hollowly.

'Yes, sir. The gentleman who worked in British Guiana. Mr Ive is prepared to pay something like ten thousand pounds – is anything the matter, sir?'

Simon Templar swallowed. 'Oh, nothing,' he said faintly. 'Nothing at all.'

They entered the living-room to interrupt a scene of

considerable excitement. Backing towards the wall, with a blank expression of alarm widening her eyes, Jacqueline Laine was staring dumbly at the small elderly gent, who was capering about in front of her like a frenzied Redskin, spluttering yard after yard of his incomprehensible adenoidal honks interspersed with wild piercing squeaks apparently expressive of intolerable joy. In each hand he held an envelope aloft like a banner.

As his interpreter came in, he turned and rushed towards him, loosing a fresh stream of noises like those of a hysterical duck.

'Mr Ive is saying, sir,' explained the interpreter, raising his voice harmoniously above the din, 'that each of those envelopes bears a perfect example of the British Guiana one-cent magenta stamp of 1856, of which only one specimen was previously believed to exist. Mr Ive is an ardent philatelist, sir, and these envelopes—'

Simon Templar blinked hazily at the small crudely printed stamp in the corner of the envelope which the little man was waving under his nose.

'You mean,' he said cautiously, 'that Mr Ive is really only interested in the envelopes?'

'Yes, sir.'

'Not the letters themselves?'

'Not the letters.'

'And he's been flapping around the house all this time trying to tell somebody about it?'

'Yes, sir.'

Simon Templar drew a deep breath. The foundations of the world were spinning giddily around his ears, but his natural resilience was inconquerable. He took out a handkerchief and mopped his brow.

'In that case,' he said contentedly, 'I'm sure we can do business. What do you say, Jacqueline?'

Jacqueline clutched his arm and nodded breathlessly.

'Hlgagtsk sweghlemlgh,' beamed Mr Ive.

The Well-Meaning Mayor

Sam Purdell never quite knew how he became Mayor. He was a small and portly man with a round blank face and a round blank mind, who had built up a moderately profitable furniture business over the last thirty-five years and acquired in the process a round pudding-faced wife, and a couple of suet dumplings of daughters.

But the inexhaustible zeal for improving the circumstances and morals of the community, that fierce drive of ambition and the twitching of the ears for the ecstatic homage of multitudes whenever he went abroad, that indomitable urge to be a leader of his people from which history's tyrants are born, was not naturally in him.

It is true that at the local reform club, of which he was a prominent member, he had often been stimulated by an appreciative audience and a large highball to lay down his views on the way in which he thought everything on earth ought to be run, but there was nothing outstandingly indicative of a political future in that.

This is a disease which is liable to attack even the most honest and respectable citizens in such circumstances. But the idea that he himself should ever occupy the position in which he might be called upon to put all those beautiful ideas into practice had never entered Sam Purdell's head in those simple early days; and if it had not been for the drive supplied by Al Eisenfeld, it might never have materialized.

'You ought to be in politics, Sam,' Al had insisted at the close of one of these perorations several years before.

Sam Purdell considered the suggestion. 'No, I wouldn't be clever enough,' he said modestly. To tell the truth, he had heard the suggestion before, had repudiated it before and had always wanted to hear it contradicted. Al Eisenfeld obliged him. It was the first time anybody had been so obliging.

This was three years before the columnist of the *Elmford News* was moved to inquire: 'How long does our mayor think he can kid reporters and deputations with his celebrated pose of injured innocence? We always thought it was a good act while it lasted; but isn't it time we had a new show?'

It was not the first time that it had been suggested in print that the naïve and childlike simplicity which was Sam Purdell's greatest charm was one of the shrewdest fronts for ingenious corruption which any politician had ever tried to put over on a batch of sane electors, but this was the nearest that any commentator had ever dared to come to saying that Sam Purdell was a crook.

It was a suggestion which left Sam a pained and puzzled man. He couldn't understand it. These adopted children of his, these citizens whose weal occupied his mind for twenty-four hours a day, were turning around to bite the hand that fed them. And the unkindest cut of all, the blow which struck at the roots of his faith in human gratitude, was that he had only tried to do his best for the city which had been delivered into his care.

For instance, there was a time when, dragged forth by the energy of one of his rotund daughters, he had climbed laboriously one Sunday afternoon to the top of the range of hills which shelter Elmford on the north. When he had got his wind and started looking around, he realized that from that vantage point there was a view which might have rejoiced the heart of any artist. Sam Purdell was no artist, but he blinked with simple pleasure at the panorama of rolling hills and wooded groves with the river winding between them like the track of a great silver snail; and when he came home again he had a beautiful idea.

'You know, we got one of the finest views in the state up there on those hills! I never saw it before, and I bet you didn't either. And why? Because there ain't no road goes up there; and when you get to my age it ain't so easy to go scrambling up through those trees and brush.'

'So what?' asked Al Eisenfeld, who was even less artistic and certainly more practical.

'So I tell you what we do,' said Sam, glowing with the ardour of his enthusiasm almost as much as with the after-effects of his unaccustomed exercise. 'We build a highway up there so they can drive out in their automobiles weekends and look around comfortably. It makes work for a lot of men, and it don't cost too much; and everybody in Elmford can get a lot of free pleasure out of it. Why, we might even get folks coming from all over the country to look at our view.'

He elaborated this inspiration with spluttering eagerness and before he had been talking for more than a quarter of an hour he had a convert.

'Sure, this is a great idea, Sam,' agreed Mr Eisenfeld warmly. 'You leave it to me. Why, I know – we'll call it the Purdell Highway . . .'

The Purdell Highway duly came into being at a cost of four million dollars. Al Eisenfeld saw to it. In the process of pushing Sam Purdell up the political tree he had engineered himself into the strategic post of Chairman of the Board of Aldermen, a position which gave him an interfering interest in practically all the activities of the city.

The fact that the cost was about twice as much as the original estimate was due to the unforeseen obstinacy of the owner of the land involved, who held out for about four times the price which it was worth. There were rumours that someone in the administration had acquired the territory under another name shortly before the deal was proposed, and had sold it to the city at his own price – rumours which shocked Sam Purdell to the core of his sensitive soul.

'Do you hear what they say, Al?' he complained, as soon as these slanderous stories reached his ears. 'They say I made one hundred thousand dollars graft out of the Purdell Highway! Now, why the hell should they say that?'

'You don't have to worry about what a few rats are saying, Sam,' replied Mr Eisenfeld soothingly. 'They're only jealous because you're so popular with the city. Hell, there are political wranglers who'd tell stories about the Archangel Gabriel himself if he was Mayor, just to try and discredit the administration so they could shove their own crooked party in. I'll look into it.'

Mr Eisenfeld's looking into it did not stop the same rumours circulating about the Purdell Bridge, which spanned the river from the southern end of the town and linked it with the State Highway, eliminating a detour of about twenty miles. What project, Sam Purdell asked, could he possibly have put forward that was more obviously designed for the convenience and prosperity of Elmford?

But there were whispers that the Bennsville Steel Company, which had obtained the contract for the bridge, had paid somebody fifty thousand dollars to see that their bid was accepted. A bid which was exactly fifty per cent higher than the one put in by their rivals.

'Do you know anything about somebody taking fifty thousand dollars to put this bid through?' demanded Sam Purdell wrathfully, when he heard about it; and Mr Eisenfeld was shocked.

'That's a wicked idea, Sam,' he protested. 'Everyone knows

this is the straightest administration Elmford ever had. Why, if I thought anybody was taking graft, I'd throw him out of the City Hall with my own hands.'

There were similar cases, each of which brought Sam a little nearer to the brink of bitter disillusion. Sometimes he said that it was only the unshaken loyalty of his family which stopped him from resigning his thankless labours and leaving Elmford to wallow in its own ungrateful slime. But most of all it was the loyalty and encouragement of Mr Eisenfeld. Mr Eisenfeld was a suave sleek man with none of Sam Purdell's rubicund and open-faced geniality, but he had a cheerful courage in such trying moments which was always ready to renew Sam Purdell's faith in human nature.

This cheerful courage shone with its old unfailing luminosity when Sam Purdell thrust the offending copy of the *Elmford News* which we have already referred to under Mr Eisenfeld's aggrieved and incredulous eyes.

'I'll show you what you do about that sort of writing, Sam,' said Mr Eisenfeld magnificently. 'You just take it like this—' He was going on to say that you tore it up, scattering the libellous fragments disdainfully to the four winds; but as he started to perform this heroic gesture his eye was arrested by the next paragraph in the same column, and he hesitated.

'Well, how do you take it?' asked the mayor peevishly.

Mr Eisenfeld said nothing for a second and the mayor looked over his shoulder to see what he was reading. 'Oh, that!' he said irritably. 'I don't know what that means. Do you know what it means, Al?'

'That' was a postscript about which Mr Purdell had some excuse to be puzzled. *'We hear that the Saint is back in this country. People who remember what he did in New York a few years ago might feel like inviting him to take a trip out here. We can promise he would find plenty of material on which to exercise his talents.'*

'What Saint are they talkin' about?' asked the mayor. 'I thought all the Saints was dead.'

'This one isn't,' said Mr Eisenfeld; but for the moment the significance of the name continued to elude him. He had an idea that he had heard it before and that it should have meant something definite to him. 'I think he was a crook who had a great run in New York a while back. No, I remember it now. Wasn't he a sort of freelance reformer who had some crazy idea he could clean up the city and put everything to right?'

He began to recall further details; and then as his memory improved he closed the subject abruptly. There were incidents among the stories that came filtering back into his recollection which gave him a vague discomfort in the pit of his stomach. It was ridiculous, of course – a cheap journalistic glorification of a common gangster; and yet, for some reason, certain stories which he remembered having read in the newspapers at the time made him feel that he would be happier if the Saint's visit to Elmford remained a theoretical proposition.

'We got lots of other more important things to think about, Sam,' he said abruptly, pushing the newspaper into the wastebasket. 'Look here – about this monument of yours on the Elmford Riviera ...'

The Elmford Riviera was the latest and most ambitious public work which the administration had undertaken up to that date. It was to be the crowning achievement in Sam Purdell's long list of benevolences toward his beloved citizens. A whole two miles of the river-bank had been acquired by the city and converted into a pleasure park which the sponsors of the scheme claimed would rival anything of its kind ever attempted.

At one end of it a beautiful casino had been erected where the citizens of Elmford might gorge themselves with food, deafen themselves with three orchestras and dance in tightly wedged ecstasy till their feet gave way. At the other end was to be provided a children's playground, staffed with trained attendants, where the infants of Elmford might be left to bawl their heads off under the most expert and scientific supervision while their elders stopped to enjoy the adult amenities of the place.

Behind the riverside drive, a concession had been arranged for an amusement park in which the populace could be shaken to pieces on a roller coaster, whirled off revolving discs, thrown about in barrels, skittered over the falls and generally enjoy all the other elaborate forms of discomfort which help to make the modern seeker after relaxation so contemptuous of the unimaginative makeshift tortures which less enlightened souls had to get along with in medieval days.

On the bank of the river itself, thousands of tons of sand had been imported to create an artificial beach where droves of holiday-makers could be herded together to blister and steam themselves into blissful imitations of the well-boiled prawn. It was, in fact, to be a place where Elmford might suffer all the horrors of Coney Island without the added torture of getting there.

And in the centre of this Elysian esplanade there was to be a monument to the man whose unquenchable devotion to the community had presented it with this last and most delightful blessing. Sam Purdell had been modestly diffident about the monument, but Mr Eisenfeld had insisted on it.

'You gotta have a monument, Sam,' he had said. 'The town owes it to you. Why, here you've been working for them all these years; and if you passed on tomorrow,' said Mr Eisenfeld, with his voice quivering at the mere thought of such a calamity, 'what would there be to show for all you've done?'

'There's the Purdell Highway,' said Sam deprecatingly, 'the Purdell Suspension Bridge, the Purdell—'

'That's nothing,' said Mr Eisenfeld largely. 'Those are just names. Why, in ten years after you die they won't mean any more than Grant or – or Pocahontas. What you oughta have is a monument of your own. Something with an inscription on it. I'll get the architect to design one.'

The monument had duly been designed – a sort of square, tapering tower eighty feet high, crowned by an eagle with outspread wings, on the base of which was to be a great marble plaque on which the beneficence and public-spiritedness of Samuel Purdell would be recorded for all time. It was about the details of the construction of this monument that Mr Eisenfeld had come to confer with the mayor.

'The thing is, Sam,' he explained, 'if this monument is gonna last, we gotta make it solid. They got the outside all built up now; but they say if we're gonna do the job properly, we got to fill it up with cement.'

'That'll take an awful lot of cement, Al,' Sam objected dubiously, casting an eye over the plans; but Mr Eisenfeld's generosity was not to be baulked.

'Well, what if it does? If the job's worth doin' at all, it's worth doin' properly. If you won't think of yourself, think of the city. Why, if we let this thing stay hollow and after a year or two it began to fall down, think what people from out of town would say!'

'What would they say?' asked Mr Purdell obtusely.

His adviser shuddered. 'They would say this was such a cheap place we couldn't even afford to put up a decent monument for our mayor. You wouldn't like people to say a thing like that about us, would you, Sam?'

The mayor thought it over. 'Okay, Al,' he said at length. 'Okay. But I don't deserve it, really I don't.'

Simon Templar would have agreed that the mayor had done nothing to deserve any more elaborate monument than a neat tombstone in some quiet worm cafeteria. But at that moment his knowledge of Elmford's politics was not so complete as it was very shortly to become.

When he saw Molly Provost slip the little automatic out of her bag he thought that the bullet was destined for the mayor; and in theory he approved. He had an engaging callousness about the value of political lives which, if universally shared, would make democracy an enchantingly simple business. But there were two policemen on motorcycles waiting to escort the mayoral car into the city, and the life of a good-looking girl struck him as being a matter for more serious consideration.

He felt that if she were really determined to solve all of Elmford's political problems by shooting the mayor in the duodenum, she should at least be persuaded to do it on some other occasion when she would have a better chance of getting away with it. Wherefore the Saint moved very quickly, so that his lean brown hand closed over hers just at the moment when she touched the trigger and turned the bullet down into the ground.

Neither Sam Purdell nor Al Eisenfeld, who were climbing into the car at that moment, even so much as looked around; and the motorcycle escort mercifully joined with them in instinctively attributing the detonation to the backfire of a passing truck.

It was such a small gun that the Saint's hand easily covered it. He held the gun and her hand together in a vice-like grip, smiling as if he were just greeting an old acquaintance, until the wail of the sirens died away.

'Have you got a licence to shoot mayors?' he inquired severely.

She had a small pale face which under a skilfully applied layer of cosmetics might have taken on a bright doll-like prettiness. It was not like that yet, but he had a sudden illuminating vision of her face as it might have been, painted and powdered, with plucked eyebrows and blackened eyelashes, subtly hardened. It was a type which he had seen often enough before, which he could recognize at once. Some of them he had seen happily married, bringing up adoring families; others . . .

For some reason the Saint thought that this girl ought not to be one of those others. Then he felt her arm go limp, and took the gun out of her unresisting hand. He put it away in his pocket.

'Come for a walk,' he said.

She shrugged dully. 'All right.'

He took her arm and led her down the block. Around the corner, out of sight of the mayor's house, he opened the door of the first of a line of parked cars. She got in resignedly. As he let in the clutch and the car slipped away under the pull of a smoothly whispering engine, she buried her face in her hands and sobbed silently.

The Saint let her have it out. He drove on thoughtfully, with a cigarette clipped between his lips, until the taller buildings of the business section rose up around them. In a quiet turning off one of the main streets of the town, he stopped the car outside a small restaurant and opened the door on her side to let her out. She dabbed her eyes and straightened her hat mechanically. As she looked around and realized where they were, she stopped with one foot on the running board.

'What have you brought me here for?' she asked stupidly.

'For lunch,' said the Saint calmly. 'If you feel like eating. For a drink, if you don't. For a chat, anyhow.'

She looked at him with fear and puzzlement still in her eyes. 'You needn't do that,' she said steadily. 'You can take me straight to the police station. We might as well get it over with.'

He shook his head. 'Do you really want to go to a police station?' he drawled. 'I'm not so fond of them myself, and usually they aren't fond of me. Wouldn't you rather have a drink?'

Suddenly she realized that the smile with which he was looking down at her wasn't a bit like the grimly triumphant smile which a detective should have worn. Nor, when she looked more closely, was there anything else about him that quite matched her idea of what a detective would be like.

It grieves the chronicle to record that her first impression was that he was too good-looking. But that was how she saw him. His tanned face was cut in a mould of rather reckless humour which didn't seem to fit in at all with the stodgy and prosaic backgrounds of the Law. He was tall, and he looked strong – her right hand still ached from the steel grip of his fingers – but it was a supple kind of strength that had no connection with mere bulk. Also he wore his clothes with a gay and careless kind of elegance which no sober police chief could have approved. The twinkle in his eyes was wholly friendly.

'Do you mean you didn't arrest me just now?' she asked uncertainly.

'I never arrested anybody in my life,' said the Saint cheerfully. 'In fact, when they shoot politicians I usually give them medals. Come on in and let's talk.'

Over a couple of martinis he explained himself further. 'My dear, I think it was an excellent scheme, on general principles. But the execution wasn't so good. When you've had as much experience in bumping people off as I have, you'll realize that it's no time to do it when a couple of cops are parked at the kerb a few yards away. I suppose you realize that they would have got you just about ten seconds after you created a vacancy for a new mayor?'

She was still staring at him rather blankly. 'I wasn't trying to do anything to the mayor,' she said. 'It was Al Eisenfeld I was going to shoot, and I wouldn't have cared if they did get me afterwards.'

The Saint frowned. 'You mean the seedy sort of bird who was with the mayor?'

She nodded. 'He's the real boss of the town. The mayor is just a figurehead.'

'Other people don't seem to think he's as dumb as he looks,' Simon remarked.

'They don't know. There's nothing wrong with Purdell, but Eisenfeld—'

'Maybe you have inside information,' said the Saint.

She looked at him over her clenched fists, dry-eyed and defiant. 'If there were any justice in the world Al Eisenfeld would be executed.'

The Saint raised his eyebrows and she read the thought in his mind and met it with cynical denial.

'Oh no – not in that way. There's no murder charge that anyone could bring against him. You couldn't bring any legal evidence in any court of law that he'd ever done any physical harm to anyone that I ever heard of. But I know that he is a murderer. He killed my father.'

And the Saint waited without interruption. The story came tumbling out in a tangle of words that bit into his brain with a burden of meaning that was one of the most profound and illuminating surprises that he had known for some considerable time. It was so easy to talk to him that before long he knew nearly as much as she did herself. He was such an easy and understanding listener that somehow it never seemed strange to her until afterwards that she had been pouring out so much to a man she had known for less than an hour.

Perhaps it was not such an extraordinary story as such stories go – perhaps many people would have shrugged it away as one of the commonplace tragedies of a hard-boiled world.

'This fellow Schmidt was a pal of Eisenfeld's. So they tried to make Dad lay off him. Dad wouldn't listen to them. He was Police Commissioner before this administration came in and he'd never listened to any politicians in his life. He always said that he went into the force as an honest man and he was going to stay that way. So when they found they couldn't keep him quiet, they framed him. They made out that he was behind practically every racket in the town. He knew the game too well to be able to kid himself. He was booked to be thrown out of the force in disgrace, and probably sent to jail as well. How could he hope to clear himself?

'The evidence which he had collected against Schmidt was in the District Attorney's office, but when Dad tried to bring that up they said that the safe had been burgled and it was gone. They even turned it around to make it look as if Dad had got rid of the evidence himself – the very thing he had told them he would never agree to do, so – I suppose he took the only way out that he could see. I suppose you'd say he was a coward to do it, but how could you ever know what he must have been suffering?'

'When was this?' asked the Saint quietly.

'Last night. He – shot himself. With his police gun. The shot woke me up. I – found him. I suppose I must have gone mad too. This morning I made up my mind. I came out to do the only thing that was left. I didn't care what happened to me after that.' She broke off helplessly. 'Oh, I must have been crazy! But I couldn't think of anything else. Why should he be able to get away with it? Why should he?' she sobbed.

'Don't worry,' said the Saint quietly. 'He won't.' He spoke with a quiet and matter-of-fact certainty which was more than a mere conventional encouragement. It made her look at him with a perplexity which she had been able to forget while he made her talk to him reawakening in her gaze.

For the first time since they had sat down, it seemed, she was able to remember that she still knew nothing about him;

that he was no more than a sympathetic stranger who had loomed up unheralded and unintroduced out of the fog which had still not completely cleared from her mind.

'Of course you aren't a detective,' she said childishly. 'I'd have recognized you if you were; but if you aren't, what are you?'

He smiled. 'I'm the guy who gives all the detectives something to work for,' he said. 'I'm the source of more aches in the heads of the ungodly than I should like to boast about. I am Trouble, Incorporated – President Simon Templar, at your service. They call me the Saint.'

'What does that mean?' she asked helplessly.

In the ordinary way Simon Templar, who had no spontaneous modesty bred into his composition, would have felt a slight twinge of disappointment that his reputation had not preceded him even to that out-of-the-way corner of the American continent. But he realized that there was no legitimate reason why she should have reacted more dramatically to the revelation of his identity, and for once he was not excessively discontented to remain unrecognized.

There were practical disadvantages to the indulgence of this human weakness for publicity which, at that particular moment and in that particular town, he was prepared to do without. He shook his head with the same lazy grin that was so extraordinarily comforting and clear-sighted.

'Nothing that you need worry about,' he said. 'Just write me down as a bloke who never could mind his own business, and give me some more of the inside dope about Al.'

'There isn't a lot more to tell you,' she said. 'I think I've already given you almost everything I know.'

'Doesn't anyone else in the town know it?'

'Hardly anybody. There are one or two people who guess how things really are, but if they tried to argue about it they'd only get laughed at. He's clever enough to have everybody believing that he's just Sam Purdell's mouthpiece; but it's the other way around. Sam Purdell really is dumb. He doesn't know what it's all about. He thinks of nothing but his highways and parks and bridges, and he honestly believes that he's only doing the best he can for the city.

'He doesn't get any graft out of it. Al gets all that; and he's clever enough to work it so that everybody thinks he's innocent and Sam Purdell is the really smart guy who's getting all the money out of it – even the Board of Aldermen think so. Dad used to talk to me about all his cases and he found out a lot about Eisenfeld while he was investigating this man Schmidt. He'd have gone after Eisenfeld himself next – if he'd been able to keep going. Perhaps Eisenfeld knew it and that made him more vicious.'

'He didn't have any evidence against Eisenfeld?'

'Only a little. Hardly anything if you're talking about legal evidence, but he knew plenty of things he might have proven if he had been given time. That's how it is, anyway.'

The Saint lighted a cigarette and gazed at her thoughtfully through a stream of smoke. 'You understood a lot more than I did, Molly,' he murmured. 'But it's a great idea . . . And the more I think of it, the more I think you must be right.'

He let his mind play around with the situation for a moment. Maybe he was too subtle himself, but there was something about that fundamental master stroke of Mr Eisenfeld's cunning that appealed to his incorrigible sense of the artistry of corruption. To be the power behind the scenes while some lifelike figurehead stood up to receive the rotten eggs was just ordinary astuteness.

But to choose for that figurehead a man who was so honest and stupid that it would take an earthquake to make him realize what was going on, and whose honest stupidity might appear to less simple-minded inquirers as an impudent disguise for double-dyed villainy – that indicated a quality of guile to which Simon Templar raised an appreciative hat. But his admiration of Mr Eisenfeld's ingenuity was purely theoretical.

He made a note of the girl's address. 'I'll keep the gun,' he said before they parted. 'You won't be needing it, and I shouldn't like you to lose your head again when I wasn't around to interfere.' His blue eyes held her for a moment with quiet confidence. 'Al Eisenfeld is going to be dealt with – I promise you that. Right at the moment I can't go into further details.'

It was one of his many mysteries that the fantastic promise failed to rouse her to utter incredulity. Afterwards she would be incredulous, after he had fulfilled the promise even more so; but while she listened at that moment there was a spell about him which made all miracles seem possible.

'What can you do?' she asked, in the blind but indescribably inspiring belief that there must be some magic which he could achieve.

'I have my methods,' said the Saint. 'I stopped off here anyhow because I was interested in the stories I'd heard about this town, and we'll call it lucky that I happened to be out trying to take a look at the mayor when you had your brainstorm. Just do one thing for me. Whatever happens, don't tell a living soul about this lunch. Forget that you ever met me or heard of me. Let me do the remembering.'

Mr Eisenfeld's memory was less retentive. When he came home a few nights later, he had completely forgotten the fleeting squirm of uneasiness which the reference to the Saint in the *Elmford News* had given him. He had almost as completely forgotten his late Police Commissioner; although when he did remember him, it was with a feeling of pleasant satisfaction that he had been so easily got rid of.

Already he had selected another occupant for that conveniently vacated office, who he was assured would prove more amenable to reason. And that night he was expecting another visitor whose mission would give him an almost equal satisfaction.

The visitor arrived punctually, and was hospitably received with a highball and a cigar. After a brief exchange of cordial commonplaces, the visitor produced a bulging wallet and slid it casually across the table. In the same casual manner Mr Eisenfeld picked it up, inspected the contents and slipped it into his pocket. After which the two men refilled their glasses and smoked for a while in companionable silence.

'We got the last of that cement delivered yesterday,' remarked the visitor, in the same way that he might have bridged a conversational hiatus with some bromidic comment on the weather.

Mr Eisenfeld nodded. 'Yeah, I saw it. They got the monument about one quarter full already – I was by there this afternoon.'

Mr Schmidt gazed vacantly at the ceiling. 'Any time you've got any other job like that, we'll still be making good cement,' he said, with the same studied casualness. 'You know we always like to look after anyone who can put a bit of business our way.'

'Sure, I'll remember it,' said Mr Eisenfeld amiably.

Mr Schmidt fingered his chin. 'Too bad about Provost, wasn't it?' he remarked.

'Yeah,' agreed Mr Eisenfeld, 'too bad.'

Half an hour later he escorted his guest out to his car. The light over the porch had gone out when he returned to the house, and without giving it any serious thought he attributed the failure to a blown fuse or a faulty bulb. He was in too good a humour to be annoyed by it; and he was actually humming complacently to himself as he groped his way up the dark steps.

The light in the hall had gone out as well, and he frowned

faintly over the idle deduction that it must have been a fuse. He pushed through the door and turned to close it; and then a hand clamped over his mouth, and something hard and uncongenial pressed into the small of his back. A gentle voice spoke chillingly in his ear.

'Just one word' – it whispered invitingly – 'just one word out of you, Al, and your life is going to be even shorter than I expected.'

Mr Eisenfeld stood still, with his muscles rigid. He was not a physical coward but the grip which held his head pressed back against the body of the unknown man behind him had a firm competence which announced that there were adequate sinews behind it to back up its persuasion in any hand-to-hand struggle.

Also, the object which prodded into the middle of his spine constituted an argument in itself which he was wise enough to understand. The clasp on his mouth relaxed tentatively and slid down to rest lightly on his throat. The same gentle voice breathed again on his right eardrum.

'Let us go out into the great open spaces and look at the night,' said the Saint.

Mr Eisenfeld allowed himself to be conducted back down the walk over which he had just returned. He had very little choice in the matter. The gun of the uninvited guest remained glued to his backbone as if it intended to take root there, and he knew that the fingers which rested so caressingly on his windpipe would have detected the first shout he tried to utter before it could reach his vocal cords. A few yards down the road a car waited with its lights out. They stopped beside it.

'Open the door and get in,' said the Saint.

Mr Eisenfeld obeyed. The gun slipped round from his back to his left side as his escort followed him into the seat behind the wheel. Simon started the engine and reached over to slip the gear lever into first. The headlights were switched on as they moved away from the curb; and Mr Eisenfeld found his first opportunity to give vent to the emotions that were chasing themselves through his system.

'What the hell's the idea of this?' he demanded violently.

'We're going for a little drive, dear old bird,' answered the Saint. 'But I promise you won't have to walk home. My intentions are more honourable than anyone like you could easily imagine.'

'If you're trying to kidnap me,' Eisenfeld blustered, 'I'm telling you you can't get away with it. I'll see that you get what's coming to you! Why, you—'

Simon let him make his speech without interruption. The lights of the residential section twinkled steadily past them, and presently even Eisenfeld's flood of outraged eloquence dwindled away before that impenetrable calm.

They drove on over the practically deserted roads – it was after midnight, and there were very few attractions in that area to induce the pious citizens of Elmford to lose their beauty sleep – and presently Mr Eisenfeld realized that their route would take them past the site of the almost completed Elmford Riviera on the bank of the river above the town.

He was right in his deduction, except for the word 'past'. As a matter of fact, the car jolted off the main highway on to the unfinished road which led down to Elmford's playground; and exactly in the middle of the two-mile esplanade, under the very shadow of the central monument which Sam Purdell had been so modestly unwilling to accept, it stopped.

'This is as far as we go,' said the Saint, and motioned politely to the door.

Mr Eisenfeld got out. He was sweating a little with perfectly natural fear, and above that there was a growing cloud of mystification through which he was trying to discover some coherent design in the extraordinary series of events which had enveloped him in those last few minutes. He seemed to be caught up in the machinery of some hideous nightmare, in which the horror was intensified by the fact that he could see no reason in the way it moved. If he was indeed the victim of an attempt at kidnapping, he couldn't understand why he should have been brought to a place like that; but just then there was no other explanation that he could see.

The spidery lines of scaffolding on the monument rose up in a futuristic filigree over his head, and at the top of it the shadowy outlines of the chute where the cement was mixed and poured into the hollow mould of stone roosted like a grotesque and angular prehistoric bird.

'Now we'll climb up and look at the view,' said the Saint.

Still wondering, Mr Eisenfeld felt himself steered towards a ladder which ran up one side of the scaffolding. He climbed mechanically, as he was ordered, while a stream of unanswerable questions drummed bewilderingly through his brain.

Once the wild idea came to him to kick downwards at the head of the man who followed him; but when he looked down he saw that the head was several rungs below his feet, keeping a safely measured distance, and when he stopped climbing, the man behind him stopped also.

Eisenfeld went on, up through the dark. He could have shouted then, but he knew that he was a mile or more from the nearest person who might have heard him.

They came out on the plank staging which ran around the top of the monument. A moment later, as he looked back, he saw the silhouette of his unaccountable kidnapper rising up against the dimly luminous background of stars and reaching the platform to lean lazily against one of the ragged ends of scaffold pole which rose above the narrow catwalk. Behind him, the hollow shaft of the monument was a square void of deep blackness in the surrounding dark.

'This is the end of your journey, Al,' said the stranger softly. 'But before you go, there are just one or two things I'd like to remind you about. Also, we haven't been properly introduced, which is probably making things rather difficult for you. You had better know me . . . I am the Saint.'

Eisenfeld started and almost overbalanced. Where had he heard that name before? Suddenly he remembered, and an uncanny chill crawled over his flesh.

'There are various reasons why it doesn't seem necessary for you to go on living,' went on that very gentle and dispassionate voice, 'and your ugly face is only one of them. This is a pretty cockeyed world when you take it all around, but people like you don't improve it. Also, I have heard a story from a girl called Molly Provost – her father was Police Commissioner until Tuesday night, I believe.'

'She's a liar,' gasped Eisenfeld hoarsely. 'You're crazy! Listen—'

He would have sworn that the stranger had never touched him except with his gun since they got into the car, but suddenly an electric flashlight spilled a tiny strip of luminance over the boards between them, and in the bright centre of the beam he saw the other's hand running through the contents of a wallet which looked somehow familiar. All at once Eisenfeld recognized it and clutched unbelievingly at his pocket. The wallet which his guest had given him an hour ago was gone; and Eisenfeld's heart almost stopped beating.

'What are you doing with that?' he croaked.

'Just seeing how much this instalment of graft is worth,' answered the Saint calmly. 'And it looks exactly like thirty thousand dollars to me. Well, it might have been more, but I suppose it will have to do. I promised Molly that I'd see she was looked after, but I don't see why it shouldn't be at your expense. Part of this is your commission for getting this cenotaph filled with cement, isn't it? . . . It seems very appropriate.'

Eisenfeld's throat constricted, and the blood began to

pound in his temples. 'I'll get you for this,' he snarled. 'You lousy crook.'

'Maybe I am a crook,' said the Saint, in a voice that was no more than a breath of sound in the still night. 'But in between times I'm something more. In my simple way I am a kind of justice ... Do you know any good reason why you should wait any longer for what you deserve?'

There is a time in every man's life when he knows beyond doubt or common fear that the threads of destiny are running out. It had happened to Al Eisenfeld too suddenly for him to understand – he had no time to look back and count the incredible minutes in which his world had been turned upside-down. Perhaps he himself had no clear idea what he was doing, but he knew that he was hearing death in the quiet voice that spoke out of the darkness in front of him. His muscles carried him away without any conscious command from his brain, and he was unaware of the queer growling cry that rattled in his throat.

There was a crash of sound in front of him, as he sprang blindly forward, and a tongue of reddish-orange flame spat out of the darkness almost in his face ...

Simon Templar steadied himself on one of the scaffold poles and stared down into the square black mould of the monument; but there was nothing that he could see, and the silence was unbroken. After a while his fingers let go the gun, and a couple of seconds later the thud of its burying itself in the wet cement at the bottom of the shaft echoed hollowly back to him.

Presently he climbed up to the chute from which the monument was being filled. He found a great mound of sacks of cement stacked beside it ready for use, and, after a little more search, a hose conveniently arranged to provide water. He was busy for three hours before he decided that he had done enough ...

'And knowing that these thoughts are beating in all our hearts,' boomed the voice of the Distinguished Personage through eight loudspeakers, 'it will always be my proudest memory that I was deemed worthy of the honour of unveiling this eternal testimonial to the man who has devoted his life to the task of making the people of Elmford proud and happy in their great city – the mayor whom you all know and love so well, Sam Purdell!'

The flag which covered the carved inscription on the base of the Purdell memorial fluttered down. A burst of well-organized cheering volleyed from five thousand throats. The cameramen dashed forward with clicking shutters. The bandmaster raised his baton. The brass and wood winds inflated their lungs. A small urchin close to the platform swallowed a piece of chewing gum, choked, and began to cry . . . The strains of 'The Star-spangled Banner' blasted throbbingly through the afternoon air.

Then, to the accompaniment of a fresh howl of cheering, Sam Purdell stepped to the microphone. He wiped his eyes and swallowed once or twice before he spoke.

'My friends,' he said, 'this is not a time when I would ask you to listen to a speech. There ain't – isn't anything I can think of worthy of this honour you have done me. I can only repeat the promise which you have all heard me make before – that while I am Mayor of this city there will be only one principle in everything over which I have control: Honesty and a square deal for every man, woman and child in Elmford.'

There was more wild applause.

The cheers followed his car as he drove away accompanied by his round perspiring wife and his round perspiring daughters. Mr. Purdell clutched his hand in a warm moist grip. 'That was such a beautiful speech you made, Sam,' she said a little tearfully.

Sam Purdell shook his head. He had one secret sorrow. 'I wish Al could have been there,' he said.

The Benevolent Burglary

'Louis Umbert?' Simon Templar repeated vaguely. 'I don't know ... I think I read something about him in a newspaper some time ago, but I'm blowed if I can remember what it was. I can't keep track of every small-time crook in creation. What's he been doing?'

'I just thought you might know something about him,' Chief Inspector Teal answered evasively.

He sat on the edge of a chair and turned his bowler hat in his pudgy hands, looking almost comically like an elephant-ine edition of an office-boy trying to put over a new excuse for taking an afternoon off. He glowered ferociously around the sunny room in which Simon was calmly continuing to eat breakfast, and racked his brain for inspiration to keep the interview going.

For the truth was that Chief Inspector Claud Eustace Teal had not called on the Saint for information about Mr Louis Umbert. Or anybody else in the same category. He had a highly efficient Records Office at his disposal down at Scotland Yard, which was maintained for the sole purpose of answering questions like that. The name was simply an excuse that he had grabbed out of his head while he was on his way up in the lift. Because there was really only one lawbreaker about whom Teal needed to go to Simon Templar for information – and that was the Saint himself.

Not that even that was likely to be very profitable, either; but Teal couldn't help it. He made the pilgrimage in the same spirit as a man who had lived under the shadow of a volcano that had been quiescent for some time might climb up to peep into the crater, with the fond hope that it might be good enough to tell him when and how it next intended to erupt. He knew he was only making a fool of himself; but that was only part of the cross he had to bear. There were times when, however hard he tried to master them, the thoughts of all the lawless mischief which that tireless buccaneer might be cooking up in secret filled his mind with such horrific nightmares that he had to do something about them or explode. The trouble was that the only thing he could think of doing was to go and have another look at the Saint in person, as if he hoped that he would be lucky enough to arrive at the very moment when Simon had decided to write out his plans on a large board and wear them round his neck. The knowledge of his own futility raised Mr Teal's blood pressure to the point that actively endangered his health; but he could no more have kept himself away from the Saint's apartment, when one of those fits of morbid uneasiness seized him, than he could have danced in a ballet.

He stuck a piece of chewing gum into his mouth and bit on it with massive violence, knowing perfectly well that the Saint knew exactly what was the matter with him, and that the Saint was probably trying politely not to laugh out loud. His smouldering eyes swivelled back to the Saint with belligerent defiance. If he caught so much as the shadow of a grin on that infernally handsome face . . .

But the Saint wasn't grinning. He wasn't paying any particular attention to Teal at all. He was reading his newspaper again; and Teal heard him murmur: 'Well, isn't that interesting?'

'Isn't what interesting?' growled the detective aggressively.

Simon folded the sheet.

'I see that the public is invited to an exhibition of Mr Elliott

Vascoe's art treasures at Mr Vascoe's house in Hammersmith. Admission will be five shillings, and all the proceeds will go to charity. The exhibition will be opened by Princess Eunice of Greece.'

Teal stiffened. He had the dizzy sense of unreality that would overwhelm a man who had been day-dreaming about what he would do if his uncle suddenly died and left him a million pounds, if a man walked straight into his office and said, 'Your uncle died and left you a million pounds.'

'Were you thinking of taking over any of those art treasures?' he inquired menacingly. 'Because if you were—'

'I've often thought about it,' said the Saint shamelessly. 'I think it's a crime for Vascoe to have so many of them. He doesn't know any more about art than a cow in a field, but he's got enough dough to buy anything his advisers tell him is worth buying, and it gives him something to swank about. It would be an act of virtue to take over his collection; but I suppose you wouldn't see it that way.'

Mr Teal's brow blackened. He could hardly believe his ears, and if he had stopped to think he wouldn't have believed them. He didn't stop.

'No, I wouldn't!' he squeaked. 'Now get this, Saint. You can get away with just so much of your line and no more. You're going to leave Vascoe's exhibition alone, or by heavens—'

'Of course I'm going to leave it alone,' said the Saint mildly. 'My paths are the paths of righteousness, and my ways are the ways of peace. You know me, Claud. Vascoe will get what's coming to him in due time, but who am I to take it upon myself to dish it out?'

'You said—'

'I said that I'd often thought about taking over some of his art treasures. But is it a crime to think? If it was, there'd be more criminals than you could build jails for. Pass the marmalade. And try not to look so disappointed.' The mockery in Simon's blue eyes was bright enough now for even Teal to realize that the Saint was deliberately taking him over the jumps once again. 'Anyone might think you wanted me to turn into a crook – and is that the right attitude for a policeman to have?'

Between Simon Templar and Mr Elliot Vascoe, millionaire and self-styled art connoisseur, no love at all was lost. Simon disliked Vascoe on principle, because he disliked all fat loud-mouthed parvenus who took care to obtain great publicity for their charitable works while they practised all kinds of small meannesses on their employees. Vascoe hated the Saint because Simon had once happened to witness a motor accident in which Vascoe was driving and a child was injured, and Vascoe had made the mistake of offering Simon a hundred pounds to forget what he had seen. That grievous error had not only failed to save Mr Vascoe a penny of the fines and damages which he was subsequently compelled to pay, but it had earned him a punch on the nose which he need not otherwise have suffered.

Vascoe had made his money quickly, and the curse of the *nouveau riche* had fallen upon him. Himself debarred for ever from the possibility of being a gentleman, either by birth or breeding or native temperament, he had made up for it by carrying snobbery to new and rarely unequalled heights. Besides works of art, he collected titles: for high-sounding names, and all the more obvious trappings of nobility, he had an almost fawning adoration. Therefore he provided lavish entertainment for any undiscriminating notables whom he could lure into his house with the attractions of his Parisian chef and his very excellent wine cellar, and contrived to get his name bracketed with those who were more discriminating by angling for them with the bait of charity, which it was difficult for them to refuse.

In a great many ways, Mr Elliot Vascoe was the type of man whose excessive wealth would have been a natural target for one of the Saint's raids on those undesirable citizens whom he included in the comprehensive and descriptive classification of 'the ungodly'; but the truth is that up till then the Saint had never been interested enough to do anything about it. There were many other undesirable citizens whose unpleasantness was no less immune from the cumbersome interference of the Law, but whose villainies were on a larger scale and whose continued putrescence was a more blatant challenge to the Saint's self-appointed mission of justice. With so much egregiously inviting material living ready to hand, it was perhaps natural that Simon should feel himself entitled to pick and choose, should tend to be what some critics might have called a trifle finicky in his selection of the specimens of ungodliness to be bopped on the bazook. He couldn't use all of them, much as he would have liked to.

But in Simon Templar's impulsive life there was a factor of Destiny that was always taking such decisions out of his hands. Anyone with a less sublime faith in his guiding star might have called it coincidence, but to the Saint that word was merely a chicken-hearted half-truth. Certain things were ordained; and when the signs pointed there was no turning back.

Two days after Teal's warning, he was speeding back to the city after an afternoon's swimming and basking in the sun at the Oaklands Park Pool, when he saw a small coupé of rather ancient vintage standing by the roadside. The bonnet of the coupé was open, and a young man was very busy with the engine; he seemed to be considerably flustered, and from the quantity of oil on his face and forearms the success of his efforts seemed to bear no relation to the amount of energy he had put into them. Near the car stood a remarkably pretty girl, and she was what really caught the Saint's eye. She seemed distressed and frightened, twisting her hands nervously together and looking as if she was on the verge of tears.

Simon had flashed past before he realized that he knew her – he had met her at a dance some weeks before. His distaste for Mr Elliot Vascoe did not apply to Vascoe's slim, auburn-haired daughter, whom Simon would have been prepared to put forward in any company as a triumphant refutation of the theories of heredity. He jammed on his brakes and backed up to the breakdown.

'Hullo, Meryl,' he said. 'Is there anything I can do?'

'If you can make this Chinese washing machine go,' said the young man, raising his smeared face from the bowels of the engine, 'you are not only a better man than I am, but I expect you can invent linotypes in your sleep.'

'This is Mr Fulton – Mr Templar.' The girl made the introduction with breathless haste. 'We've been here for three-quarters of an hour—'

The Saint started to get out.

'I never was much of a mechanic,' he murmured. 'But if I can unscrew anything or screw anything up . . .'

'That wouldn't be any good – Bill knows everything about cars, and he's already taken it to pieces twice.' The girl's voice was shaky with dawning hope. 'But if you could take me home yourself . . . I've simply *got* to be back before seven! Do you think you could do it?'

Her tone was so frantic that she made it sound like a matter of life and death.

Simon glanced at his watch, and at the milometer on the dashboard. It would be about fifteen miles to Hammersmith, and it was less than twenty minutes to seven.

'I can try,' he said, and turned to Fulton. 'What about you – will you come on this death-defying ride?'

Fulton shook his head. He was a few years older than the girl, and Simon liked the clean-cut good looks of him.

'Don't worry about me,' he said. 'You try to get Meryl back. I'm going to make this prehistoric wreck move under its own steam if I stay here all night.'

Meryl Vascoe was already in the Saint's car; and Simon returned to the wheel with a grin and a shrug. For a little while he was completely occupied with finding out just how high an unlawful speed he could make through traffic. When the Saint set out to do some fast travelling it was a hair-raising performance; but Meryl Vascoe's hair was fortunately raise-proof. She spent some minutes repairing various imperceptible details of her almost flawless face, and then she touched his knee anxiously.

'When we get there, just put me down at the corner,' she said. 'I'll run the rest of the way. You see, if Father saw you drive up to the door he'd be sure to ask questions.'

' "What are you doing with that scoundrel?" ' Simon said melodramatically. ' "Don't you know that he can't be trusted with a decent woman?" '

She laughed.

'That isn't what I'm worried about,' she said. 'Though I don't suppose he'd be very enthusiastic about our being together – I haven't forgotten what a scene we had about that dance where you picked me up and took me off to the Café de Paris for the rest of the night. But the point is that I don't want him to know that I've been out driving at all.'

'Why not?' asked the Saint, reasonably. 'The sun is shining. London is beginning to develop its summer smell. What could you do that would be better and healthier than taking a day in the country?'

She looked at him guardedly, hesitating.

'Well – then I ought to have gone out in my own car, with one of the chauffeurs. But he'd be furious if he knew I'd been out with Bill Fulton, so when I went out this afternoon I told him that I was going shopping with an old school friend.'

Simon groaned.

'That old school friend – she does work long hours,' he protested. 'I should have thought you could have invented something better than that. However, I take it that Papa doesn't like Bill Fulton, and you do, so you meet him on the quiet. That's sensible enough. But what's your father got against him? He looked good enough to me. Does he wash, or something?'

'You don't have to insult my father when I'm listening,' she said stiffly; and then, in another moment, the emotions inside overcame her loyalty. 'I suppose it's because Bill isn't rich and hasn't got a title or anything . . . And then there's the Comte de Beaucroix—'

Simon swerved the car dizzily under the arm of a policeman who was trying to hold them up.

'Who?' he demanded.

'The Comte de Beaucroix – he's staying with us just now. He had to go and see some lawyers this afternoon, but he'll be back for dinner; and if I'm not home and dressed when they ring the gong, Father'll have a fit.'

'Poor little rich girl,' said the Saint sympathetically. 'So you have to dash home to play hostess to another of your father's expensive phonies.'

'Oh, no; this one's perfectly genuine. He's quite nice, really, only he's so wet. But Father's been caught too often before. He got hold of this Count's passport and took it down to the French Consulate, and they said it was quite all right.'

'The idea being,' Simon commented shrewdly, 'that Papa doesn't want any comebacks after he's made you the Countess de Beaucroix.'

She didn't answer at once; and Simon himself was busy with the task of passing a truck on the wrong side, whizzing over a crossing while the lights changed from amber to red, and making a skidding turn under the nose of a taxi at the next red light. But there was something about him that had always had an uncanny knack of unlocking other people's conventional reserves; and besides, they had once danced together and talked much delightful nonsense while all the conventional inhabitants of London slept.

She found herself saying: 'You see, all Bill's got is his radio business, and he's invented a new valve that's going to make him a fortune but I got Father to lend him the five thousand pounds Bill needed to develop it. Father gave him the money, but he made Bill sign a sort of mortgage that gave Father the right to take his invention away from him if the money isn't paid back. Now Father says that if Bill tries to marry me he'll foreclose, and Bill wouldn't have anything left. I know how Bill's getting on, and I know if he only has a few months more he'll be able to pay Father back ten times over.'

'Can't you wait those few months?' asked the Saint. 'If Bill's on to something as good as that—'

She shook her head.

'But Father says that if I don't marry the Comte de Beaucroix as soon as he asks me to – and I know he's going to – he'll foreclose on Bill anyway, and Bill won't get a penny for all his work.' Her voice broke, and when Simon glanced at her quickly he saw the shine of tears in her eyes. 'Bill doesn't know – if you tell him, I'll kill you! But he can't understand what's the matter with me. And I – I—' Her lovely face tightened with a strange bitterness. 'I always thought these things only happened in pictures,' she said huskily. 'How can any man *be* like that?'

'You wouldn't know, darling,' said the Saint gently.

That was all he said at the time but at the same moment he resolved that he would invest five of his shillings in an admission to Mr Elliot Vascoe's exhibition. Certain things were indubitably Ordained . . .

He arrived just after the official opening, on the first day.

The rooms in which the exhibition was being held were crowded with aspiring and perspiring socialites, lured there either in the hope of collecting one of Mr Vascoe's bacchanalian invitations to dinner, or because they hoped to be recognized by other socialites, or because they hoped to be mistaken for connoisseurs of Art, or just because they hadn't the courage to let anyone think that they couldn't spend five shillings on charity just as easily as anyone else. Simon Templar shouldered his way through them until he sighted Vascoe. He had done some thinking since he drove Meryl home, and it had only confirmed him in his conviction that Nemesis was due to overtake Mr Vascoe at last. At the same time, Simon saw no reason why he shouldn't deal himself in on the party.

With Vascoe and Meryl was a tall and immaculately dressed young man with a pink face whose amiable stupidity was accentuated by a chin that began too late and a forehead that stopped too soon. Simon had no difficulty in identifying him as the Comte de Beaucroix, and that was how Meryl introduced him before Vascoe turned round and recognized his unwelcome visitor.

'How did you get in here?' he brayed.

'Through the front door,' said the Saint genially. 'I put down my five bob, and they told me to walk right in. It's a public exhibition, I believe. Did you come in on a free pass?'

Vascoe recovered himself with difficulty, but his large face remained an ugly purple.

'Come to have a look round, have you?' he asked offensively. 'Well, you can look as much as you like. I flatter myself this place is burglar-proof.'

Meryl turned white; and the Count tittered. Other guests who were within earshot hovered expectantly – some of them, one might have thought, hopefully. But if they were waiting for a prompt and swift outbreak of violence, or even a sharp and candid repartee, they were doomed to disappointment. The Saint smiled with unruffled good humour.

'Burglar-proof, is it?' he said tolerantly. 'You really think it's burglar-proof. Well, well, *well!*' He patted Mr Vascoe's bald head affectionately. 'Now I'll tell you what I'll do, Fatty. I'll bet you five thousand pounds it's burgled within a week.'

For a moment Vascoe seemed to be in a tangle with his own vocal cords. He could only stand there and gasp like a fish.

'You – you have the effrontery to come here and tell me you're going to burgle my house?' he spluttered. 'You – you ruffian! I'll have you handed over to the police! I never heard of such – such – such—'

'I haven't committed any crime yet, that I know of,' said the Saint patiently. 'I'm simply offering you a sporting bet. Of course, if you're frightened of losing—'

'Such damned insolence!' howled Vascoe furiously. 'I've got detectives here—'

He looked wildly around for them.

'Or if five thousand quid is too much for you . . .' Simon continued imperturbably.

'I'll take your five thousand pounds,' Vascoe retorted viciously. 'If you've got that much money. I'd be glad to break you as well as see you sent to jail. And if anything happens after this, the police will know who to look for!'

'That will be quite a chance for them,' said the Saint. 'And now, in the circumstances, I think we ought to have a stakeholder.'

He scanned the circle of faces that had gathered round them, and singled out a dark cadaverous-looking man who was absorbing the scene from the background with an air of disillusioned melancholy.

'I see Morgan Dean of the *Daily Mail* over there,' he said. 'Suppose we each give him our cheques for five thousand pounds. He can pay them into his own bank and write a cheque for ten thousand when the bet's settled. Then there won't be any difficulty about the winner collecting. What about it, Dean?'

The columnist rubbed his chin.

'Sure,' he drawled lugubriously. 'My bank'll probably die of shock, but I'll chance it.'

'Then we're all set,' said the Saint, taking out his cheque-book. 'Unless Mr Vascoe wants to back out—'

Mr Vascoe stared venomously from face to face. It was dawning on him that he was in a corner. If he had seen the faintest encouragement anywhere to laugh off the situation, he would have grabbed at the opportunity with both hands but he looked for the encouragement in vain. He hadn't a single real friend in the room, and he was realist enough to know it. Already he could see heads being put together, could hear whispers ... He knew just what would be said if he backed down ... and Morgan Dean would put the story on the front page ...

Vascoe drew himself up, and a malignant glitter came into his small eyes.

'It suits me,' he said swaggeringly. 'Mr Dean will have my cheque this afternoon.'

He stalked away, still fuming; and Morgan Dean's sad face came closer to the Saint.

'Son,' he said, 'I like a good story as much as anyone. And I like you. And nobody'd cheer louder than me if Vascoe took a toss. But don't you think you've bitten off more than you can chew? I know how much Vascoe loves you, and I'd say he'd almost be glad to spend five thousand pounds to see you in jail. Besides, it wouldn't do you any good. You couldn't sell stuff like this.'

'You could sell it without the slightest trouble,' Simon contradicted him. 'There are any number of collectors who aren't particular how they make their collections, and who don't care if they can't show them to the public. And I've never been in jail, anyway – one ought to try everything once.'

He spent the next hour going slowly round the exhibition, making careful notes about the exhibits in his catalogue, while Vascoe watched him with his rage rising to the brink of apoplexy. He also examined all the windows and showcases, taking measurements and drawing diagrams with a darkly conspiratorial air, and only appearing to notice the existence of the two obvious detectives who followed him everywhere when he politely asked them not to breathe so heavily down his neck.

Teal saw the headlines, and nearly blew all the windows out of Scotland Yard. He burst into the Saint's apartment like a whirling dervish.

'What's the meaning of this?' he bugled brassily, thrusting a crumped copy of the *Daily Mail* under the Saint's nose. 'Come on – what is it?'

Simon looked at the quivering paper.

'"Film Star Says She Prefers Love"', he read from it innocently. 'Well, I suppose it means just that Claud. Some people are funny that way.'

'I mean *this!*' blared the detective, dabbing at Morgan Dean's headline with a stubby forefinger. 'I've warned you once, Templar; and if you try to win this bet I'll get you for it if it's the last thing I do!'

The Saint lighted a cigarette and leaned back.

'Aren't you being just a little bit hasty?' he inquired reasonably; but his blue eyes were twinkling with imps of mockery that sent cold shivers up and down the detective's spine. 'All I've done is to bet that there'll be a burglary at Vascoe's within a week. It may be unusual, but is it criminal? If I were an insurance company—'

'You aren't an insurance company,' Teal said pungently.

'But you wouldn't make a bet like that if you thought there was any risk of losing it.'

'That's true. But that still doesn't make me a burglar. Maybe I was hoping to put the idea into somebody else's head. Now if you want to give your nasty suspicious mind something useful to work on, why don't you find out something about Vascoe's insurance?'

For a moment the audacity of the suggestion took Teal's breath away. And then incredulity returned to his rescue.

'Yes – and see if I can catch him burgling his own house so he can lose five thousand pounds!' he hooted. 'Do you know what would happen if I let my suspicious mind have its own way? I'd have you arrested as a suspected person and keep you locked up for the rest of the week!'

The Saint nodded enthusiastically.

'Why don't you do that?' he suggested. 'It'd give me a gorgeous alibi.'

Teal glared at him thoughtfully. The temptation to take the Saint at his word was almost overpowering. But the tantalizing twinkle in the Saint's eyes, and the memory of many past encounters with the satanic guile of that debonair freebooter filled Teal's heated brain with a gnawing uneasiness that paralysed him. The Saint must have considered that contingency: if Teal carried out his threat, he might be doing the very thing that the Saint expected and wanted him to do – he might be walking straight into a baited trap that would elevate him to new pinnacles of ridiculousness before it turned him loose. The thought made him go hot and cold all over.

Which was exactly what Simon meant it to do.

'When I put you in the cooler,' Teal proclaimed loudly, 'you're going to stay there for more than a week.'

He stormed out of the apartment and went to interview Vascoe.

'With your permission, sir,' he said, 'I'd like to post enough men round this house to make it impossible for a mouse to get in.'

Vascoe shook his head.

'I haven't asked for protection,' he said coldly. 'If you did that, the Saint would be forced to abandon the attempt. I should prefer him to make it. The Ingerbeck Agency is already employed to protect my collection. There are two armed guards in the house all day, and another man on duty all night. And the place is fitted with the latest burglar alarms. The only way it could be successfully robbed would be by an armed gang, and we know that the Saint doesn't work that way. No, Inspector. Let him get in. He won't find it so easy to get out again. And then I'll be glad to send for you.'

Teal argued; but Vascoe was obstinate. He almost succeeded in convincing the detective of the soundness of his reasoning. There would be no triumph or glory in merely preventing the Saint from getting near the house; but to catch him red-handed would be something else again. Nevertheless, Teal would have felt happier if he could have convinced himself that the Saint was possible to catch.

'At least, you'd better let me post one of my own men outside,' he said.

'You will do nothing of the sort,' Vascoe said curtly. 'The Saint would recognize him a mile off. The police have had plenty of opportunities to catch him before this, and I don't remember your making any brilliant use of them.'

Teal left the house in an even sourer temper than he had entered it, and if he had been a private individual he would have assured himself that anything that happened to Vascoe or his art treasures would be richly deserved. Unfortunately his duty didn't allow him to dispose of the matter so easily. He had another stormy interview with the Assistant Commissioner, who for the first time in history was sympathetic.

'You've done everything you could, Mr Teal,' he said. 'If Vascoe refuses to give us any assistance, he can't expect much.'

'The trouble is that if anything goes wrong, that won't stop him squawking,' Teal said gloomily.

Of all the persons concerned, Simon Templar was probably the most untroubled. For two days he peacefully followed the trivial round of his normal law-abiding life; and the plain-clothes men whom Teal had set to watch him, in spite of his instructions, grew bored with their vigil.

At about two o'clock in the morning of the third day his telephone rang.

'This is Miss Vascoe's chauffeur, sir,' said the caller. 'She couldn't reach a telephone herself, so she asked me to speak to you. She said that she must see you.'

Simon's blood ran a shade faster – he had been half expecting such a caller.

'When and where?' he asked crisply.

'If you can be in Regent's Park near the Zoo entrance in an hour's time, sir – she'll get there as soon as she has a chance to slip away.'

'Tell her I'll be there,' said the Saint.

He hung up the instrument and looked out of the window. On the opposite pavement, a man paced wearily up and down as he had done for two nights before, wondering why he should have been chosen for a job that kept him out of bed to so little purpose.

But on this particular night the monotony of the sleuth's existence was destined to be relieved. He followed his quarry on a brief walk which led to Soho and into one of the many night haunts which crowd a certain section of that fevered district, where the Saint was promptly ushered to a favoured table by a beaming head waiter. The sleuth, being an unknown and unprofitable-looking stranger, was ungraciously hustled into an obscure corner. The Saint sipped a drink and watched the dancing for a few minutes, and then got up and sauntered back through the darkened room towards the exit. The sleuth, noting with a practised eye that he had still left three-quarters of his drink and a fresh packet of cigarettes on the table, and that he had neither asked for nor paid a bill, made the obvious deduction and waited without anxiety for his return. After a quarter of an hour he began to have faint doubts of his wisdom, after half an hour he began to sweat; and in forty-five minutes he was in a panic. The lavatory attendant didn't remember noticing the Saint, and certainly he wasn't in sight when the detective arrived; the doorman was quite certain that he had gone out nearly an hour ago, because he had left him ten shillings to pay the waiter.

An angry and somewhat uncomfortable sleuth went back to the Saint's address and waited for some time in agony before the object of his attention came home. As soon as he was relieved at eight o'clock, he telephoned headquarters to report the tragedy; but by then it was too late.

Chief Inspector Teal's blue eyes swept scorchingly over the company that had collected in Vascoe's drawing-room. It consisted of Elliot Vascoe himself, Meryl, the Comte de Beaucroix, an assortment of servants, and the night guard from Ingerbeck's.

'I might have known what to expect,' he complained savagely. 'You wouldn't help me to prevent anything like this happening, but after it's happened you expect me to clean up the mess. It'd serve you right if I told you to let your precious Ingerbeck do the cleaning up. If the Saint was here—'

He broke off, with his jaw dropping and his eyes rounding into reddened buttons of half-unbelieving wrath.

The Saint was there. He was drifting through the door like a pirate entering a captured city, with an impotently protesting butler fluttering behind him like a flustered vulture

– sauntering coolly in with a cigarette between his lips and blithe brows slanted banteringly over humorous blue eyes. He nodded to Meryl, and smiled over the rest of the congregation.

'Hullo, souls,' he murmured. 'I heard I'd won my bet, so I toddled over to make sure.'

For a moment Vascoe himself was gripped in the general petrification; and then he stepped forward, his face crimson with fury.

'There you are,' he burst out incoherently. 'You come here – you—There's your man, Inspector. Arrest him!'

Teal's mouth clamped up again.

'You don't have to tell me,' he said grimly.

'And just why,' Simon inquired lazily, as the detective moved towards him, 'am I supposed to be arrested?'

'Why?' screamed the millionaire. 'You – you stand there and ask *why?* I'll tell you why. Because you've been too clever for once, Mr Smarty. You said you were going to burgle this house, and you've done it – and now you're going to prison where you belong!'

The Saint leaned back against an armchair, ignoring the handcuffs that Teal was dragging from his pocket.

'Those are harsh words, Comrade,' he remarked reproachfully. 'Very harsh. In fact, I'm not sure that they wouldn't be actionable. I must ask my lawyer. But would anybody mind telling me what makes you so sure that I did this job?'

'I'll tell you why.' Teal spoke. 'Last night the guard got tired of working so hard and dozed off for a while.' He shot a smoking glance at the wretched private detective who was trying to obliterate himself behind the larger members of the crowd. 'When he woke up, somebody had opened that window, cut the alarms, opened that centre showcase, and taken about twenty thousand pounds' worth of small stuff out of it. And that somebody couldn't resist leaving his signature.' He jerked out a piece of Vascoe's own notepaper, on which had been drawn a spidery skeleton figure with an elliptical halo poised at a rakish angle over its round blank head. 'You wouldn't recognize it, would you?' Teal jeered sarcastically.

Even so, his voice was louder than it need have been. For in spite of everything, at the back of his mind there was a horrible little doubt. The Saint had tricked him so many times, had led him up the garden path so often and then left him freezing in the snow, that he couldn't make himself believe that anything was certain. And that horrible doubt made his head swim as he saw the Saint's critical eyes rest on the drawing.

'Oh, yes,' said the Saint patiently. 'I can see what it's meant to be. And now I suppose you'd like me to give an account of my movements last night.'

'If you're thinking of putting over another of your patent alibis,' Teal said incandescently, 'let me tell you before you start that I've already heard how you slipped the man I had watching you – just about the time that this job was done.'

Simon nodded.

'You see,' he said, 'I had a 'phone message that Miss Vascoe wanted to see me very urgently, and I was to meet her at the entrance of the Zoo in Regent's Park.'

The girl gasped as everyone suddenly looked at her.

'But Simon – I didn't—'

Her hands flew to her mouth.

Teal's eyes lighted with triumph as they swung back to the Saint.

'That's fine,' he said exultantly. 'And Miss Vascoe doesn't know anything about it. So who else is going to testify that you spent your time waiting there – the man in the moon?'

'No,' said the Saint. 'Because I didn't go there.'

Teal's eyes narrowed with the fog that was starting to creep into his brain.

'Well, what—'

'I was expecting some sort of call like that,' said the Saint. 'I knew somebody was going to knock off this exhibition – after the bet I'd made with Vascoe, the chance of getting away with it and having me take the rap was too good to miss. I meant it to look good – that's why I made the bet. But of course, our friend had to be sure I wouldn't have an alibi, and he was pretty cunning about it. He guessed that you'd be having me shadowed, but he knew that a message like he sent me would make me shake my shadow. And then I'd have a fine time trying to prove that I spent an hour or so standing outside the Zoo at that hour of the night. Only I'm pretty cunning myself, when I think about it; so I didn't go. I came here instead.'

Teal's mouth opened again.

'You—'

'What are we wasting *time* for?' snorted Vascoe. 'He admits he was here—'

'I was here,' said the Saint coolly. 'You know how the back of the house goes practically down to the river, and you have a little private garden there and a landing stage? I knew that if anything was happening, it'd happen on that side – it'd be too risky to do anything on the street frontage, where anybody might come and see it. Well, things were happening. There was a man out there, but I beat him over the head and tied him up before he could make a noise. Then I waited around; and somebody opened the window from *inside* and threw out a parcel. So I picked it up and took it home. Here it is.'

He took it out of his hip pocket – it was a very large parcel.

Vascoe let out a hoarse yell, jumped at it, and wrenched it out of his hands. He ripped it open with clawing fingers.

'My miniatures!' he sobbed. 'My medallions – my cameos! My—'

'Here, wait a minute!'

Teal thrust himself forward again, taking possession of the package.

'It's a fine story,' he said raspily. 'But this is one time you're not going to get away with it. Yes, I get the idea. You pull the job so you can win your bet, and then you bring the stuff back with that fairy tale and think everything's going to be all right. Well, you're not going to get away with it! What happened to the fellow you say you knocked out and tied up, and who else saw him, and who else saw all these things happen?'

The Saint smiled.

'I left him locked up in the garage,' he said. 'He's probably still there. As for who else saw him, Martin Ingerbeck was with me.'

'Who?'

'Ingerbeck himself. The detective bloke. You see, I happened to help him with a job once, so I didn't see why I shouldn't help him with another. So as soon as I guessed what was going to happen I called him up, and he met me at once and came along with me. He even recognized the bloke who opened the window, too.'

'And who was that?' Teal demanded derisively; but somehow his derision sounded hollow.

The Saint bowed.

'I'm afraid,' he said, 'it was the Comte de Beaucroix.'

The Count stared at him pallidly.

'I think you must be mad,' he said.

'It's preposterous!' spluttered Vascoe. 'I happen to have made every enquiry about the Comte de Beaucroix. There isn't the slightest doubt that he's—'

'Of course he is,' said the Saint calmly. 'But he wasn't always. They do it the same way in France as we do in England – a fellow can go around with one name for most of his life, and then he inherits a title and changes his name without any legal formalities. It's funny that you should have been asking me about him, Claud. His name used to be Charles Umbert. As soon as Meryl mentioned the Comte de Beaucroix, I remembered what it was that I'd read about him in the papers. I'd noticed that he came into the title when his uncle died. That's why I thought something like this might happen, and that's why I made that bet with Vascoe.'

The night guard fizzed suddenly out of retirement.

'That's right!' he exploded suddenly. 'I'll bet it was him. I wondered why I went off to sleep like that. Well, about two o'clock *he* came downstairs – said he was looking for something to read because he couldn't get to sleep – and got me to have a drink with him. It was just after he went upstairs that I fell off. That drink must've been doped!'

De Beaucroix looked from side to side, and his face twitched. He made a sudden grab at his pocket; but Teal was too quick for him.

Simon Templar hitched himself off the armchair as the brief scuffle subsided.

'Well, that seems to be that,' he observed languidly. 'You'll have to wait for another chance, Claud. Go home and take some lessons in detecting, and you may do better next time.' He looked at Vascoe. 'I'll see my lawyers later and find out what sort of a suit we can cook up on account of all the rude things you've been saying, but meanwhile I'll collect my cheque from Morgan Dean.' Then he turned to Meryl. 'I'm going to lend Bill Fulton the profits to pay off his debts with,' he said. 'I shall expect a small interest in his invention, and a large slice of wedding cake.'

Before she could say anything he was gone. Thanks didn't interest him: he wanted breakfast.

The Star Producers

INTRODUCTION BY LESLIE CHARTERIS[1]

Ever since I can remember, I have been feebly protesting against the criticism most commonly levelled at the Saint stories, which is that my plots are farfetched and implausible. It has done me little good to insist that in truth I have a rather poor imagination, and that therefore I find it much easier to steal plots from the newspapers than to dream them up. Obviously, I give them some artistic distortions and trimmings; but far more often than not the hard core of the story is something that intrigued me in real life.

I have even given my sources, sometimes, which is the kind of excuse that I don't think a writer really ought to make. But the brand is still on me, and I think my good friend 'Ellery Queen' is the only critic who has ever acknowledged my defence.

And now I am going to take my protest a stage further.

I solemnly assert that even when I do write a story out of pure imagination, my mind works with such a faultless sense of realism that life itself will sometimes be constrained to make my story come true.

This story is one of those.

I will not spoil the story be giving away the surprise ending before you start it. But I have to tell you, and the fact can be verified by anyone who cares to take the trouble, that soon after I wrote this story a gentleman in London (who

[1] From *The Second Saint Omnibus* (1952)

was, however, completely honest, and in no other way resembled my Star Producers) wrote and produced a play of similar calibre to the opus which I invented in my story, only it was called *Young England*, and the result was exactly the same as you read of here.

Mr Homer Quarterstone was not, to be candid, a name to conjure with in the world of the Theatre. It must be admitted that his experience behind the footlights was not entirely confined to that immortal line: 'Dinner is served.' As a matter of fact, he had once said 'The Baron is here' and 'Will there be anything further, Madam?' in the same act; and in another never-to-be-forgotten drama which had run for eighteen performances on Broadway, he had taken part in the following classic dialogue:

NICK: Were you here?
JENKINS: (Mr Homer Quarterstone): No, sir.
NICK: Did you hear anything?
JENKINS: No, sir.
NICK: A hell of a lot of use you are.
JENKINS: Yes, sir.
    (Exit, carrying tray.)

In the executive line, Mr Quarterstone's career had been marked by the same magnanimous emphasis on service rather than personal glory. He had not actually produced any spectacles of resounding success but he had contributed his modest quota to their triumph by helping to carry chairs and tables on to the stage and arrange them according to the orders of the scenic director. And although he had not actually given his personal guidance to any of the financial manœuvres associated with theatrical production, he had sat in the box office at more than one one-night stand, graciously controlling the passage over the counter of those fundamental monetary items without which the labours of more egotistical financiers would have been fruitless.

Nevertheless, while it is true that the name of Quarterstone had never appeared in any headlines, and that his funeral cortège would never have attracted any distinguished pall-bearers, he had undoubtedly found the Theatre more profitable than many other men to whom it had given fame.

He was a man of florid complexion and majestic bearing, with a ripe convexity under his waistcoat and a forehead that arched glisteningly back to the scruff of his neck; and he had a taste for black Homburgs and astrakhan-collared overcoats which gave an impression of great artistic prosperity. This prosperity was by no means illusory, for Mr Homer Quarterstone, in his business capacity, was now the principal, president, director, owner and twenty-five per cent of the staff of the Supremax Academy of Dramatic Art, which according to its frequent advertisements had been the training ground, the histrionic hothouse, so to speak, of many stars whose names were now household words from the igloos of Greenland to the tents of the wandering Bedouin. And the fact that Mr Quarterstone had not become the principal, president, director, owner, etc., of the Supremax Academy until several years after the graduation of those illustrious personages, when in a period of unaccustomed affluence and unusually successful borrowing he had purchased the name and good will of an idealistic but moribund concern, neither deprived him of the legal right to make that claim in his advertising nor hampered the free flow of his imagination when he was expounding his own experience and abilities to prospective clients.

Simon Templar, who sooner or later made the acquaintance

of practically everyone who was collecting too much money with too little reason, heard of him first from Rosalind Hale, who had been one of those clients; and she brought him her story for the same reason that many other people who had been foolish would often come to Simon Templar with their troubles, as if the words 'The Saint' had some literally super-natural significance, instead of being merely the nickname with which he had once incongruously been christened.

'I thought it was the only sensible thing to do – to get some proper training – and his advertisements looked genuine. You wouldn't think those film stars would let him use their names for a fraud, would you? . . . I suppose I was a fool, but I'd played in some amateur things, and people who weren't trying to flatter me said I was good, and I really believed I'd got it in me, sort of instinctively. And some of the people who believe they've got it in them must be right, and they must do something about it, or else there wouldn't be any actors and actresses at all, would there? And really I'm – I – well, I don't make you shudder when you look at me, do I?'

This at least was beyond argument, unless the looker was a crusted misogynist, which the Saint very firmly was not. She had an almost childishly heart-shaped face, with small features that were just far enough from perfection to be exciting, and her figure had just enough curves in just the right places.

The Saint smiled at her without any cynicism.

'And when you came into this money . . .'

'Well, it looked just like the chance I'd been dreaming about. But I still wanted to be intelligent about it and not go dashing off to Hollywood to turn into a waitress, or spend my time sitting in producers' waiting rooms hoping they'd notice me and just looking dumb when they asked if I had experi-ence, or anything like that. That's why I went to Quarterstone. And he said I'd got everything, and I only wanted a little schooling. I paid him five hundred dollars for a course of lessons, and then another five hundred for an advanced course, and then another five hundred for a movie course and by that time he'd been talking to me so that he'd found out all about that legacy, and that was when his friend came in and they got me to give them four thousand dollars to put that play on.'

'In which you were to play the lead.'

'Yes, and—'

'The play never did go on.'

She nodded, and the moistness of her eyes made them shine like jewels. She might not have been outstandingly intelligent, she might or might not have had any dramatic talent, but her own drama was real. She was crushed, frightened, dazed, wounded in the deep and desperate way that a child is hurt when it has innocently done something disastrous, as if she were still too stunned to realize what she had done.

Some men might have laughed, but the Saint didn't laugh. He said in his quiet friendly way: 'I suppose you checked up on your legal position?'

'Yes. I went to see a lawyer. He said there wasn't anything I could do. They'd been too clever. I couldn't prove that I'd been swindled. There really was a play and it could have been put on, only the expenses ran away with all the money before that, and I hadn't got any more, and apparently that often happens, and you couldn't prove it was a fraud. I just hadn't read the contracts and things properly when I signed them, and Urlaub – that's Quarterstone's friend – was entitled to spend all that money, and even if he was careless and stupid you couldn't prove it was criminal . . . I suppose it was my own fault and I've no right to cry about it, but it was everything I had, and I'd given up my job as well, and – well, things have been pretty tough. You know.'

He nodded, straightening a cigarette with his strong brown fingers.

All at once the consciousness of what she was doing now seemed to sweep over her, leaving her tongue-tied. She had to make an effort to get out the last words that everything else had inevitably been leading up to.

'I know I'm crazy and I've no right, but could you – could you think of anything to do about it?'

He went on looking at her thoughtfully for a moment, and then, incredulously, she suddenly realized that he was smiling, and that his smile was still without satire.

'I could try,' he said.

He stood up, long immaculately tailored legs gathering themselves with the lazy grace of a tiger, and all at once she found something in his blue eyes that made all the legends about him impossible to question. It was as if he had lifted all the weight off her shoulders without another word when he stood up.

'One of the first things I should prescribe is a man-sized lunch,' he said. 'A diet of doughnuts and coffee never produced any great ideas.'

When he left her it was still without any more promises, and yet with a queer sense of certainty that was more comforting than any number of promises.

The Saint himself was not quite so certain; but he was interested, which perhaps meant more. He had that impetuously human outlook which judged an adventure on its artistic quality rather than on the quantity of boodle which it might contribute to his unlawful income. He liked Rosalind Hale, and he disliked such men as Mr Homer Quarterstone and Comrade Urlaub sounded as if they would be; more than that, perhaps, he disliked rackets that preyed on people to whom a loss of four thousand dollars was utter tragedy. He set out that same afternoon to interview Mr Quarterstone.

The Supremax Academy occupied the top floor and one room on the street level of a sedate old-fashioned building in the West Forties; but the entrance was so cunningly arranged and the other intervening tenants so modestly unheralded that any impressionable visitor who presented himself first at the ground-floor room labelled 'Inquiries' and who was thence whisked expertly into the elevator and upwards to the rooms above, might easily have been persuaded that the whole building was taken up with various departments of the Academy, a hive buzzing with ambitious Thespian bees. The brassy but once luscious blonde who presided in the Inquiry Office lent tone to this idea by saying that Mr Quarterstone was busy, very busy, and that it was customary to make appointments with him days in advance; when she finally organized the interview it was with the regal generosity of a slightly flirtatious goddess performing a casual miracle for an especially favoured and deserving suitor – a beautifully polished routine that was calculated to impress prospective clients from the start with a gratifying sense of their own importance.

Simon Templar was always glad of a chance to enjoy his own importance, but on this occasion he regretfully had to admit that so much flattery was undeserved, for instead of his own name he had cautiously given the less notorious name of Tombs. This funereal anonymity, however, cast no shadow over the warmth of Mr Quarterstone's welcome.

'My dear Mr Tombs! Come in. Sit down. Have a cigarette.'

Mr Quarterstone grasped him with large warm hands, wrapped him up, transported him tenderly and installed him in an armchair like a collector enshrining a priceless piece of fragile glass. He fluttered anxiously around him, pressing a cigarette into the Saint's mouth and lighting it before he retired reluctantly to his own chair on the other side of the desk.

'And now, my dear Mr Tombs,' said Mr Quarterstone at last, clasping his hands across his stomach, 'how can I help you?'

Simon looked at his hands, his feet, the carpet, the wall and then at Mr Quarterstone.

'Well,' he said bashfully, 'I wanted to inquire about some dramatic lessons.'

'Some – ah – oh, yes. You mean a little advanced coaching. A little polishing of technique?'

'Oh, no,' said the Saint hastily. 'I mean, you know your business, of course, but I'm only a beginner.'

Mr Quarterstone sat up a little straighter and gazed at him.

'You're only a beginner?' he repeated incredulously.

'Yes.'

'You mean to tell me you haven't any stage experience?'

'No. Only a couple of amateur shows.'

'You're not joking?'

'Of course not.'

'Well!'

Mr Quarterstone continued to stare at him as if he were something rare and strange. The Saint twisted his hat-brim uncomfortably. Mr Quarterstone sat back again, shaking his head.

'That's the most extraordinary thing I ever heard of,' he declared.

'But why?' Simon asked, with not unreasonable surprise.

'My dear fellow, anyone would take you for a professional actor! I've been in the theatrical business all my life – I was on Broadway for ten years, played before the King of England, produced hundreds of shows – and I'd have bet anyone I could pick out a professional actor every time. The way you walked in, the way you sat down, the way you use your hands, even the way you're smoking that cigarette – it's amazing! Are you sure you're not having a little joke?'

'Absolutely.'

'May I ask what is your present job?'

'Until a couple of days ago,' said the Saint ingenuously, 'I was working in a bank. But I'd always wanted to be an actor, so when my uncle died and left me twenty thousand dollars I thought it was a good time to start. I think I could play parts like William Holden,' he added, looking sophisticated.

Mr Quarterstone beamed like a cat full of cream.

'Why not?' he demanded oratorically. 'Why ever not? With that natural gift of yours . . .' He shook his head again, clicking his tongue in eloquent expression of his undiminished awe and admiration. 'It's the most amazing thing! Of course, I sometimes see fellows who are nearly as good-looking as you are, but they haven't got your manner. Why, if you took a few lessons—'

Simon registered the exact amount of glowing satisfaction which he was supposed to register.

'That's what I came to you for, Mr Quarterstone. I've seen your advertisements—'

'Yes, yes!'

Mr Quarterstone got up and came around the desk again. He took the Saint's face in his large warm hands and turned it this way and that, studying it from various angles with increasing astonishment. He made the Saint stand up and studied him from a distance, screwing up one eye and holding up a finger in front of the other to compare his proportions. He stalked up to him again, patted him here and there and felt his muscles. He stepped back again and posed in an attitude of rapture.

'Marvellous!' he said 'Astounding!'

Then, with an effort, he brought himself out of his trance.

'Mr Tombs,' he said firmly, 'there's only one thing for me to do. I must take you in charge myself. I have a wonderful staff here, the finest staff you could find in any dramatic academy in the world, past masters, everyone of 'em – but they're not good enough. I wouldn't dare to offer you anything but the best that we have here. I offer you myself. And because I only look upon it as a privilege – nay, a sacred duty – to develop this God-given talent you have, I shall not try to make any money out of you. I shall only make a small charge to cover the actual value of my time. Charles Laughton paid me five thousand dollars for one hour's coaching in a difficult scene. Marlon Brando took me to Hollywood and paid me fifteen thousand dollars to criticize him in four rehearsals. But I shall only ask you for enough to cover my out-of-pocket expenses – let us say, one thousand dollars – for a course of ten special, personal, private, exclusive lessons . . . No,' boomed Mr Quarterstone, waving one hand in a magnificent gesture, 'don't thank me! Were I to refuse to give you the benefit of all my experience, I should regard myself as a traitor to my calling, a very – ah – Ishmael!'

If there was one kind of acting in which Simon Templar had graduated from a more exacting academy than was dreamed of in Mr Quarterstone's philosophy, it was the art of depicting the virgin sucker yawning hungrily under the baited hook. His characterization was pointed with such wide-eyed and unsullied innocence, such eager and open-mouthed receptivity, such a succulently plastic amenability to suggestion, such a rich response to flattery – in a word, with such a sublime absorptiveness to the old oil – that men such as Mr Quarterstone, on becoming conscious of him for the first time, had been known to wipe away a furtive tear as they dug down into their pockets for first mortgages on the Golden Gate Bridge and formulae for extracting radium from old toothpaste tubes. He used all of that technique on Mr Homer Quarterstone, so effectively that his enrolment in the Supremax Academy proceeded with the effortless ease of a stratospherist returning to terra firma a short head in front of his punctured balloon. Mr Quarterstone did not actually brush away an unbidden tear, but he did bring out an enormous leather-bound ledger and enter up particulars of his newest student with a gratifying realization that Life, in spite of the pessimists, was not wholly without its moments of unshadowed joy.

'When can I start?' asked the Saint, when that had been done.

'Start?' repeated Mr Quarterstone, savouring the word. 'Why, whenever you like. Each lesson lasts a full hour, and you can divide them up as you wish. You can start now if you want to. I had an appointment . . .'

'Oh.'

'But it is of no importance, compared with this.' Mr Quarterstone picked up the telephone. 'Tell Mr Urlaub I shall be too busy to see him this afternoon,' he told it. He hung up. 'The producer,' he explained, as he settled back again. 'Of course you've heard of him. But he can wait. One day he'll be waiting on your doorstep, my boy.' He dismissed Mr Urlaub, the producer with a majestic *ademán*. 'What shall we take first – elocution?'

'You know best, Mr Quarterstone,' said the Saint eagerly.

Mr Quarterstone nodded. If there was anything that could have increased his contentment it was a pupil who had no doubt that Mr Quarterstone knew best. He crossed his legs and hooked one thumb in the armhole of his waistcoat.

'Say, "Eee." '

'Eee.'

'Ah.'

Simon went on looking at him expectantly.

'Ah,' repeated Mr Quarterstone.

'I beg your pardon?'

'I said "Ah." '

'Oh.'

'No, ah.'

'Yes, I—'

'Say it after me, Mr Tombs. "Aaaah." Make it ring out. Hold your diaphragm in, open your mouth and bring it up from your chest. This is a little exercise in the essential vowels.'

'Oh. Aaaah.'

'Oh.'

'Oh.'

'I.'

'I.'

'Ooooo.'

'Ooooo.'

'Wrong.'

'I'm sorry . . .'

'Say "Wrong," Mr Tombs.'

'Wrong.'

'Right,' said Mr Quarterstone.

'Right.'

'Yes, yes,' said Mr Quarterstone testily. 'I—'

'Yes, yes, I.'

Mr Quarterstone swallowed.

'I don't mean you repeat every word I say,' he said. 'Just the examples. Now let's try the vowels again in a sentence. Say this: "Faar skiies looom O-ver meee." '

'Faaar skiiies looom O-ver meee.'

'Daaark niight draaws neeear.'

'The days are drawing in,' Simon admitted politely.

Mr Quarterstone's smile became somewhat glassy, but whatever else he may have been he was no quitter.

'I'm afraid he is a fraud,' Simon told Rosalind Hale when he saw her the next day. 'But he has a beautiful line of sugar for the flies. I was the complete gawky goof, the perfect bank clerk with dramatic ambitions – you could just see me going home and leering in the mirror and imagining myself making love to Brigitte Bardot – but he told me just couldn't believe how anyone with my poise couldn't have had any experience.'

The girl's white teeth showed on her lower lip.

'But that's just what he told me!'

'I could have guessed it, darling. And I don't suppose you were the first, either . . . I had two lessons on the spot, and I've had another two today; and if he can teach anyone anything worth knowing about acting, then I can train ducks to write shorthand. I was so dumb that anyone with an ounce of artistic feeling would have thrown me out of the window, but when I left him this afternoon he almost hugged me and told me he could hardly wait to finish the course before he rushed out to show me to John Van Druten.'

She moved her head a little, gazing at him with big sober eyes.

'He was just the same with me, too. Oh, I've been such a fool!'

'We're all fools in our own way,' said the Saint consolingly. 'Boys like Homer are my job, so they don't bother me. On the other hand, you've no idea what a fool I can be with soft lights and sweet music. Come on to dinner and I'll show you.'

'But now you've given Quarterstone a thousand dollars, and what are you going to do about it?'

'Wait for the next act of the stirring drama.'

The next act was not long in developing. Simon had two more of Mr Quarterstone's special, personal, private, exclusive lessons the next day, and two more the day after – Mr Homer Quarterstone was no apostle of the old-fashioned idea of making haste slowly, and by getting in two lessons daily he was able to double his temporary income, which then chalked up at the very pleasing figure of two hundred dollars per diem, minus the overhead of which the brassy blonde was not the smallest item. But this method of gingering up the flow of revenue also meant that its duration was reduced from ten days to five, and during a lull in the next day's first hour (Diction, Gesture and Facial Expression) he took the opportunity of pointing out that Success, while already certain, could never be too certain or too great, and therefore that a supplementary series of lessons in the Art and Technique of the Motion Picture, while involving only a brief delay, could only add to the magnitude of Mr Tombs's ultimate inevitable triumph.

On this argument, for the first time, Mr Tombs disagreed.

'I want to see for myself whether I've mastered the first lessons,' he said. 'If I could get a small part in a play, just to try myself out . . .'

He was distressingly obstinate, and Mr Quarterstone, either because he convinced himself that it would only be a waste of time, or because another approach to his pupil's remaining nineteen thousand dollars seemed just as simple, finally yielded. He made an excuse to leave the studio for a few minutes, and Simon knew that the next development was on its way.

It arrived in the latter part of the last hour (Declamation with Gestures, Movement and Facial Expression – The Complete Classical Scene).

Mr Quarterstone was demonstrating.

'To be,' trumpeted Mr Quarterstone, gazing ceilingwards with an ecstatic expression, the chest thrown out, the arms slightly spread, 'or not to be.' Mr Quarterstone ceased to be. He slumped, the head bowed, the arms hanging listlessly by the sides, the expression doleful. 'That – is the question.' Mr Quarterstone pondered it, shaking his head. The suspense was awful. He elaborated the idea. 'Whether 'tis nobler' – Mr Quarterstone drew himself nobly up, the chin lifted, the right arm turned slightly across the body, the forearm parallel with the ground – 'in the mind' – he clutched his brow, where he kept his mind – 'to suffer' – he clutched his heart, where he did his suffering – 'the slings' – he stretched out his left hand for the slings – 'and arrows' – he flung out his right hand for the arrows – 'of outrageous fortune' – Mr Quarterstone rolled the insult lusciously around his mouth and spat it out with defiance – 'or to take arms' – he drew himself up again, the shoulders squared, rising slightly on tiptoe – 'against a sea of troubles' – his right hand moved over a broad panorama, undulating symbolically – 'and by opposing' – the arms rising slightly from the elbows, fists clenched, shoulders thrown back, chin drawn in – 'end them!' – the forearms striking down again with a fierce chopping movement, expressive of finality and knocking a calendar off the table.

'Excuse me,' said the brassy blonde, with her head poking around the door. 'Mr Urlaub is here.'

'Tchah!' said Mr Quarterstone, inspiration wounded in mid-flight. 'Tell him to wait.'

'He said—'

Mr Quarterstone's eyes dilated. His mouth opened. His hands lifted a little from his sides, the fingers tense and parted rather like plump claws, the body rising. He was staring at the Saint.

'Wait!' he cried. 'Of course! The very thing! The very man you've got to meet! One of the greatest producers in the world today! Your chance!'

He leapt a short distance off the ground and whirled on the blonde, his arm flung out, pointing quiveringly.

'Send him in!'

Simon looked wildly breathless.

'But – but will he—'

'Of course he will! You've only got to remember what I've taught you. And sit down. We must be calm!'

Mr Quarterstone sank into a chair, agitatedly looking

calm, as Urlaub bustled in. Urlaub trotted quickly across the room.

'Ah, Homer.'

'My dear Waldemar? How's everything?'

'Terrible! I came to ask for your advice . . .'

Mr Urlaub leaned across the desk. He was a smallish, thin, bouncy man with a big nose and sleek black hair. His suit fitted him as tightly as an extra skin, and the stones in his tiepin and his rings looked enough like diamonds to actually be diamonds. He moved as if he were hung on springs, and his voice was thin and spluttery like the exhaust of an anaemic motorcycle.

'Niementhal has quit. Let me down at the last minute. He wanted to put some goddam gigolo into the lead. Some ham that his wife's got hold of. I said to him, "Aaron, your wife is your business and this play is my business." I said, "I don't care if it hurts your wife's feelings and I don't care if she gets mad at you, I can't afford to risk my reputation on Broadway and my investment in this play by putting that ham in the lead." I said, "Buy her a box of candy or a diamond bracelet or anything or send her to Paris or something, but don't ask me to make her happy by putting that gigolo in this play." So he quit. And me with everything set, and the rest of the cast ready to start rehearsing next week, and he quits. He said, "All right, then use your own money." I said, "You know I've got fifty thousand dollars in this production already, and all you were going to put in is fifteen thousand, and for that you want me to risk my money and my reputation by hiring that ham. I thought you said you'd got a good actor." "Well, you find yourself a good actor and fifteen thousand dollars," he says, and he quits. Cold. And I can't raise another cent – you know how I just tied up half a million to save those aluminium shares.'

'That's tough, Waldemar,' said Mr Quarterstone anxiously.

'Waldemar, that's tough! . . .. Ah – by the way – pardon me – may I introduce a student of mine? Mr Tombs . . .'

Urlaub turned vaguely, apparently becoming aware of the Saint's presence for the first time. He started forward with a courteously extended hand as the Saint rose.

But their hands did not meet at once. Mr Urlaub's approaching movement died slowly away, as if paralysis had gradually overtaken him, so that he finally came to rest just before they met, like a clockwork toy that had run down. His eyes became fixed, staring. His mouth opened.

Then, very slowly, he revived himself. He pushed his hand onwards again and grasped the Saint's as if it were something precious, shaking it slowly and earnestly.

'A pupil of yours, did you say, Homer?' he asked in an awestruck voice.

'That's right. My star pupil, in fact. I might almost say . . .'

Mr Urlaub paid no attention to what Quarterstone might almost have said. With his eyes still staring, he darted suddenly closer, peered into the Saint's face, took hold of it, turned it from side to side, just as Quarterstone had once done. Then he stepped back and stared again, prowling around the Saint like a dog prowling around a tree. Then he stopped.

'Mr Tombs,' he said vibrantly, 'will you walk over to the door, and then walk back towards me?'

Looking dazed, the Saint did so.

Mr Urlaub looked at him and gulped. Then he hauled a wad of typescript out of an inside pocket, fumbled through it and thrust it out with one enamelled fingernail dabbing at a paragraph.

'Read that speech – read it as if you were acting it.'

The Saint glanced over the paragraph, drew a deep breath and read with almost uncontrollable emotion.

'No, do not lie to me. You have already given me the answer

for which I have been waiting. I am not ungrateful for what you once did for me, but I see now that that kind act was only a part of your scheme to ensnare my better nature in the toils of your unhallowed passions, as though pure love were a thing that could be bought like merchandise. Ah, yes, I loved you, but I did not know that that pretty face was only a mask for the corruption beneath. How you must have laughed at me! Ha, ha. I brought you a rose, but you turned it into a nest of vipers in my bosom. They have stabbed my heart! (Sobs)'

Mr Urlaub clasped his hands together. His eyes bulged and rolled upwards.

'My God,' he breathed hoarsely.

'What?' said the Saint.

'Why?' said Mr Quarterstone.

'But it's like a miracle!' squeaked Waldemar Urlaub. 'He's the man! The type! The face! The figure! The voice! The manner! He is a genius! Homer, where did you find him? The women will storm the theatre.' He grasped the Saint by the arm, leaning as far as he could over the desk and over Mr Quarterstone. 'Listen. He must play that part. He must. He is the only man. I couldn't put anyone else in it now. Not after I've seen him. I'll show Aaron Niementhal where he gets off. Quit, did he? Okay. He'll be sorry. We'll have a hit that'll make history!'

'But Waldemar . . .'

Mr Urlaub dried up. His clutching fingers uncoiled from Simon's arm. The fire died out of his eyes. He staggered blindly back and sank into a chair and buried his face in his hands.

'Yes,' he whispered bitterly. 'I'd forgotten. The play can't go on. I'm sunk, Homer – just for a miserable fifteen grand. And now, of all times, when I've just seen Mr Tombs!'

'You know I'd help you if I could, Waldemar,' said Mr Quarterstone earnestly. 'But I just bought my wife a fur coat, and she wants a new car, and that ranch we just bought in California set me back a hundred thousand.'

Mr Urlaub shook his head.

'I know. It's not your fault. But isn't it just the toughest break?'

Quarterstone shook his head in sympathy. And then he looked at the Saint.

It was quite a performance, that look. It started casually, beheld inspiration, blazed with triumph, winked, glared significantly, poured out encouragement, pleaded, commanded and asked and answered several questions, all in a few seconds. Mr Quarterstone had not at any period in his career actually held down the job of prompter, but he more than made up with enthusiasm for any lack of experience. Only a man who had been blind from birth could have failed to grasp the idea that Mr Quarterstone was suggesting, and the Saint had not strung along so far in order to feign blindness at the signal for his entrance.

Simon cleared his throat.

'Er – did you say you only needed another fifteen thousand dollars to put on this play?' he asked diffidently, but with a clearly audible note of suppressed excitement.

After that he had to work no harder than he would have had to work to get himself eaten by a pair of hungry lions. Waldemar Urlaub, once the great light had dawned on him, skittered about like a pea on a drum in an orgy of exultant planning. Mr Tombs would have starred in the play anyhow, whenever the remainder of the necessary wind had been raised – Urlaub had already made up his mind to that – but if Mr Tombs had fifteen thousand dollars as well as his genius and beauty, he would be more than a star. He could be co-producer as well, a sharer in the profits, a friend and equal, in every way the heir to the position which the great Aaron Niementhal would have occupied. His name would go on the billing with double force – Urlaub grabbed a piece of paper and a pencil to illustrate it:

Sebastian Tombs

and

Waldemar Urlaub

present

Sebastian Tombs

in

'Love – The Redeemer'

There would also be lights on the theatre, advertisements, photographs, newspaper articles, news items, gossip paragraphs, parties, movie rights, screen tests, Hollywood, London, beautiful and adoring women . . . Mr Urlaub built up a luminous picture of fame, success and fortune, while Mr Quarterstone nodded benignly and slapped everybody on the back and beamed at the Saint at intervals with a sublimely smug expression of 'I told you so.'

'And they did all that to me, too,' said Rosalind Hale wryly. 'I was practically Sarah Bernhardt when they'd finished . . . But I told you just how they did it. Why do you have to let yourself in for the same mess that I got into?'

'The easiest way to rob a bank is from the inside,' said the Saint cryptically. 'I suppose you noticed that they really have got a play?'

Yes. I read part of it – the same as you did.'

'Did you like it?'

She made a little grimace.

'You've got a right to laugh at me. I suppose that ought to have been warning enough, but Urlaub was so keen about it, and Quarterstone had already made me think he was a great producer, so I couldn't say that I thought it was awful. And then I wondered if it was just because I didn't know enough about plays.'

'I don't know much about plays myself,' said the Saint. 'But the fact remains that Comrade Urlaub has got a complete play, with three acts and everything, god-awful though it is. I took it away with me to read it over and the more I look at it the more I'm thinking that something might be done with it.'

Rosalind was aghast.

'You don't mean to say you'd really put your money into producing it?'

'Stranger things have happened,' said the Saint thoughtfully. 'How bad can a play be before it becomes good? And how much sense of humour is there in the movie business? Haven't you seen those reprints of old two-reelers that they show sometimes for a joke, and haven't you heard the audience laughing itself sick . .? Listen. I only wish I knew who wrote *Love – the Redeemer*. I've got an idea . . .'

Mr Homer Quarterstone could have answered his question for him, for the truth was that the author of *Love – the Redeemer* resided under the artistic black Homburg of Mr Homer Quarterstone. It was a matter of considerable grief to Mr Quarterstone that no genuine producer had ever been induced to see eye to eye with him on the subject of the superlative merits of that amorous masterpiece, so that after he had grown weary of collecting rejections, Mr Quarterstone had been reduced to the practical expedient of using his magnum opus as one of the props in the more profitable but by no means less artistic drama from which he and Mr Urlaub derived their precarious incomes; but his loyalty to the child of his brain had never been shaken.

It was therefore with a strange squirmy sensation in the pit of his stomach that Mr Quarterstone sat in his office a few mornings later and gazed at a card in the bottom left-hand corner of which were the magic words, '*Paragon Pictures, Inc., Hollywood,*

Calif.' A feeling of fate was about him, as if he had been unexpectedly reminded of a still-cherished childhood dream.

'Show her in,' he said with husky magnificence.

The order was hardly necessary, for she came in at once, shepherded by a beaming Waldemar Urlaub.

'Just thought I'd give you a surprise, Homer,' he explained boisterously. 'Did your heart jump when you saw that card? Well, so did mine. Still, it's real. I fixed it all up. Sold her the play. "You can't go wrong," I said, "with one of the greatest dramas ever written."'

Mr. Wohlbreit turned her back on him coldly and inspected Mr Quarterstone. She looked nothing like the average man's conception of a female from Hollywood, being gaunt and masculine with a sallow lined face and gold-rimmed glasses and mousey hair plastered back above her ears, but Mr Quarterstone had at least enough experience to know that women were used in Hollywood in executive positions which did not call for the decorative qualities of more publicized employees.

She said in her cold masculine voice: 'Is this your agent?'

Mr Quarterstone swallowed.

'Ah—'

'Part owner,' said Mr Urlaub eagerly. 'That's right, isn't it, Homer? You know our agreement – fifty-fifty in everything. Eh? Well, I've been working on this deal—'

'I asked you,' said Mr. Wohlbreit penetratingly, 'because I understand that you're the owner of this play we're interested in. There are so many chisellers in this business that we make it our policy to approach the author first direct – if he wants to take in any ten-percenters afterwards, that's his affair. A Mr Tombs brought me the play first, and told me he had an interest in it. I found out that he got it from Mr Urlaub, so I went to him. Mr Urlaub told me that you were the original author. Now, who am I to talk business with?'

Mr Quarterstone saw his partner's mouth opening for another contribution.

'With -- with us,' he said weakly.

It was not what he might have said if he had had time to think, but he was too excited to be particular.

'Very well,' said Mr. Wohlbreit. 'We've read this play, *Love – the Redeemer*, and we think it would make a grand picture. If you haven't done anything yet about the movie rights . . .'

Mr Quarterstone drew himself up. He felt as if he was in a daze from which he might be rudely awakened at any moment, but it was a beautiful daze. His heart was thumping, but his brain was calm and clear. It was, after all, only the moment with which he had always known that his genius must ultimately be rewarded.

'Ah – yes,' he said with resonant calm. 'The movie rights are, for the moment, open to – ah – negotiation. Naturally, with a drama of such quality, dealing as it does with a problem so close to the lives of every member of the thinking public, and appealing to the deepest emotions and beliefs of every intelligent man and woman—'

'We thought it would make an excellent farce,' said Mr. Wohlbreit blandly. 'It's just the thing we've been looking for for a long time.' But before the stricken Mr Quarterstone could protest, she had added consolingly: 'We could afford to give you thirty thousand dollars for the rights.'

'Ah – quite,' said Mr Quarterstone bravely.

By the time that Mr. Wohlbreit had departed, after making an appointment for the contract to be signed and the cheque paid over at the Paragon offices the following afternoon, his wound had healed sufficiently to let him take Mr Urlaub in his arms, as soon as the door closed, and embrace him fondly in an impromptu rumba.

'Didn't I always tell you that play was a knockout?' he crowed. 'It's taken 'em years to see it, but they had to wake up in the end. Thirty thousand dollars! Why, with that money I can—' He sensed a certain stiffness in his dancing partner and hastily corrected himself: 'I mean, we – we can—'

'Nuts,' said Mr Urlaub coarsely. He disengaged himself and straightened the creases out of his natty suit. 'What you've got to do now is sit down and figure out a way to crowbar that guy Tombs out of this.'

Mr Quarterstone stopped dancing suddenly and his jaw dropped.

'Tombs?'

'Yeah! He wasn't so dumb. He had the sense to see that that play of yours was the funniest thing ever written. When we were talking about it in here he must have thought we thought it was funny, too.'

Mr Quarterstone was appalled as the idea of duplicity struck him.

'Waldemar – d'you think he was trying to—'

'No. I pumped the old battle-axe on the way here. He told her he only had a part interest, but he wanted to do something for the firm and give us a surprise – he thought he could play the lead in the picture, too.'

'Has she told him—'

'Not yet. You heard what she said. She gets in touch with the author first. But we got to get him before he gets in touch with her. Don't you remember those contracts we signed yesterday? Fifty per cent of the movie rights for him!'

Mr Quarterstone sank feebly on to the desk.

'Fifteen thousand dollars!' he groaned. Then he brightened tentatively. 'But it's all right, Waldemar. He agreed to put fifteen thousand dollars into producing the play, so we just call it quits and we don't have to give him anything.'

'You great fat lame-brained slob,' yelped Mr Urlaub affectionately. 'Quits! Like hell it's quits! D'you think I'm not going to put that play on, after this? It took that old battle-axe to see it, but she's right. They'll be rolling in the aisles!' He struck a Quarterstoneish attitude. ' "I brought you a rose," ' he uttered tremulously, ' "but you turned it into a nest of vipers in my bosom. They have stabbed my heart!" My God! It's a natural! I'm going to put it on Broadway whatever we have to do to raise the dough – but we aren't going to cut that mug Tombs in on it.'

Mr Quarterstone winced.

'It's all signed up legal,' he said dolefully. 'We'll have to spend our own dough and buy him out.'

'Get your hat,' said Mr Urlaub shortly. 'We'll cook up a story on the way.'

When Rosalind Hale walked into the Saint's apartment at the Waldorf-Astoria that afternoon, Simon Templar was counting crisp new hundred-dollar bills into neat piles.

'What have you been doing?' she said. 'Burgling a bank?'

The Saint grinned.

'The geetus came out of a bank, anyway,' he murmured. 'But Comrades Quarterstone and Urlaub provided the cheques. I just went out and cashed them.'

'You mean they bought you out?'

'After a certain amount of haggling and squealing – yes. Apparently Aaron Niementhal changed his mind about backing the show, and Urlaub didn't want to offend him on account of Aaron offered to cut him in on another and bigger and better proposition at the same time; so they gave me ten thousand dollars to tear up the contracts, and the idea is that I ought to play the lead in Niementhal's bigger and better show.'

She pulled off her hat and collapsed into a chair. She was no longer gaunt and masculine and forbidding, for she had changed out of a badly fitting tweed suit and removed her sallow make-up and thrown away the gold-rimmed glasses and fluffed out her hair again so that it curled in its usual soft brown waves around her face, so that her last resemblance to anyone by the name of Wohlbreit was gone.

'Ten thousand dollars,' she said limply. 'It doesn't seem possible. But it's real. I can see it.'

'You can touch it, if you like,' said the Saint. 'Here.' He pushed one of the stacks over the table towards her. 'Fifteen hundred that you paid Quarterstone for tuition.' He pushed another. 'Four thousand that you put into the play.' He drew a small sheaf towards himself. 'One thousand that I paid for my lessons. Leaving three thousand and five hundred drops of gravy to be split two ways.'

He straightened the remaining pile, cut it in two and slid half of it on to join the share that was accumulating in front of her.

She stared at the money helplessly for a second or two, reached out and touched it with the tips of her fingers, and then suddenly she came round the table and flung herself into his arms. Her cheek was wet where it touched his face.

'I don't know how to say it,' she said shakily. 'But you know what I mean.'

'There's only one thing bothering me,' said the Saint some time later, 'and that's whether you're really entitled to take back those tuition fees. After all, Homer made you a good enough actress to fool himself. Maybe he was entitled to a percentage, in spite of everything.'

His doubts, however, were set at rest several months afterwards, when he had travelled a long way from New York and many other things had happened, when one day an advertisement in a New York paper caught his eye:

14th Week!
Sold out 3 months ahead!
The Farce Hit of the Season:

LOVE – THE REDEEMER

by Homer Quarterstone

IMPERIAL THEATRE

A Waldemar Urlaub Production

Simon Templar was not often at a loss for words, but on this occasion he was tongue-tied for a long time. And then, at last, he lay back and laughed helplessly.

'Oh, well,' he said. 'I guess they earned it.'

The Charitable Countess

Simon Templar's mail, like that of any other celebrity, was a thing of infinite variety. Perhaps it was even more so than that of most celebrities, for actors and authors and the other usual recipients of fan mail are of necessity a slightly smaller target for the busy letter-writer than a man who has been publicized at frequent intervals as a twentieth-century Robin Hood, to the despair and fury of the police officials at whose expense the publicity has been achieved. Of those correspondents who approached him under his better-known *nome de guerre* of 'The Saint', about half were made up of people who thought that the nickname should be taken literally, and half of people who suspected that it stood for the exact opposite.

There were, of course, the collectors of autographs and signed photos. There were the hero-worshipping schoolboys whose ideas of a future profession would have shocked their fathers, and the romantic schoolgirls whose ideals of a future husband would have made their mothers swoon. There were also romantic maidens who were not so young, who supplied personal data of sometimes startling candour and whose proportions were correspondingly more concrete.

And then there were the optimists who thought that the Saint would like to finance a South American revolution, a hunt for buried treasure on the Spanish Main, a new night club or an invention for an auxiliary automatic lighter to light automatic lighters with. There were the plodding sportsmen who could find a job in some remote town, thereby saving their wives and children from immiment starvation, if only the Saint would lend them the fare. There were the old ladies who thought that the Saint might be able to trace their missing Pomeranians, and the old gentleman who thought that he might be able to exterminate the damned Socialists. There were crooks and cranks, fatheads and fanatics, beggars, liars, romancers, idiots, thieves, rich men, poor men, the earnest, the flippant, the gay, the lonely, the time-wasters and the genuine tragedies, all that strange and variegated section of humanity that writes letters to total strangers; and then sometimes the letters were not from one stranger to another, but were no less significant, like a letter that came one morning from a man named Marty O'Connor:

I should of written you before but I didn't want you to think I was asking for a handout. I stuck at that job in Canada and we were doing fine. I thought we were all set but the guy was playing the markit, I didn't know he was that dumb, so the nex thing is hes bust, the garage is sold up and Im out a job. I could not get nothing else there, but I hear the heat is off in New York now so me and Cora hitchike back, I got a job as chaufer and hold that 3 weeks til the dame hears I got a police record, she won't believe Im going strait now. I got the bums rush, havent found nothing since, but Cora does odd jobs and I may get a job any day. When I do you got to come see us again, we never fergot what you done for us and would do the same for you anytime if we burn for it . . .

That was a reminder of two people whom he had helped because he liked them and because he thought they were worth helping, in one of those adventures that made all his lawlessness seem worthwhile to him, whatever the moralists might say. Marty O'Connor, who put off writing to his friend for fear of being suspected of begging, was a very different character from many others who wrote with no such scruples and with less excuse – such as the Countess Jannowicz, whose letter came in the same mail.

The smile which Simon had had for Marty's letter turned cynical as he read it. On the face of it, it was a very genteel and dignified epistle, tastefully engraved under an embossed coronet, and printed on expensive handmade paper. The Countess Jannowicz, it said, requested the pleasure of Mr Simon Templar's company at a dinner and dance to be held at the Waldorf-Astoria on the twentieth of that month, in aid of the National League for the Care of Incurables, R.S.V.P. That in itself would have been harmless enough, but the catch came in very small copperplate at the foot of the invitation, in the shape of the words, '*Tickets* $25' – and in the accompanying printed pamphlet describing the virtues of the League and its urgent need of funds.

Simon had heard from her before, as had many other people in New York, for she was a busy woman. Born as Maggie Oaks in Weehawken, New Jersey, resplendent later as Margaretta Olivera in a place of honour in the nuder tableaux at the Follies, she had furred her nest with a notable collection of skins, both human and animal, up to the time when she met and married Count Jannowicz, a Polish boulevardier of great age and reputedly fabulous riches. Disdaining such small stuff as alimony, she had lived with him faithfully and patiently until the day of his death, which in defiance of all expectations he had postponed for an unconscionable time through more and more astounding stages of senility, only to discover after the funeral that he had been living for all that time on an annuity which automatically ceased its payments forthwith; so that after nineteen years of awful fidelity his widowed countess found herself the proud inheritor of a few more furs, a certain amount of jewellery, a derelict castle already mortgaged for more than its value and some seven-teen kopeks in hard cash.

Since she was then forty-four, and her outlines had lost the voluptuousness which had once made them such an asset to the more artistic moments of the Follies, many another woman might have retired to the companionable obscurity of her fellow unfortunates in some small Riviera pension. Not so Maggie Oaks, who had the stern marrow of Weehawken in her bones. At least she had the additional intangible asset of a genuine title, and during her spouse's doggedly declining years she had whiled away the time consolidating the social position which her marriage had given her; so that after some sober consideration which it would have educated a bishop to hear, she was able to work out a fairly satisfactory solution to her financial problems.

Unlike Mr Elliot Vascoe, of whom we have heard before, who used charity to promote his social ambitions, she used her social position to promote charities. What the charities were did not trouble her much, so long as they paid her the twenty-five per cent of the proceeds which was her standard fee. She had been known to sponsor, in the same day, a luncheon in aid of the Women's Society for the Prosecution of Immorality, and a ball in aid of the Free Hospital for Unmarried Mothers. As a means of livelihood it had been a triumphant inspiration. Social climbers fought to serve, expensively, on her committees; lesser snobs scrambled to attend her functions and get their names in the papers in such distinguished company; charitable enterprises, strug-gling against depressions, were only too glad to pass over some of the labour of extracting contributions from the public to such a successful organizer; and the Countess Jannowicz, née Maggie Oaks, lived in great comfort on Park Avenue and maintained a chauffeur-driven Cadillac out of her twenty-five per cents, eked out by other percentages which various restaurants and hotels were only too glad to pay her for bringing them the business.

The Saint had had his piratical eye on her for a long time; and now, with the apt arrival of that last invitation at a period when he had no other more pressing business on his hands, it seemed as if the discounting of the charitable countess was a pious duty which could no longer be postponed. He called on her the same afternoon at her apartment, for when once the Saint had made up his mind to a foray the job was as good as done. A morning's meditation had been enough for him to sketch out a plan of campaign, and after that he saw no good reason to put it aside while it grew whiskers.

But what the plan was is of no importance, for he never used it. He had sent in a card bearing his venerable alias of Sebastian Tombs, but when the countess sailed into the luxuriously modernistic drawing-room in which the butler had parked him, she came towards him with outstretched hand and a grim smile that promised surprises a split second before she spoke. 'Mr Templar?' she said coolly. 'I'm sorry I had to keep you waiting.'

It would be unfair to say that the Saint was disconcerted – in a buccaneer's life nothing could be foreseen, anyway, and you had to be schooled to the unexpected. But a perceptible instant went by before he answered. 'Why, hullo, Maggie,' he murmured. 'I was going to break it to you gently.'

'A man with your imagination should have been able to do better. After all, Mr Sebastian Tombs is getting to be almost as well known as the great Simon Templar – isn't he?'

The Saint nodded, admitting his lapse, and making a mental note that the time had come to tear himself finally away from the alter ego to which he had clung with perverse devotion for too many years. 'You keep pretty well up-to-date,' he remarked.

'Why not?' she returned frankly. 'I've had an idea for some time that I'd be getting a visit from you one day.'

'Would that be the voice of conscience?'

'Just common sense. Even you can't have a monopoly on thinking ahead.'

Simon studied her interestedly. The vats of champagne which had sparkled down her gullet in aid of one charity or another over the past six years had left their own thin dry tang in her voice, but few of her other indulgences had left their mark. The cargoes of caviar, the schools of smoked salmon, the truckloads of *foie gras*, the coveys of quail, the beds of oysters and the regiments of lobsters which had marched in eleemosynary procession through her intestines, had resolved themselves into very little solid flesh. Unlike most of her kind, she had not grown coarse and flabby; she had aged with a lean and arid dignity. At fifty, Maggie Oaks, late of Weehawken and the Follies, really looked like a countess, even if it was a rather tart and desiccated countess. She looked like one of those brittle fishblooded aristocrats who stand firm for kindness to animals and discipline for the lower classes. She had hard bright eyes and hard lines cracked into the heavy layers of powder and enamel on her face, and she was a hard bad woman in spite of her successful sophistication.

'At least that saves a lot of explanations,' said the Saint, and she returned his gaze with her coldly quizzical stare.

'I take it that I was right – that you've picked me for your next victim.'

'Let's call it "contributor",' suggested the Saint mildly.

She shrugged. 'In plain language, I'm either to give you, or have stolen from me, whatever sum of money you think fit to assess as a fine for what you would call my misdeeds.'

'Madam, you have a wonderful gift of coming to the point.'

'This money will be supposedly collected for charity,' she

went on, 'but you will take your commission for collecting it before you pass it on.'

'That was the general idea, Maggie.'

She lighted a cigarette. 'I suppose I shouldn't be allowed to ask why it's a crime for me to make a living in exactly the same way as you do?'

'There is a difference. I don't set myself up too seriously as a public benefactor. As a matter of fact, most people would tell you that I was a crook. If you want that point of view, ask a policeman.'

Her thin lips puckered with watchful mockery. 'That seems to make me smarter than you are, Mr Templar. The policeman would arrest you, but he'd tip his hat to me.'

'That's possible,' Simon admitted imperturbably. 'But there are other differences.'

'Meaning what?'

'Mathematical ones. A matter of simple economy. When I collect money, unless I'm trying to put things right for someone else who's been taken for a mug, between seventy-five and ninety per cent of it really does go to charity. Now suppose you collect ten thousand dollars in ticket sales for one of your parties. Twenty-five hundred bucks go straight into your pocket – you work on the gross. Other organizing expenses take up at least a thousand dollars more. Advertising, prizes, decorations, publicity and what not probably cost another ten per cent. Then there's the orchestra, hire of rooms and waiters and the cost of a lot of fancy food that's much too good for the people who eat it – let's say four thousand dollars. And the caterers give you a five-hundred-dollar cut on that. The net result is that you take in three thousand dollars and a nice big dinner, and the good cause gets maybe fifteen hundred. In other words, every time one of your suckers buys one of your fifty-dollar tickets, to help to save fallen women or something like that, he gives you twice as much as he gives the fallen women, which might not be exactly what he had in mind. So I don't think we really are in the same class.'

'You don't mean that I'm in a better class?' she protested sarcastically.

The Saint shook his head. 'Oh no,' he said. 'Not for a moment . . . But I do think that some of these differences ought to be adjusted.'

Her mouth was as tight as a trap. 'And how will that be done?'

'I thought it'd be an interesting change if you practised a little charity yourself. Suppose we set a donation of fifty thousand dollars—'

'Do you really think I'd give you fifty thousand dollars?'

'Why not?' asked the Saint reasonably. 'Other people have. And the publicity alone would be almost worth it. Ask your press agent. Besides, it needn't really even cost you anything. That famous diamond necklace of yours, for instance – even in the limited markets I could take it to, it'd fetch fifty thousand dollars easily. And, if you bought yourself a good imitation hardly anyone would know the difference.'

For a moment her mouth stayed open at the implication of what he was saying, and then she burst into a deep cackle of laughter. 'You almost scared me,' she said. 'But people have tried to bluff me before. Still, it was nice of you to give me the warning.' She stood up. 'Mr Templar, I'm not going to threaten you with the police because I know that would only make you laugh. Besides, I think I can look after myself. I'm not going to give you fifty thousand dollars, of course, and I'm not going to let you steal my necklace. If you can get either, you'll be a clever man. Will you come and see me again when you've hatched a plot?'

The Saint stood up also, and smoothed the clothes over

his sinewy seventy-four inches. His lazy blue eyes twinkled. 'That sounds almost like a challenge.'

'You can take it as one if you like.'

'I happen to know that your necklace isn't insured – no company in the country will ever carry you for a big risk since that fraudulent claim that got you a suspended sentence when you were in the Follies. Insurance company black lists don't fade.'

Her thin smile broadened. 'I got ten thousand dollars, just the same, and that's more than covered any losses I've had since,' she said calmly. 'No, Mr Templar, I'm not worried about insurance. If you can get what you're after I'll be the first to congratulate you.'

Simon's brows slanted at her with an impudent humour that would have given her fair warning if she had been less confident. He had completely recovered from the smither-eening of his first ingenious plans, and already his swift imagination was playing with a new and better scheme. 'Is that a bet?' he said temptingly.

'Do you expect me to put it in writing?'

He smiled back at her. 'I'll take your word for it . . . We must tell the newspapers.'

He left her to puzzle a little over that last remark, but by the time she went to bed she had forgotten it. Consequently she had a second spell of puzzlement a couple of mornings later when she listened to the twittering voice of one of her society acquaintances on the telephone. 'My *dear*, how *too* original! Quite the *cleverest* thing I ever heard of! . . . Oh, now you're just playing innocent! Of *course* it's in all the papers! And on the front page, too . . .! How *did* you manage it? My dear, I'm *madly* jealous! The Saint could steal anything I've got, and I mean *anything*! He must be the most *fascinating* man – isn't he?'

'He is, darling, and I'll tell him about your offer,' said the countess instinctively. She hung up the microphone and said: 'Silly old cow!' There had been another ball the night before, in aid of a seamen's mission or a dogs' hospital or something, and she had had to deal with the usual charitable ration of champagne and brandy; at that hour of the morning after her reactions were not as sharp as they became later in the day. Nevertheless, a recollection of the Saint's parting words seeped back into her mind with a slight shock. She took three aspirins in a glass of whisky and rang for some newspapers.

She didn't even have to open the first one. The item pricked her in the eyes just as the sheet was folded:

SAINT WILL ROB COUNTESS FOR CHARITY
'It's a Bet,' says Society Hostess

NEW YORK, October 12. – Simon Templar, better known as 'The Saint', famous 20th-century Robin Hood, added yesterday to his long list of audacities by announcing that he had promised to steal for charity the $100,000 necklace of Countess Jannowicz, the well-known society leader.

But for once the police have not been asked to prevent the intended crime. Templar called on the countess personally last Tuesday to discuss his scheme, and was told that she would be the first to congratulate him if he could get away with it.

The twist in the plot is that Countess Jannowicz is herself an indefatigable worker for charity, and the organizer of countless social functions through which thousands of dollars are annually collected for various hospitals and humane societies.

Those who remember the countess's many triumphs in roping in celebrities as a bait for her charities believe that she has surpassed herself with her latest 'catch'. It was whispered that the sensational stunt launching of some new

(*continued on page nine*)

The countess read it all through, and then she put her head back on the pillows and thought about it some more and began to shake with laughter. The vibration made her feel as if the top of her head was coming off but she couldn't stop it. She was still quivering among her curlers when the telephone exploded again.

'It's someone from Police Headquarters,' reported her maid. 'Inspector Fernack.'

'What the hell does he want?' demanded the countess. She took over the instrument. 'Yes,' she squawked.

'This is Inspector Fernack of Centre Street,' clacked the diaphragm. 'I suppose you've seen that story about the Saint and yourself in the papers?'

'Oh yes,' said the countess sweetly. 'I was just reading it. Isn't it simply delightful?'

'That isn't for me to say,' answered the detective in a laboured voice. 'But if this is a serious threat we shall have to take steps to protect your property.'

'Take steps— Oh, but I don't want to make it *too* easy for him. He always seems to get away with everything when the police are looking out for him.'

There was a strangled pause at the other end of the wire. Then: 'You mean that this is really only a publicity stunt?'

'Now, now,' said the countess coyly. 'That would be telling, wouldn't it? Good-bye, Inspector.' She handed the telephone back to her maid. 'If that damn flatfoot calls again, tell him I'm out,' she said. 'Get me some more aspirin and turn on my bath.'

It was typical of her that she dismissed Fernack's offer without a moment's uneasiness. After she had bathed and swallowed some coffee, however, she did summon the sallow and perspiring Mr Ullbaum who lived a feverish life as her press agent and vaguely general manager. 'There'll be some reporters calling for interviews,' she said. 'Some of 'em have been on the phone already. Tell 'm anything that comes into your head, but keep it funny.'

Mr Ullbaum spluttered, which was a habit of his when agitated, which was most of the time. 'But what's so funny if he does steal the necklace?'

'He isn't going to get the necklace – I'll take care of that. But I hope he tries. Everybody he's threatened to rob before has gone into hysterics before he's moved a finger, and they've been licked before he starts. I'm going to lick him and make him look as big as a flea at the same time – and all without even getting out of breath. We'll treat it as a joke now, and after he's made a fool of himself and it really *is* a joke, it'll be ten times funnier. For God's sake go away and use your own brain. That's what I pay you for. I've got a headache.'

She was her regal self again by cocktail time, when the Saint saw her across the room at the Pavilion with a party of friends, immaculately groomed from the top of her tight-waved head to the toes of her tight-fitting shoes and looking as if she had just stepped out of an advertisement for guillotines. He sauntered over in answer to her imperiously beckoning forefinger. 'I see your press agent didn't waste any time, Mr Templar.'

'I don't know,' said the Saint innocently. 'Are you sure you didn't drop a hint to your own publicity man?'

She shook her head. 'Mr Ullbaum was quite upset when he heard about it.'

The Saint smiled. He knew the permanently flustered Mr Ullbaum. 'Then it must have been my bloke,' he murmured. 'How did you like the story?'

'I thought it was rather misleading in places, but Mr

Ullbaum is going to put that right . . . Still, the police are quite interested. I had a phone call from a detective this morning before I was really awake.'

A faint unholy glimmer crossed the Saint's eyes. 'Would that be Inspector Fernack, by any chance?'

'Yes.'

'What did you tell him?'

'I told him to leave me alone.'

Simon seemed infinitesimally disappointed, but he grinned. 'I was wondering why he hadn't come paddling around to see me and add some more fun to the proceedings. I'm afraid I'm going to miss him. But it's nice to play with someone like you who knows the rules.'

'I know the rules, Mr Templar,' she said thinly. 'And the first rule is to win. Before you're finished you're going to wish you hadn't boasted so loudly.'

'You're not worried?'

She moved one jewel-encrusted hand indicatively. 'Did you notice those two men at that table in the corner?'

'Yes – have they been following you? I'll call a cop and have them picked up if you like.'

'Don't bother. Those are my bodyguards. They're armed and they have orders to shoot at the drop of a hat. Are you sure, *you* aren't worried?'

He laughed. 'I never drop my hat.' He buttoned his coat languidly, and the impudent scapegrace humour danced in his eyes like sunlight on blue water. 'Well – I've got to go on with my conspiring, and I'm keeping you from your friends . . .'

There was a chorus of protest from the other women at the table, who had been craning forward with their mouths open, breathlessly eating up every word. 'Oh *no*!' . . .

'Countess, you *must* introduce us!' . . . 'I've been *dying* to meet him!'

The countess's lips curled. 'Of course, my dears,' she said, with the sugariness of arsenic. 'How rude of me!' She performed the introductions. 'Lady Instock was telling me only this morning that you could steal *anything* from her,' she added spikily.

'*Anything*,' confirmed Lady Instock, gazing at the Saint rapturously out of her pale protruding eyes.

Simon looked at her thoughtfully. 'I won't forget it,' he said.

As he returned to his own table he heard her saying to a unanimous audience: 'Isn't he the most *thrilling*—'

Countess Jannowicz watched his departure intently, ignoring the feminine palpitations around her. She had a sardonic sense of humour, combined with a scarcely suppressed contempt for the climbing sycophants who crawled around her, that made the temptation to elaborate the joke too attractive to resist. Several times during the following week she was impelled to engineer opportunities to refer to 'that Saint person who's trying to steal my necklace'; twice again, when their paths crossed in fashionable restaurants, she called him to her table for the express pleasure of twitting him about his boast. To demonstrate her contempt for his reputation by teasing him on such friendly terms, and at the same time to enjoy the awed reactions of her friends, flattered something exhibitionistic in her that gave more satisfaction than any other fun she had had for years. It was like having a man-eating tiger for a pet and tweaking its ears.

This made nothing any easier for Mr Ullbaum. The countess was already known as a shrewd collector of publicity and the seeds of suspicion had been firmly planted by the opening story. Mr Ullbaum tried to explain to groups of sceptical reporters that the Saint's threat was perfectly genuine but that the countess was simply treating it with the disdain which it deserved; at the same time he tried to carry out his instructions to 'keep it funny', and the combination was too much for his mental powers. The cynical cross-examinations he had to submit to usually reduced him to ineffectual spluttering. His disclaimers were duly printed, but in contexts that made them sound more like admissions.

The countess, growing more and more attached to her own joke, was exceptionally tolerant. 'Let 'em laugh,' she said. 'It'll make it all the funnier when he flops.'

She saw him a third time at supper at '21' and invited him to join her party for coffee. He came over, smiling and immaculate, as much at ease as if he had been her favourite nephew. While she introduced him – a briefer business now, for he had met some of the party before – she pointedly fingered the coruscating rope of diamonds on her neck. 'You see I've still got it on,' she said as he sat down.

'I noticed that the lights seemed rather bright over here,' he admitted. 'You've been showing it around quite a lot lately, haven't you? Are you making the most of it while you've got it?'

'I want to make sure that you can't say I didn't give you plenty of chances.'

'Aren't you afraid that some ordinary grab artist might get it first? You know I have my competitors.'

She looked at him with thinly veiled derision. 'I'll begin to think there is a risk of that if you don't do something soon. And the suspense is making me quite jittery. Haven't you been able to think of a scheme yet?'

Simon's eyes rested on her steadily for a moment while he drew on his cigarette. 'That dinner and dance you were organizing for Friday – you sent me an invitation,' he said. 'Is it too late for me to get a ticket?'

'I've got some in my bag. If you've got twenty-five dollars—'

He laid fifty dollars on the table. 'Make it two – I may want someone to help me carry the loot.'

Her eyes went hard and sharp for an instant before a buzz of excited comment from her listening guests shut her off from him. He smiled at them all inscrutably and firmly changed the subject while he finished his coffee and smoked another cigarette. After he had taken his leave, she faced a bombardment of questions with stony preoccupation. 'Come to the dance on Friday,' was all she would say. 'You may see some excitement.'

Mr Ullbaum, summoned to the Presence again the next morning, almost tore his hair. 'Now will you tell the police?' he gibbered.

'Don't be so stupid,' she snapped. 'I'm not going to lose anything, and he's going to look a bigger fool than he has for years. All I want you to do is see that the papers hear that Friday is the day – we may sell a few more tickets.'

Her instinct served her well in that direction at least. The stories already published, vague and contradictory as they were, had boosted the sale of tickets for the Grand Ball in aid of the National League for the Care of Incurables beyond her expectations, and the final announcement circulated to the press by the unwilling Mr Ullbaum caused a flurry of last-minute buying that had the private ballroom hired for the occasion jammed to overflowing by eight o'clock on the evening of the twentieth. It was a curious tribute to the legends that had grown up around the name of Simon Templar, who had brought premature grey hairs to more police officers than could easily have been counted. Everyone who could read knew that the Saint had never harmed any innocent person, and there were enough sensation-seekers with clear consciences in New York to fill the spacious suite beyond capacity. Countess Jannowicz, glittering with diamonds, took her place calmly at the head table beside the chairman. He was the aged and harmlessly doddering bearer of a famous name who served in the same honorary position in several charitable societies and boards of directors without ever knowing much more about them than was entailed in presiding over occasional public meetings convened by energetic organizers like the countess; and he was almost stone deaf, an ailment which was greatly to his advantage in view of the speeches he had to listen to.

'What's this I read about some fella goin' to steal your necklace?' he mumbled, as he shakily spooned his soup.

'It wouldn't do you any good if I told you, you dithering old buzzard,' said the countess with a gracious smile.

'Oh yes. Mm. Ha. Extraordinary.'

She was immune to the undercurrents of excitement that ebbed and flowed through the room like leakages of static electricity. Her only emotion was a slight anxiety lest the Saint should cheat her, after all, by simply staying away.

After all the build-up, that would certainly leave her holding the bag. But it would bring him no profit, and leave him deflated on his own boast at the same time; it was impossible to believe that he would be satisfied with such a cheap anticlimax as that.

What else he could do and hope to get away with, on the other hand, was something that she had flatly given up trying to guess. Unless he had gone sheerly cuckoo, he couldn't hope to steal so much as a spoon that night, after his intentions had been so widely and openly proclaimed, without convicting himself on his own confession. And yet the Saint had so often achieved things that seemed equally impossible that she had to stifle a reluctant eagerness to see what his uncanny ingenuity would devise. Whatever that might be, the satisfaction of her curiosity could cost her nothing – for one very good reason. The Saint might have been able to accomplish the apparently impossible before, but he would literally have to perform a miracle if he was to open the vaults of the Vandrick National Bank. For that was where her diamond necklace lay that night and where it had lain ever since he paid his first call on her. The string she had been wearing ever since was a first-class imitation, worth about five hundred dollars. That was her answer to all the fanfaronading and commotion – a precaution so obvious and elementary that no one else in the world seemed to have thought of it, so flawless and unassailable that the Saint's boast was exploded before he even began, so supremely ridiculously simple that it would make the whole earth quake with laughter when the story broke.

Even so, ratcheted notch after notch by the lurking fear of a fiasco, tension crept up on her as the time went by without a sign of the Saint's elegant slender figure and tantalizing blue eyes. He was not there for the dinner or the following speeches, nor did he show up during the interval while some of the tables were being whisked away from the main ballroom to make room for the dancing. The dancing started without him, went on through long-drawn expectancy while impatient questions leapt at the countess spasmodically from time to time like shots from ambush.

'He'll come," she insisted monotonously, while news photographers roamed restively about with their fingers aching on the triggers of their flashlights.

At midnight the Saint arrived. No one knew how he got in; no one had seen him before; but suddenly he was there. The only announcement of his arrival was when the music stopped abruptly in the middle of a bar. Not all at once, but gradually, in little groups, the dancers shuffled to stillness, became frozen to the floor as the first instinctive turning of eyes towards the orchestra platform steered other eyes in the same direction.

He stood in the centre of the dais, in front of the microphone. No one had a moment's doubt that it was the Saint, although his face was masked. The easy poise of his athletic figure in the faultlessly tailored evening clothes was enough introduction, combined with the careless confidence with which he stood there, as if he had been a polished master of ceremonies preparing to make a routine announcement. The two guns he held, one in each hand, their muzzles shifting slightly over the crowd, seemed a perfectly natural part of his costume.

'May I interrupt for a moment, ladies and gentlemen?' he said. He spoke quietly but the loud-speakers made his voice audible in every corner of the room. Nobody moved or made any answer. His question was rather superfluous. He *had* interrupted, and everyone's ears were strained for what he had to say. 'This is a hold-up,' he went on in the same easy conversational tone. 'You've all been expecting it, so none of you should have heart failure. Until I've finished, none of you may leave the room – a friend of mine is at the other end of the hall to help to see that this order is carried out.'

A sea of heads screwed round to where a shorter, stockier man, in evening clothes that seemed too tight for him, stood blocking the far entrance, also masked and also with two guns in his hands. 'So long as you all do exactly what you're told, I promise that nobody will get hurt. You two' – one of his guns flicked towards the countess's bodyguards, who were standing stiff-fingered where they had been caught when they saw him – 'come over here. Turn your backs, take out your guns slowly and drop them on the floor.'

His voice was still quiet and matter-of-fact but both men obeyed like automatons. 'O.K. Now turn around – and kick them towards me ... That's fine. You can stay where you are, and don't try to be heroes if you want to live to boast about it.'

A smile touched his lips under the mask. He pocketed one of his guns and picked up a black bag from the dais and tossed it out on the floor. Then he put a cigarette between his lips and lighted it with a match flicked on the thumbnail of the same hand. 'The hold-up will now proceed,' he remarked affably. 'The line forms on the right, and that means everybody except the waiters. Each of you will put a contribution in the bag as you pass by. Lady Instock, that's a nice pair of earrings . . .'

Amazed, giggling, white-faced, surly, incredulous, according to their different characters, the procession began to file by and drop different articles into the bag under his directions. There was nothing much else that they could do. Each of them felt that gently waving gun centred on his own body, balancing its bark of death against the first sign of resistance. To one red-faced man who started to bluster, a waiter said tremulously: 'Better do what he says. Tink of all da ladies. Anybody might get hit if he start shooting.' His wife shed a pearl necklace and hustled him by. Most of the gathering had the same idea. Anyone who had tried to to be a hero would probably have been mobbed by a dozen others who had no wish to die for his glory. Nobody really thought much beyond that. This wasn't what they had expected, but they couldn't analyse their reactions. Their brains were too numbed to think very much.

Two brains were not numbed. One of them belonged to the chairman who had lost his glasses, adding dimsightedness to his other failings. From where he stood he couldn't distinguish anything as small as a mask or a gun but somebody seemed to be standing up on the platform and was probably making a speech. The chairman nodded from time to time with an expression of polite interest, thinking busily about the new corn plaster that somebody had recommended to him. The other active brain belonged to the Countess Jannowicz but there seemed to be nothing useful that she could do with it. There was no encouraging feeling of enterprise to be perceived in the guests around her, no warm inducement to believe that they would respond to courageous leadership.

'Can't you see he's bluffing?' she demanded in a hoarse bleat. 'He wouldn't dare to shoot!'

'I should be terrified,' murmured the Saint imperturbably, without moving his eyes from the passing line. 'Madame, that looks like a very fine emerald ring . . .'

Something inside the countess seemed to be clutching at her stomach and shaking it up and down. She had taken care to leave her own jewels in a safe place but it hadn't occurred to her to give the same advice to her guests. And now the Saint was robbing them under her nose – almost under her own roof. Social positions had been shattered overnight on slighter grounds. She grabbed the arm of a waiter who was standing near. 'Send for the police, you fool!' she snarled. He looked at her and drew down the corners of his mouth in what might have been a smile or a sneer, or both, but he made no movement.

Nobody made any movement except as the Saint directed. The countess felt as if she were in a nightmare. It was amazing to her that the hold-up could have continued so long without interruption – without some waiter opening a service door and seeing what was going on, or someone outside in the hotel noticing the curious quietness and giving the alarm. But the ballroom might have been spirited away on to a desert island. The last of the obedient procession passed by the Saint and left its contribution in the bag and joined the silent staring throng of those who had already contributed. Only the chairman and the countess had not moved – the chairman because he hadn't heard a word and didn't know what was going on.

The Saint looked at her across the room. 'I've been saving Countess Jannowicz to the last,' he said, 'because she's the star turn that you've all been waiting for. Will you step up now, Countess?'

Fighting a tangle of emotions, but compelled by a fascination that drove her like a machine, she moved towards the platform. And the Saint glanced at the group of almost frantic photographers. 'Go ahead, boys,' he said kindly. 'Take your pictures. It's the chance of a lifetime . . . Your necklace, Countess.'

She stood still, raised her hands a little way, dropped them, raised them again, slowly, to her neck. Magnesium bulbs winked and splashed like a barrage of artificial lightning as she unfastened the clasp and dropped the necklace on top of the collection in the bag. 'You can't get away with this,' she said whitely.

"Let me show you how easy it is,' said the Saint calmly. He turned his gun to the nearest man to the platform. 'You, sir – would you mind closing the bag, carefully, and taking it down to my friend at the other end of the room? Thank you.' He watched the bag on its way down the room until it was in the hands of the stocky man at the far entrance. 'O.K., partner,' he said crisply. 'Scram.'

As if the word had been a magical incantation, the man vanished. A kind of communal gasp like a sigh of wind swept over the assembly, as if the final unarguable physical disappearance of their property had squeezed the last long-held breath out of their bodies. Every eye had been riveted on it in its last journey through their midst, every eye had blinked to the shock of its ultimate vanishment, and then every eye dragged itself dazedly back to the platform from which those catastrophes had been dictated.

Almost to their surprise, the Saint was still standing there. But his other gun had disappeared and he had taken his mask off. In some way, the aura of subtle command that had clung to him before in spite of his easy casualness had gone, leaving the easy casualness alone. He was still smiling. For an instant the two bodyguards were paralysed. And then with muffled choking noises they made a concerted dive for their guns. The Saint made no move except a slight deprecating motion of the hand that held his cigarette. 'Ladies and gentlemen,' he said into the microphone, 'I must now make my apologies, and an explanation.'

The bodyguards straightened up, with their guns held ready. And yet something in his quiet voice, unarmed as he was, gripped them in spite of themselves, as it had gripped everyone else in the room. They looked questioningly towards the countess. She gave them no response. She was rigid, watching the Saint with the first icy grasp of an impossible premonition closing in on her.

Somehow the Saint was going to get away with it. She knew it with a horrible certainty, even while she was wildly trying to guess what he would say. He could never have been so insane as to believe that he could pull a public hold-up like that without being arrested an hour after he left the hotel, unless he had had some trick up his sleeve to immobilize the hue and cry. And she knew that she was now going to hear the trick she had not thought of.

'You have just been the victims of a hold-up,' he was saying. 'Probably to nearly all of you that was a novel experience. But it is something that might happen to any of you tonight, tomorrow, at any time – so long as there are men at large to whom that seems like the best way of making a living. You came here tonight to help the National League for the Care of Incurables. That is a good and humane work. But I have taken this opportunity – with the kind co-operation of Countess Jannowicz – to make you think of another equally good, perhaps even more constructive work: the Care of Curables. I am talking about a class of whom I may know more than most of you – a section of those unfortunates who are broadly and discriminatingly called criminals.

'Ladies and gentlemen, not every lawbreaker is a

brutalized desperado, fit only for swift extermination. I know that there are men of that kind, and you all know that I have been more merciless with them than any officer of the law. But there are others. I mean the men who steal through ignorance, through poverty, through misplaced ambition, through despair, through lack of better opportunity, I mean also men who have been punished for their crimes, and who are now at the crossroads. One road takes them deeper and deeper into crime, into becoming real brutalized desperadoes. The other road takes them back to honesty, to regaining their self-respect, to becoming good and valuable citizens. All they need is the second chance which society is often so unwilling to give them. To give these men their second chance, has been founded the Society for the Rehabilitation of Delinquents – rather an elaborate name for a simple and straightforward thing. I am proud to be the first president of that society. We believe that money spent on this object is far cheaper than the money spent on keeping prisoners in jail, and at the same time is less than the damage that these men would do to the community if they were left to go on with their crimes. We ask you to believe the same thing, and to be generous.

'Everything that has been taken from you tonight can be found tomorrow at the office of the Society, which is in the Missouri Trust Building on Fifth Avenue. If you wish to leave your property there, to be sold for the benefit of the Society, we shall be grateful. If it has too great a sentimental value to you, and you wish to buy it back, we shall be glad to exchange it for a cheque. And if you object to us very seriously, and simply want it back, we shall of course have to give it back. But we hope that none of you will demand that.

'That is why we ventured to take the loot away tonight. Between now and tomorrow morning, we want you to have time to think. Think of how different this hold-up would have been if it had been real. Think of your feelings when you saw your jewellery vanishing out of that door. Think of how little difference it would really make to your lives' – he looked straight at the countess – 'if you were wearing imitation stones, while the money that has been locked up idly in the real ones was set free to do good and useful work. Think, ladies and gentlemen, and forgive us the melodramatic way in which we have tried to bring home our point.'

He stepped back, and there was a moment of complete silence. The chairman had at last found his glasses. He saw the speaker retiring with a bow from the microphone. Apparently the speech was over. It seemed to be the chairman's place to give the conventional lead. He raised his hands and clapped loudly. It is things like that that turn tides and start revolutions. In another second the whole ball was clattering with hysterical applause.

'My dear, how *do* you think of these things—' 'The most *divinely* thrilling—' 'I was really *petrified* . . .'

The Countess Jannowicz wriggled dazedly free from the shrill jabber of compliments, managed somehow to snatch the Saint out of a circle of clamorous women of which Lady Instock was the most gushing leader. In a comparatively quiet corner of the room she faced him. 'You're a good organizer, Mr Templar. The head waiter tells me that Mr Ullbaum telephoned this afternoon and told the staff how they were to behave during the hold-up.'

He was cheerfully appreciative. 'I must remember to thank him.'

'Mr Ullbaum did no such thing.'

He smiled. 'Then he must have been impersonated. But the damage seems to be done.'

'You know that for all your talking you've still committed a crime?'

'I think you'd be rather a lonely prosecutor.'

Rage had made her a little incoherent. 'I shall not come to your office. You've made a fool of yourself. My necklace is in the bank—'

'Countess,' said the Saint patiently, 'I'd guessed that much. That's why I want you to be sure and bring me the real one. Lady Instock is going to leave her earrings and send a cheque as well, and all the rest of your friends seem to be sold on the idea. You're supposed to be the number one patron. What would they think of you if after all the advertising you let yourself out with a five-hundred-dollar string of cut glass?'

'I can disclaim—'

'I know you can. But your name will still be mud. Whereas at the moment you're tops. Why not make the best of it and charge it to publicity?'

She knew she was beaten – that he had simply turned a trick with the cards that for days past she had been busily forcing into his hand. But she still fought with the bitterness of futility. 'I'll have the police investigate this phony charity—'

'They'll find that it's quite legally constituted, and so long as the funds last they'll be administered with perfect good faith.'

'And who'll get the benefit of them besides yourself?'

Simon smiled once again. 'Our first and most urgent case will be a fellow named Marty O'Connor. He helped me with the collection tonight. You ought to remember him – he was your chauffeur for three weeks. Anyone like yourself, Countess,' said the Saint rather cruelly, 'ought to know that charity begins at home.'

The Mug's Game

The stout jovial gentleman in the shapeless suit pulled a card out of his wallet and pushed it across the table. The printing on it said 'J. J. Naskill.'

The Saint looked at it and offered his cigarette case.

'I'm afraid I don't carry any cards,' he said. 'But my name is Simon Templar.'

Mr Naskill beamed, held out a large moist hand to be shaken, took a cigarette, mopped his glistening forehead and beamed again.

'Well, it's a pleasure to talk to you, Mr Templar,' he said heartily. 'I get bored with my own company on these long journeys and it hurts my eyes to read on a train. Hate travelling, anyway. It's a good thing my business keeps me in one place most of the time. What's your job, by the way?'

Simon took a pull at his cigarette while he gave a moment's consideration to his answer. It was one of the few questions that ever embarrassed him. It wasn't that he had any real objection to telling the truth, but that the truth tended to disturb the tranquil flow of ordinary casual conversation. Without causing a certain amount of commotion, he couldn't say to a perfect stranger, 'I'm a sort of benevolent brigand. I raise hell for crooks and racketeers of all kinds, and make life miserable for policemen, and rescue damsels in distress and all that sort of thing.' The Saint had often thought of it as a deplorable commentary on the stodgy unadventurousness of the average mortal's mind; but he knew that it was beyond his power to alter.

He said apologetically: 'I'm just one of those lazy people. I believe they call it "independent means." '

This was true enough for an idle moment. The Saint could have exhibited a bank account that would have dazzled many men who called themselves wealthy, but it was on the subject of how that wealth had been accumulated that several persons who lived by what they had previously called their wits were inclined to wax profane.

Mr Naskill sighed.

'I don't blame you,' he said. 'Why work if you don't have to? Wish I was in your shoes myself. Wasn't born lucky, that's all. Still, I've got a good business now, so I shouldn't complain. Expect you recognize the name.'

'Naskill?' The Saint frowned slightly. When he repeated it, it did have a faintly familiar ring. 'It sounds as if I ought to know it—'

The other nodded.

'Some people call it Noskill,' he said. 'They're about right, too. That's what it is. Magic for amateurs. Look.'

He flicked a card out of his pocket on to the table between them. It was the ace of diamonds. He turned it over and immediately faced it again. It was the nine of clubs. He turned it over again and it was the queen of hearts. He left it lying face down on the cloth and Simon picked it up curiously and examined it. It was the three of spades, but there was nothing else remarkable about it.

'Used to be a conjuror myself,' Naskill explained. 'Then I got rheumatism in my hands, and I was on the rocks. Didn't know any other job, so I had to make a living teaching other people tricks. Most of 'em haven't the patience to practise sleight of hand, so I made it easy for 'em. Got a fine trade now, and a two-hundred-page catalogue. I can make anybody into just as good a magician as the money they like to spend, and they needn't practise for five minutes. Look.'

He took the card that the Saint was still holding, tore it into small pieces, folded his plump fingers on them for a moment and spread out his hands – empty. Then he broke open the cigarette he was smoking and inside it was a three of spades rolled into a tight cylinder, crumpled but intact.

'You can buy that one for a dollar and a half,' he said. 'The first one I showed you is two dollars. It's daylight robbery, really, but some people like to show off at parties, and they give me a living.'

Simon slid back his sleeve from his wrist watch and glanced out of the window at the speeding landscape. There was still about an hour to go before they would be in Miami, and he had nothing else to take up his time. Besides, Mr Naskill was something novel and interesting in his experience; and it was part of the Saint's creed that a modern brigand could never know too much about the queerer things that went on in the world.

He caught the eye of a waiter at the other end of the dining car and beckoned him over.

'Could you stand a drink?' he suggested.

'Scotch for me,' said Mr Naskill gratefully. He wiped his face again while Simon duplicated the order. 'But I'm still talking about myself. If I'm boring you—'

'Not a bit of it.' The Saint was perfectly sincere. 'I don't often meet anyone with an unusual job like yours. Do you know any more tricks?'

Mr Naskill polished a pair of horn-rimmed spectacles, fitted them on his nose and hitched himself forward.

'Look,' he said eagerly.

He was like a child with a new collection of toys. He dug into another of his sagging pockets, which Simon was now deciding were probably loaded with enough portable equipment to stage a complete show, and hauled out a pack of cards which he pushed over to the Saint.

'You take 'em. Look 'em over as much as you like. See if you can find anything wrong with 'em . . . All right. Now shuffle 'em. Shuffle 'em all you want.' He waited. 'Now spread 'em out on the table. You're doing this trick, not me. Take any card you like. Look at it – don't let me see it. All right. Now, I haven't touched the cards at all, have I, except to give 'em to you? You shuffled 'em and you picked a card without me helping you. I couldn't have forced it on you or anything. Eh? All right. Well, I could put any trimmings I wanted on this trick – any fancy stunts I could think up to make it look more mysterious. They'd all be easy because I know what card you've got all the time. You've got the six of diamonds.'

Simon turned the card over. It was the six of diamonds.

'How's that?' Naskill demanded gleefully.

The Saint grinned. He drew a handful of cards towards him, face downwards as they lay, and pored over the backs for two or three minutes before he sat back again with a rueful shrug.

Mr Naskill chortled.

'There's nothing wrong with your eyes,' he said. 'You could go over 'em with a microscope and not find anything. All the same, I'll tell you what you've got. The king of spades, the two of spades, the ten of hearts—'

'I'll take your word for it,' said the Saint resignedly. 'But how on earth do you do it?'

Naskill glowed delightedly.

'Look,' he said.

He took off his glasses and passed them over. Under the flat lenses Simon could see the notations clearly printed in the corners of each card – KS, 2S, 10H. They vanished as soon as he moved the glasses and it was impossible to find a trace of them with the naked eye.

'I've heard of that being done with coloured glasses,' said the Saint slowly, 'but I noticed that yours weren't coloured.'

Naskill shook his head.

'Coloured glasses are old stuff. Too crude. Used to be used a lot by sharpers but too many people got to hear about 'em. You couldn't get into a card game with coloured glasses these days. No good for conjuring, either. But this is good. Invented it myself. Special ink and special kind of glass. There is a tint in it, of course, but it's too faint to notice.' He shoved the cards over the cloth. 'Here. Keep the lot for a souvenir. You can have some fun with your friends. But don't go asking 'em in for a game of poker, mind.'

Simon gathered the cards together.

'It would be rather a temptation,' he admitted. 'But don't you get a lot of customers who buy them just for that?'

'Sure. A lot of professionals use my stuff. I know 'em all. Often see 'em in the shop. Good customers – they buy by the dozen. Can't refuse to serve 'em – they'd only get 'em some other way or buy somewhere else. I call it a compliment to the goods I sell. Never bothers my conscience. Anybody who plays cards with strangers is asking for trouble, anyway. It isn't only professionals, either. You'd be surprised at some of the people I've had come in and ask for a deck of readers – that's the trade name for 'em. I remember one fellow . . .'

He launched into a series of anecdotes that filled up the time until they had to separate to their compartments to collect their luggage. Mr Naskill's pining for company was understandable after only a few minutes' acquaintance; it was clear that he was constitutionally incapable of surviving for long without an audience.

Simon Templar was not bored. He had already had his money's worth. Whether his friends would allow him to get very far with a programme of card tricks if he appeared before them in an unaccustomed set of horn-rimmed windows was highly doubtful; but the trick was worth knowing, just the same.

Almost every kind of craftsman has specialized journals to inform him of the latest inventions and discoveries and technical advances in his trade, but there is as yet no publication called the *Grafter's Gazette and Weekly Skulldugger* to keep a professional freebooter abreast of the newest devices for separating the sucker from his dough, and the Saint was largely dependent on his own researches for the encyclopedic knowledge of the wiles of the ungodly that had brought so much woe to the *chevaliers d'Industrie* of two hemispheres. Mr Naskill's conversation had yielded a scrap of information that would be filed away in the Saint's well-stocked memory against the day when it would be useful. It might lie fallow for a month, a year, five years, before it produced its harvest: the Saint was in no hurry. In the fullness of time he would collect his dividend – it was one of the cardinal articles of his faith that nothing of that kind ever crossed his path without a rendezvous for the future, however distant that future might be. But one of the things that always gave the Saint a particular affection for this story was the promptness with which his expectations were fulfilled.

There were some episodes in Simon Templar's life when all the component parts of a perfectly rounded diagram fell into place one by one with such a sweetly definitive succession of crisp clicks that mere coincidence was too pallid and anaemic a theory with which to account for them – when he almost felt as if he were reclining passively in an armchair and watching the oiled wheels of Fate roll smoothly through the convolutions of a supernaturally engineered machine.

Two days later he was relaxing his long lean body on the private beach of the Hispaniola, revelling in the clean sharp bite of the sun on his brown skin and lazily debating the comparative attractions of iced beer or a Pimm's Cup as a noon refresher, when two voices reached him sufficiently clearly to force themselves into his drowsy consciousness. They belonged to a man and a girl, and it was obvious that they were quarrelling.

Simon wasn't interested. He was at peace with the world. He concentrated on digging up a small sand castle with his toes and tried to shut them out. And then he heard the girl say: 'My God, are you so dumb that you can't see that they must be crooks?'

It was the word 'crooks' that did it. When the Saint heard that word, he could no more have concentrated on sand castles than a rabid Egyptologist could have remained aloof while gossip of scarabs and sarcophagi shuttled across his head. A private squabble was one thing, but this was something else that to the Saint made eavesdropping not only pardonable but almost a moral obligation.

He rolled over and looked at the girl. She was only a few feet from him and even at that range it was easier to go on looking than to look away. From her loose raven hair down to her daintily enamelled toe-nails there wasn't an inch of her that didn't make its own demoralizing demands on the eye, and the clinging silk swimsuit she wore left very few inches any secret.

'Why must they be crooks?' asked the man stubbornly. He was young and tow-headed but the Saint's keen survey traced hard and haggard lines in his face. 'Just because I've been out of luck—'

'Luck!' The girl's voice was scornful and impatient. 'You were out of luck when you met them. Two men that you know nothing about, who pick you up in a bar and suddenly discover that you're the bosom pal they've been looking for all their lives – who want to take you out to dinner every night, and take you out fishing every day, and buy you drinks and show you the town – and you talk about luck! D'you think they'd do all that if they didn't know they could get you to play cards with them every night and make you lose enough to pay them back a hundred times over?'

'I won plenty from them to begin with.'

'Of course you did! They let you win – just to encourage you to play higher. And now you've lost all that back and a lot more that you can't afford to lose. And you're still going on, making it worse and worse.' She caught his arm impulsively and her voice softened. 'Oh, Eddie, I hate fighting with you like this, but can't you see what a fool you're being?'

'Well, why don't you leave me alone if you hate fighting? Anyone might think I was a kid straight out of school.'

He shrugged himself angrily away from her, and as he turned he looked straight into the Saint's eyes. Simon was so interested that the movement caught him unprepared, still watching them, as if he had been hiding behind a curtain and it had been abruptly torn down.

It was much too late for Simon to switch his eyes away without looking even guiltier that he had to go on watching, and the young man went on scowling at him and said uncomfortably: 'We aren't really going to cut each other's throats, but there are some things that women can't understand.'

'If a man told him that elephants laid eggs he'd believe it, just because it was a man who told him,' said the girl petulantly, and she also looked at the Saint. 'Perhaps if *you* told him—'

'The trouble is, she won't give me credit for having any sense—'

'He's such a baby—'

'If she didn't read so many detective stories—'

'He's so damned pig-headed—'

The Saint held up his hands.

'Wait a minute,' he pleaded. 'Don't shoot the referee – he doesn't know what it's all about. I couldn't help hearing what you were saying, but it isn't my fight.'

The young man rubbed his head shamefacedly, and the girl bit her lip.

Then she said quickly: 'Well, please, won't you *be* a referee? Perhaps he'd listen to you. He's lost fifteen thousand dollars already, and it isn't all his own money—'

'For God's sake,' the man burst out savagely, 'are you trying to make me look a complete heel?'

The girl caught her breath, and her lip trembled. And then, with a sort of sob, she picked herself up and walked quickly away without another word.

The young man gazed after her in silence, and his fist clenched on a handful of sand as if he would have liked to hurt it.

'Oh hell,' he said expressively.

Simon drew a cigarette out of the packet beside him and tapped it meditatively on his thumbnail while the awkward hiatus made itself at home. His eyes seemed to be intent on following the movements of a small fishing cruiser far out on the cobalt waters of the Gulf Stream.

'It's none of my damn business,' he remarked at length, 'but isn't there just a chance that the girl friend may be right? It's happened before; and a resort like this is rather a happy hunting ground for all kinds of crooks.'

'I know it is,' said the other sourly. He turned and looked at the Saint again miserably. 'But I *am* pig-headed, and I can't bear to admit to her that I could have been such a mug. She's my fiancée – I suppose you guessed that. My name's Mercer.'

'Simon Templar is mine.'

The name had a significance for Mercer that it apparently had not had for Mr Naskill. His eyes opened wide.

'Good God, you don't mean—You're not the Saint?'

Simon smiled. He was still immodest enough to enjoy the sensation that his name could sometimes cause.

'That's what they call me.'

'Of course I've read about you, but— Well, it sort of . . .' The young man petered out incoherently. 'And I'd have argued with you about crooks . . . But – well, you ought to know. Do *you* think I've been a mug?'

The Saint's brows slanted sympathetically.

'If you took my advice,' he answered, 'you'd let these birds find someone else to play with. Write it off to experience, and don't do it again.'

'But I can't!' Mercer's response was desperate. 'She – she was telling the truth. I've lost money that wasn't mine. I've only got a job in an advertising agency that doesn't pay very much, but her people are pretty well off. They've found me a better job here, starting in a couple of months, and they sent us down here to find a home, and they gave us twenty thousand dollars to buy it and furnish it, and that's the money I've been playing with. Don't you see? I've *got* to go on and win it back!'

'Or go on and lose the rest.'

'Oh, I know. But I thought the luck must change before that. And yet—But everybody who plays cards isn't a crook, is he? And I don't see how they could have done it. After she started talking about it, I watched them. I've been looking for it. And I couldn't catch them making a single move that wasn't above-board. Then I began to think about marked cards – we've always played with their cards. I sneaked away one of the packs we were using last night, and I've been look- ing at it this morning. I'll swear there isn't a mark on it. Here, I can show you.'

He fumbled feverishly in a pocket of his beach robe and pulled out a pack of cards. Simon glanced through them. There was nothing wrong with them that he could see; and it was then that he remembered Mr J. J. Naskill.

'Does either of these birds wear glasses?' he asked.

'One of them wears pince-nez,' replied the mystified young man. 'But—'

'I'm afraid,' said the Saint thoughtfully, 'that it looks as if you are a mug.'

Mercer swallowed.

'If I am,' he said helplessly, 'what on earth am I going to do?'

Simon hitched himself up.

'Personally, I'm going to have a dip in the pool. And you're going to be so busy apologizing to your fiancée and making friends again that you won't have time to think about anything else. I'll keep these cards and make sure about them, if you don't mind. Then suppose we meet in the bar for a cocktail about six o'clock, and maybe I'll be able to tell you something.'

When he returned to his own room the Saint put on Mr Naskill's horn-rimmed glasses and examined the cards again. Every one of them was clearly marked in the diagonally opposite corners with the value of the card and the initial of the suit, exactly like the deck that Naskill had given him; and it was then that the Saint knew that his faith in Destiny was justified again.

Shortly after six o'clock he strolled into the bar and saw that Mercer and the girl were already there. It was clear that they had buried their quarrel.

Mercer introduced her: 'Miss Grange – or you can just call her Josephine.'

She was wearing something in black and white taffeta, with a black and white hat and black and white gloves and a black and white bag, and she looked as if she had just stepped out of a fashion plate. She said: 'We're both ashamed of ourselves for having a scene in front of you this afternoon, but I'm glad we did. You've done Eddie a lot of good.'

'I hadn't any right to blurt out all my troubles like that,' Mercer said sheepishly. 'You were damned nice about it.'

The Saint grinned.

'I'm a pretty nice guy,' he murmured. 'And now I've got something to show you. Here are your cards.'

He spread the deck out on the table and then he took the horn-rimmed glasses out of his pocket and held them over the cards so that the other two could look through them. He slid the cards under the lenses one by one, face downwards, and turned them over afterwards, and for a little while they stared in breathless silence.

The girl gasped.

'I told you so!'

Mercer's fists clenched.

'By God, if I don't murder those swine—'

She caught his wrist as he almost jumped up from the table.

'Eddie, that won't do you any good.'

'It won't do them any good either! When I've finished with them—'

'But that won't get any of the money back.'

'I'll beat it out of them.'

'But that'll only get you in trouble with the police. That wouldn't help . . . Wait!' She clung to him frantically. 'I've got it. You could borrow Mr Templar's glasses and play them at their own game. You could break Yoring's glasses – sort of accidentally. They wouldn't dare to stop playing on account of that. They'd just have to trust to luck, like you've been doing, and anyway, they'd feel sure they were going to get it all back again later. And you could win everything back and never see them again.' She shook his arm in her excitement. 'Go on, Eddie. It'd serve them right. I'll let you play just once more if you'll do that!'

Mercer's eyes turned to the Saint, and Simon pushed the glasses across the table towards him.

The young man picked them up slowly, looked at the cards through them again. His mouth twitched. And then, with a sudden hopeless gesture, he thrust them away and passed a shaky hand over his eyes.

'It's no good,' he said wretchedly. 'I couldn't do it. They know I don't wear glasses. And I – I've never done anything like that before. I'd only make a mess of it. They'd spot me in five minutes. And then there wouldn't be anything I could say. I – I wouldn't have the nerve. I suppose I'm just a mug after all—'

The Saint leaned back and put a light to a cigarette and sent a smoke-ring spinning through the fronds of a potted palm. In all his life he had never missed a cue, and it seemed that this was very much like a cue. He had come to Miami Beach to bask in the sun and be good, but it wasn't his fault if business was thrust upon him.

'Maybe someone with a bit of experience could do it better,' he said. 'Suppose you let me meet your friends.'

Mercer looked at him, first blankly, then incredulously; and the girl's dark eyes slowly lighted up.

Her slim fingers reached impetuously for the Saint's hand.

'You wouldn't really do that – help Eddie to win back what he's lost—'

'What would you expect Robin Hood to do?' asked the Saint quizzically. 'I've got a reputation to keep up – and I might even pay my own expenses while I'm doing it.' He drew the revealing glasses towards him and tucked them back in his pocket. 'Let's go and have some dinner and organize the details.'

But actually there were hardly any details left to organize, for Josephine Grange's inspiration had been practically complete in its first outline. The Saint, who never believed in expending any superfluous effort, devoted most of his attention to some excellent lobster thermidor; but he had a pleasant sense of anticipation that lent an edge to his appetite. He knew, even then, that all those interludes of virtue in which he had so often tried to indulge, those brief intervals in which he played at being an ordinary respectable citizen and promised himself to forget that there was such a thing as crime, were only harmless self-deceptions – that for him the only complete life was still the ceaseless hair-trigger battle in which he had found so much delight. And this episode had everything that he asked to make a perfect cameo.

He felt like a star actor waiting for the curtain to rise on the third act of an obviously triumphant first night when they left the girl at the Hispaniola and walked over to the Runaway Bar – 'that's where we usually meet,' Mercer explained. And a few minutes later he was being introduced to the other two members of the cast.

Mr Yoring, who wore the pince-nez, was a small pear-shaped man in a crumpled linen suit, with white hair and bloodhound jowls and a pathetically frustrated expression. He looked like a retired businessman whose wife took him to the opera. Mr Kilgarry, his partner, was somewhat taller and younger, with a wide mouth and a rich nose and a raffish manner: he looked like the kind of man that men like Mr Yoring wish they could be. Both of them welcomed Mercer with an exuberant bonhomie that was readily expanded to include the Saint. Mr Kilgarry ordered a round of drinks.

'Having a good time here, Mr Templar?'

'Pretty good.'

'Ain't we all having a good time?' crowed Mr Yoring. 'I'm gonna buy a drink.'

'I've just ordered a drink,' said Mr Kilgarry.

'Well, I'm gonna order another,' said Mr Yoring defiantly. No wife was going to take him to the opera tonight.

'You in business, Mr Templar?' asked Mr Kilgarry interestedly.

The Saint smiled.

'My business is letting other people make money for me,'

he said, continuing strictly in the vein of truth. He patted his pockets significantly. 'The market's been doing pretty well these days.'

Mr Kilgarry and Mr Yoring exchanged glances, while the Saint picked up his drink. It wasn't his fault if they misunderstood him; but it had been rather obvious that the conversation was doomed to launch some tactful feelers into his financial status, and Simon saw no need to add to their coming troubles by making them work hard for their information.

'Well, that's fine,' said Mr Yoring happily. 'I'm gonna buy another drink.'

'You can't,' said Mr Kilgarry. 'It's my turn.'

Mr Yoring looked wistful, like a small boy who has been told that he can't go out and play with his new air gun. Then he wrapped an arm around Mercer's shoulders.

'You gonna play tonight, Eddie?'

'I don't know,' Mercer said hesitantly. 'I've just been having dinner with Mr Templar—'

'Bring him along,' boomed Mr Kilgarry heartily. 'What's the difference? Four's better than three, any day. D'you play cards, Mr Templar?'

'Most games,' said the Saint cheerfully.

'That's fine,' said Mr Kilgarry. 'Fine,' he repeated, as if he wanted to leave no doubt that he thought it was fine.

Mr Yoring looked dubious.

'I dunno. We play rather high stakes, Mr Templar.'

'They can't be too high for me,' said the Saint boastfully.

'Fine,' said Mr Kilgarry again, removing the last vestige of uncertainty about his personal opinion. 'Then that's settled. What's holding us back?'

There was really nothing holding them back except the drinks that were lined up on the bar, and that deterrent was eliminated with a discreetly persuasive briskness. Under Mr

Kilgarry's breezy leadership they piled into a taxi and headed for one of the smaller hotels on Ocean Drive, where Mr Yoring proclaimed that he had a bottle of Scotch that would save them from the agonies of thirst while they were playing. As they rode up in the elevator he hooked his arm affectionately through the Saint's.

'Say, you're awright, ole man,' he announced. 'I like to meet a young feller like you. You oughta come out fishin' with us. Got our own boat here, hired for the season, an' we just take out fellers we like. You like fishin'?'

'I like catching sharks,' said the Saint, with unblinking innocence.

'You ought to come out with us,' said Mr Kilgarry hospitably.

The room was large and uncomfortable, cluttered with that hideous hodge-podge of gilt and lacquer and brocade, assembled without regard to any harmony of style or period, which passes for the height of luxury in American hotel furnishing. In the centre of the room there was a card table already set up, adding one more discordant note to the cacophony of junk, but still looking as if it belonged there. There were bottles and a pail of ice and a pea-green and old-rose butterfly table of incredible awfulness.

Mr Kilgarry brought up chairs, and Mr Yoring patted Mercer on the shoulder.

'You fix a drink, Eddie,' he said. 'Let's all make ourselves at home.'

He lowered himself into a place at the table, took off his pince-nez, breathed on them and began to polish them with his handkerchief.

Mercer's tense gaze caught the Saint's for an instant. Simon nodded imperceptibly and settled his own glasses more firmly on the bridge of his nose.

'How's the luck going to be tonight, Eddie?' chaffed

Kilgarry, opening two new decks of cards and spilling them on the cloth.

'You'll be surprised,' retorted the young man. 'I'm going to give you two gasbags a beautiful beating tonight.'

'Attaboy,' chirped Yoring encouragingly.

Simon had taken one glance at the cards, and that had been enough to assure him that Mr Naskill would have been proud to claim them as his product. After that, he had been watching Mercer's back as he worked over the drinks. Yoring was still polishing his pince-nez when Mercer turned to the table with a glass in each hand. He put one glass down beside Yoring, and as he reached over to place the other glass in front of the Saint the cuff of his coat sleeve flicked the pince-nez out of Yoring's fingers and sent them spinning. The Saint made a dive to catch them, missed, stumbled and brought his heel down on the exact spot where they were in the act of hitting the carpet. There was a dull scrunching sound, and after that there was a thick and stifling silence.

The Saint spoke first.

'That's torn it,' he said weakly.

Yoring blinked at him as if he was going to burst into tears.

'I'm terribly sorry,' said the Saint.

He bent down and tried to gather up some of the debris. Only the gold bridge of the pince-nez remained in one piece, and that was bent. He put it on the table, started to collect the scraps of glass and then gave up the hopeless task.

'I'll pay for them, of course,' he said.

'I'll split it with you,' said Mercer. 'It was my fault. We'll take it out of my winnings.'

Yoring looked from one to another with watery eyes.

'I – I don't think I can play without my glasses,' he mumbled.

Mercer flopped into the vacant chair and raked in the cards.

'Come on,' he said callously. 'It isn't as bad as all that. You can show us your hand and we'll tell you what you've got.'

'Can't you manage?' urged the Saint. 'I was going to enjoy this game, and it won't be nearly so much fun with only three.'

The silence came back, thicker than before. Yoring's eyes shifted despairingly from side to side. And then Kilgarry crushed his cigar butt violently into an ashtray.

'You can't back out now,' he said, and there was an audible growl in the fruity tones of his voice.

He broke the other pack across the baize with a vicious jerk of the hand that was as eloquent as a movement could be.

'Straight poker. Cut for deal. Let's go.'

To Simon Templar the game had the same dizzy unreality that it would have had if he had been supernaturally endowed with a genuine gift of clairvoyance. He knew the value of every card as it was dealt, knew what was in his own hand before he picked it up. Even though there was nothing mysterious about it, the effect of the glasses he was wearing gave him a sensation of weirdness that was too instinctive to overcome. It was mechanically childish, and yet it was an unforgettable experience. When he was out of the game, watching the others bet against each other, it was like being a cat watching two blind men looking for each other in the dark.

For nearly an hour, curiously enough, the play was fairly even: when he counted his chips he had only a couple of hundred dollars more than when he started. Mercer, throwing in his hand whenever the Saint warned him by a pressure of his foot under the table that the opposition was too strong, had done slightly better; but there was nothing sensational in their advantage. Even Mr Naskill's magic lenses had no influence over the run of the cards, and the luck of the deals slightly favoured Yoring and Kilgarry. The Saint's clairvoyant knowledge saved him from making any disastrous errors, but now and again he had to bet out a hopeless hand to avoid giving too crude an impression of infallibility.

He played a steadily aggressive game, waiting patiently for the change that he knew must come as soon as the basis of the play had had time to settle down and establish itself. His nerves were cool and serene, and he smiled often with an air of faint amusement; but something inside him was poised and gathered like a panther crouched for a spring.

Presently Kilgarry called Mercer on the third raise and lost a small jackpot to three nines. Mercer scowled as he stacked the handful of chips.

'Hell, what's the matter with this game?' he protested. 'This isn't the way we usually play. Let's get some life into it.'

'It does seem a bit slow,' Simon agreed. 'How about raising the ante?'

'Make it a hundred dollars,' Mercer said sharply. 'I'm getting tired of this. Just because my luck's changed we don't have to start playing for peanuts.'

Simon drew his cigarette to a bright glow.

'It suits me.'

Yoring plucked at his lower lip with fingers that were still shaky.

'I dunno, ole man——'

'Okay.' Kilgarry pushed out two fifty-dollar chips with a kind of fierce restraint. 'I'l play for a hundred.'

He had been playing all the time with grim concentration, his shoulders hunched as if he had to give some outlet to a seethe of violence in his muscles, his jaw thrust out and tightly clamped, and as the time went by he seemed to have been regaining confidence. 'Maybe the game is on the level,' was the idea expressed by every line of his body, 'but I can still take a couple of mugs like this in any game.'

He said, almost with a resumption of his former heartiness:

'Are you staying long, Mr Templar?'

'I expect I'll be here for quite a while.'

'That's fine! Then after Mr Yoring's got some new glasses we might have a better game.'

'I shouldn't be surprised,' said the Saint amiably.

He was holding two pairs. He took a card, and still had two pairs. Kilgarry stood pat on three kings. Mercer drew three cards to a pair, and was no better off afterwards. Yoring took two cards and filled a flush.

'One hundred,' said Yoring nervously.

Mercer hesitated, threw in his hand.

'And two hundred,' snapped Kilgarry.

'And five,' said the Saint.

Yoring looked at them blearily. He took a long time to make up his mind. And then, with a sigh, he pushed his hand into the discard.

'See you,' said Kilgarry.

With a wry grin, the Saint faced his hand. Kilgarry grinned also, with a sudden triumph, and faced his.

Yoring made a noise like a faint groan.

'Fix us another drink, Eddie,' he said huskily.

He took the next pack and shuffled it clumsily. His fingers were like sausages strung together. Kilgarry's mouth opened on one side and he nudged the Saint as he made the cut.

'Lost his nerve,' he said. 'See what happens when they get old.'

'Who's old?' said Mr Yoring plaintively. 'There ain't more 'n three years—'

'But you've got old ideas,' Kilgarry jeered. 'You could have beaten both of us.'

'You never had to wear glasses—'

'Who said you wanted glasses to play poker? It isn't always the cards that win.'

Kilgarry was smiling, but his eyes were almost glaring at

Yoring as he spoke. Yoring avoided his gaze guiltily and squinted at the hand he had dealt himself. It contained the six, seven, eight and nine of diamonds, and the queen of spades. Simon held two pairs again but the card he drew made it a full house. He watched while Yoring discarded the queen of spades and felt again that sensation of supernatural omniscience as he saw that the top card of the pack, the card Yoring had to take, was the ten of hearts.

Yoring took it, fumbled his hand to the edge of the table, and turned up the corners to peep at them. For a second he sat quite still, with only his mouth working. And then, as if the accumulation of all his misfortunes had at last stung him to a wild and fearful reaction like the turning of a worm, a change seemed to come over him. He let the cards flatten out again with a defiant click and drew himself up. He began to count off hundred-dollar chips . . .

Mercer, with only a pair of sevens, bluffed recklessly for two rounds before he fell out in response to the Saint's kick under the table.

There were five thousand dollars in the pool before Kilgarry, with a straight, shrugged surrenderingly and dropped his hand in the discard.

The Saint counted two stacks of chips and pushed them in. 'Make it another two grand,' he said.

Yoring looked at him waveringly. Then he pushed in two stacks of his own.

'There's your two grand.' He counted the chips he had left, swept them with a sudden splash into the pile. 'And twenty-nine hundred more,' he said.

Simon had twelve hundred left in chips. He pushed them in, opened his wallet and added crisp new bills.

'Making three thousand more than that for you to see me,' he said coolly.

Mercer sucked in his breath and whispered: 'Oh boy!'

Kilgarry said nothing, hunching tensely over the table.

Yoring blinked at him.

'Len' me some chips, ole man.'

'Do you know what you're doing?' Kilgarry asked in a harsh strained voice.

Yoring picked up his glass and half emptied it. His hand wobbled so that some of it ran down his chin.

'I know,' he snapped.

He reached out and raked Kilgarry's chips into the pile.

'Eighteen hunnerd,' he said. 'I gotta buy some more. I'll write you a cheque—'

Simon shook his head.

'Im sorry,' he said quietly. 'I'm playing table stakes. We agreed on that when we started.'

Yoring peered at him.

'You meanin' something insultin' about my cheque?'

'I don't mean that,' Simon replied evenly. 'It's just a matter of principle. I believe in sticking to the rules. I'll play you a credit game some other time. Tonight we're putting it on the line.'

He made a slight gesture towards the cigar box where they had each deposited five thousand-dollar bills when they bought their chips.

'Now look here,' Kilgarry began menacingly.

The Saint's clear blue eyes met his with sapphire smoothness.

'I said cash, brother. Is that clear?'

Yoring groped through his pockets. One by one he untangled crumpled bills from various hiding places until he had built his bet up to thirty-two hundred and fifty dollars. Then he glared at Kilgarry.

'Len' me what you've got.'

'But—'

'All of it!'

Reluctantly Kilgarry passed over a roll. Yoring licked his thumb and numbered it through. It produced a total raise of four thousand one hundred and fifty dollars. He gulped down the rest of his drink and dribbled some more down his chin.

'Go on,' he said thickly. 'Raise that.'

Simon counted out four thousand-dollar bills. He had one more, and he held it poised. Then he smiled.

'What's the use?' he said. 'You couldn't meet it. I'll take the change and see you.'

Yoring's hand went to his mouth. He didn't move for a moment, except for the wild swerve of his eyes.

Then he picked up his cards. With trembling slowness he turned them over one by one. The six, seven, eight, nine – and ten of *diamonds*.

Nobody spoke; and for some seconds the Saint sat quite still. He was summarizing the whole scenario for himself, in all its inspired ingenuity and mathematical precision, and it is a plain fact that he found it completely beautiful. He was aware that Mercer was shaking him inarticulately and that Yoring's rheumy eyes were opening wider on him with a flame of triumph.

And suddenly Kilgarry guffawed and thumped the table.

'Go to it,' he said. 'Pick it up, Yoring. I take it all back. You're not so old, either!'

Yoring opened both his arms to embrace the pool.

'Just a minute,' said the Saint.

His voice was softer and gentler than ever, but it stunned the room to another immeasurable silence. Yoring froze as he moved, with his arms almost shaped into a ring. And the Saint smiled very kindly.

Certainly it had been a good trick, and an education, but the Saint didn't want the others to fall too hard. He had those moments of sympathy for the ungodly in their downfall.

He turned over his own cards, one by one. Aces. Four of them. And a joker. Simon thought they looked pretty. He had collected them with considerable care, which may have prejudiced him.

'My pot, I think,' he remarked apologetically.

Kilgarry's chair was the first to grate back.

'Here,' he snarled, 'that's not—'

'The hand he dealt me?' The texture of Simon's mockery was like gossamer. 'And he wasn't playing the hand I thought he had, either. I thought he'd have some fun when he got used to being without his glasses,' he added cryptically.

He tipped up the cigar box and added its contents to the stack of currency in front of him, and stacked it into a neat sheaf.

'Well, I'm afraid that sort of kills the game for tonight,' he murmured, and his hand was in his side pocket before Kilgarry's movement was half started. Otherwise he gave no sign of perturbation, and his languid self-possession was as smooth as velvet. 'I suppose we'd better call it a day,' he said without any superfluous emphasis.

Mercer recovered his voice first.

'That's right,' he said jerkily. 'You two have won plenty from me other nights. Now we've got some of it back. Let's get out of here, Templar.'

They walked along Ocean Drive, past the variegated modernistic shapes of the hotels, with the rustle of the surf in their ears.

'How much did you win on that last hand?' asked the young man.

'About fourteen thousand dollars,' said the Saint contentedly.

Mercer said awkwardly: 'That's just about what I'd lost to them before . . . I don't know how I can ever thank you for getting it back. I'd never have had the nerve to do it alone . . .

And then when Yoring turned up that straight flush – I don't know why – I had an awful moment thinking you'd made a mistake.'

The Saint put a cigarette in his mouth and struck his lighter.

'I don't make a lot of mistakes,' he said calmly. 'That's where a lot of people go wrong. It makes me rather tired, sometimes. I suppose it's just professional pride, but I hate to be taken for a mug. And the funny thing is that with my reputation there are always people trying it. I suppose they think that my reactions are so easy to predict that it makes me quite a set-up for any smart business.' The Saint sighed, deploring the inexplicable optimism of those who should know better. 'Of course I knew that a switch like that was coming – the whole idea was to make me feel so confident of the advantage I had with those glasses that I'd be an easy victim of any ordinary card-sharping. And then, of course, I wasn't supposed to be able to make any complaint because that would have meant admitting that I was cheating, too. It was a grand idea, Eddie – at least you can say that for it.'

Mercer had taken several steps before all the implications of what the Saint had said really hit him.

'But wait a minute,' he got out. 'How do you mean they knew you were wearing trick glasses?'

'Why else do you imagine they planted that guy on the train to pretend he was J. J. Naskill?' asked the Saint patiently. 'That isn't very bright of you, Eddie. Now, I'm nearly always bright. I was so bright that I smelt a rat directly you lugged that pack of marked cards out of your beach robe – that was really carrying it a bit too far, to have them all ready to produce after you'd got me to listen in on your little act with Josephine. I must say you all played your parts beautifully, otherwise; but it's little details like that that spoil the effect. I told you at the time that you were a mug,' said the Saint reprovingly. 'Now why don't you paddle off and try to comfort Yoring and Kilgarry? I'm afraid they're going to be rather hurt when they hear that you didn't at least manage to make the best of a bad job and get me to hand you my winnings.'

But Mercer did not paddle off at once. He stared at the Saint for quite a long time, understanding why so many other men who had once thought themselves clever had learned to regard that cool and smiling privateer as something closely allied to the devil himself. And wondering, as they had, why the death penalty for murder had ever been invented.

The Man Who Liked Ants

INTRODUCTION BY LESLIE CHARTERIS[1]

In the sacred cause of accuracy, and out of selfless devotion to what I grandiloquently call My Public, I have done many weird and laborious things in order to protect the readers of the Saint Saga, so far as possible, from anything misleading or synthetic.

I have travelled to distant and insanitary places, bored myself with a multitude of dull and dangerous characters, learned to fly airplanes, crawled around the bottom of the sea in diving suits, consumed large quantities of alcohol, and generally left no gallstone unturned to ensure that my vicarious adventurers shall receive the greatest authenticity I can deliver.

In order to get the background for this short story I did nothing so glamorous. I merely browsed through some twenty volumes on the subject of ants and kindred insects. And I am here obliged to admit that even that concentrated course of study was not enough.

Two or three important entomologists with alphabets after their names have taken the trouble to write and point out to me certain biological impossibilities in the background of this story.

I mention this merely in order to impress upon the amateur and professional entomologists in the audience that I am now thoroughly bored with the subject, and that I

---

[1] From *The Second Saint Omnibus* (1952)

do not want any more heckling or quibbling from the bleachers.

Here is the story for what it is worth, and if you don't like it you can feed it to your termites.

I still like it as an experiment. In the course of a frightening number of Saint stories, I have tried to project him into as many established story styles as possible. This is my one attempt to put the Saint into a pure horror-science story; and those readers who like *Frankenstein* and *Dracula* may get a pleasant goose-pimple out of my ants.

'I wonder what would have happened if you had gone into a respectable business, Saint,' Ivar Nordsten remarked one afternoon.

Simon Templar smiled at him so innocently that for an instant his nickname might almost have seemed justified – if it had not been for the faint lazy twinkle of unsaintly mockery that stirred at the back of his blue eyes.

'The question is too farfetched, Ivar. You might as well speculate about what would have happened if I'd been a Martian or a horse.'

They sat on the veranda of the house of Ivar Nordsten – whose name was not really Ivar Nordsten, but who was alive that day and the master of fabulous millions only because the course of one of the Saint's lawless escapades had once crossed his path at a time when death would have seemed a happy release. He of all living men should have had no wish to change the history of that twentieth-century Robin Hood, whose dark reckless face could be found photographed in half the police archives of the world, and whose gay impudence of outlawry had in its time set the underworlds of five continents buzzing like nests of infuriated wasps. But in that mood of idle fantasy which may well come with the after-lunch contentment of a warm Florida afternoon, Nordsten would have put forward almost any preposterous premise that might give him the pleasure of listening to his friend.

'It isn't as farfetched as that,' he said. 'You will never admit it, but you have many respectable instincts.'

'But I have so many more disreputable ones to keep them under control,' answered the Saint earnestly. 'And it's always been so much more amusing to indulge the disreputable instincts . . . No, Ivar, I mustn't let you make a paragon out of me. If I were quite cynically psycho-analysing myself, I should probably say that the reason why I only soak the more obvious excrescences on the human race is because it makes everything okay with my respectable instincts and lets them go peacefully to sleep. Then I can turn all my disreputable impulses loose on the mechanical problem of soaking this obvious excrescence in some satisfyingly novel and juicy manner, and get all the fun of original sin out of it without any qualms of conscience.'

'But you contradict yourself. The mere fact that you speak in terms of what you call "an obvious excrescence on the human race" proves that you have some moral standards by which you judge him, and that you have some idealistic interest in the human race itself.'

'The human race,' said the Saint sombrely, 'is a repulsive, dull, bloated, ill-conditioned and ill-favoured mass of dimly conscious meat, the chief justification for whose existence is that it provides a contrasting background against which my beauty and spiritual perfections can shine with a lustre only exceeded by your own.'

'You have a natural modesty which I have never suspected,' Nordsten observed gravely, and they both laughed. 'But,' he added, 'I think you will get on well with Dr Sardon.'

'Who is he?'

'A neighbour of mine. We are dining with him tonight.'

Simon frowned.

'I warned you that I was travelling without any dress clothes,' he began, but Nordsten shook his head maliciously.

'Dr Sardon likes dress clothes even less than you do. And you never warned me that you were coming here at all. So what could I do? I accepted his invitation a week ago, so when you arrived I could only tell Sardon what had happened. Of course he insisted that you must come with me. But I think he will interest you.'

The Saint sighed resignedly and swished the Peter Dawson gently around in his glass so that the ice clinked.

'Why should I be interested in any of your neighbours?' he protested. 'I didn't come here to commit any crimes; and I'm sure all these people are as respectable as millionaires can be.'

'Dr Sardon is not a millionaire. He is a very brilliant biologist.'

'What else makes him interesting?'

'He is very fond of ants,' said Nordsten seriously, and the Saint sat up.

Then he finished his drink deliberately and put down the glass.

'Now I know that this climate doesn't agree with you,' he said. 'Let's get changed and go down to the tennis court. I'll put you in your place before we start the evening.'

Nevertheless he drove over to Dr Sardon's house that evening in a mood of open-minded curiosity. Scientists he had known before, men who went down thousands of feet into the sea to look at globigerina ooze and men who devised laboratories to manufacture gold; but this was the first time that he had heard of a biologist who was fond of ants. Everything that was out of the ordinary was prospective material for the Saint. It must be admitted that in simplifying his own career to elementary equations by which obvious excrescences on the human race could be soaked, he did himself less than justice.

But there was nothing about the square smooth-shaven man who was introduced to him as Dr Sardon to take away the breath of any hardened outlaw. He might perhaps have been an ordinary efficient doctor, possibly with an exclusive and sophisticated practice; more probably he could have been a successful stockbroker, or the manager of any profitable commercial business. He shook hands with them briskly and almost mechanically, seeming to summarize the Saint in one sweeping glance through his crisp-looking rimless pince-nez.

'No, you're not a bit late, Mr Nordsten. As a matter of fact I was working until twenty minutes ago. If you had come earlier I should have been quite embarrassed.'

He introduced his niece, a dark slender girl with a quiet and rather aloof beauty which would have been chilling if it had not been relieved by the friendly humour of her brown eyes. About her, Simon admitted, there might certainly have been things to attract the attention of a modern buccaneer.

'Carmen has been assisting me. She has a very good degree from Columbia.'

He made no other unprompted reference to his researches, and Simon recognized him as the modern type of scientist whose carefully cultivated pose of matter-of-fact worldliness is just as fashionable an affectation as the mystical and bearded eccentricity of his predecessors used to be. Dr Sardon talked about politics, about his golf handicap and about the art of Walt Kelly. He was an entertaining and effective conversationalist, but he might never had heard of such a thing as biology until towards the close of dinner Ivar Nordsten skilfully turned a discussion of gardening to the subject of insect pests.

'Although, of course,' he said, 'you would not call them that.'

It was strange to see the dark glow that came into Sardon's eyes.

'As a popular term,' he said in his deep vibrant voice, 'I

suppose it is too well established for me to change it. But it would be much more reasonable for the insects to talk about human pests.'

He turned to Simon.

'I expect Mr Nordsten has already warned you about the— bee in my bonnet,' he said; but he used the phrase without smiling. 'Do you by any chance know anything about the subject?'

'I had a flea once,' said the Saint reminiscently. 'I called him Goebbels. But he left me.'

'Then you would be surprised to know how many of the most sensational achievements of man were surpassed by the insects hundreds of years ago without any artificial aids.' The finger tips of his strong nervous hands played a tattoo against each other. 'You talk about the Age of Speed and Man's Conquest of the Air; and yet the fly *Cephenomia*, the swiftest living creature, can outpace many of your boasted aeroplanes. What is the greatest scientific marvel of the century? Probably you would say radio. But Count Arco, the German radio expert, has proved the existence of a kind of wireless telegraphy, or telepathy, between certain species of beetle, which makes nothing of a separation of miles. Lakhovsky claims to have demonstrated that this is common to several other insects. When the *Redemanni* termites build their twenty-five-foot conical towers topped with ten-foot chimneys they are performing much greater marvels of engineering than building an Empire State Building. To match them, in proportion to our size, we should have to put up skyscrapers four thousand feet high – and do it without tools.'

'I knew the ants would come into it,' said Nordsten *sotto voce*.

Sardon turned on him with his hot piercing gaze.

'Termites are not true ants – the term "white ants" is a misnomer. Actually they are related to the cockroach. I merely mentioned them as one of the most remarkable of the lower insects. They have a superb social organization, and they may even be superior strategists to the true ants, but they were never destined to conquer the globe. The reason is that they cannot stand light and they cannot tolerate temperatures below twenty degrees centigrade. Therefore, their fields of expansion are for ever limited. They are one of Nature's false beginnings. They are a much older species than man, and they have evolved as far as they are likely to evolve . . . It is not the same with the true ants.'

He leaned forward over the table, with his face white and transfigured as if in a kind of trance.

'The true ant is the destined ruler of the earth. Can you imagine a state of society in which there was no idleness, no poverty, no unemployment, no unrest? We humans would say that it was an unattainable Utopia; and yet it was in existence among the ants when man was a hairy savage scarcely distinguishable from an ape. You may say that it is incompatible with progress – that it could only be achieved in the same way that it is achieved by domestic cattle. But the ant has the same instincts which have made man the tyrant of creation in his time. *Lasius fuliginosus* keeps and milks its own domestic cattle, in the form of plant lice. *Polyergus rufescens* and *Formica sanguinea* capture slaves and put them to work. *Messor barbarus*, the harvesting ant, collects and stores grain. The *Attüni* cultivate mushrooms in underground forcing houses. And all these things are done, not for private gain, but for the good of the whole community. Could man in any of his advances ever boast of that?'

'But if ants have so many advantages,' said the Saint slowly, 'and they've been civilized so much longer than man, why haven't they conquered the earth before this?'

'Because Nature cheated them. Having given them so much, she made them wait for the last essential – pure physical bulk.'

'The brontosaurus had enough of that,' said Nordsten, 'and yet man took its place.'

Sardon's thin lips curled.'

'The difference in size between man and brontosaurus was nothing compared with the difference in size between man and ant. There are limits to the superiority of brain over brawn – even to the superiority of the brain of an ant, which in proportion to its size is twice as large as the brain of a man. But the time is coming . . .'

His voice sank almost to a whisper, and in the dim light of candles on the table the smouldering luminousness of his eyes seemed to leave the rest of his face in deep shadow.

'With the ant, Nature overreached herself. The ant was ready to take his place at the head of creation before creation was ready for him – before the solar system had progressed far enough to give him the conditions in which his body, and his brain with it, his brain which in all its intrinsic qualities is so much finer than the brain of man, could grow to the brute size at which all its potentialities could be developed. Nevertheless, when the solar system is older, and the sun is red because the white heat of its fire is exhausted, and the red light which will accelerate the growth of all living cells is stronger, the ant will be waiting for his turn. Unless Nature finds a swifter instrument than Time to put right her miscalculation . . .'

'Does it matter?' asked the Saint lightly, and Sardon's face seemed to flame at him.

'It matters. That is only another thing which we can learn from the ant – that individual profit and ambition should count for nothing beside more enduring good. Listen. When I was a boy I loved small creatures. Among them I kept a colony of ants. In a glass box. I watched them in their busy lives, I studied them as they built their nest, I saw how they divided their labour and how they lived and died so that their common life could go on. I loved them because they were so much better than everyone else I knew. But the other boys could not understand. They thought I was soft and stupid. They were always tormenting me. One day they found my glass box where the ants lived. I fought them, but there were so many of them. They were big and cruel. They made a fire and they put my box on it, while they held me. I saw the ants running, fighting, struggling insanely—' The hushed voice tightened as he spoke until it became thin and shrill like a suppressed scream. 'I saw them curling up and shrivelling, writhing, tortured. I could hear the hiss of their seething agony in the flames. I saw them going mad, twisting – sprawling – blackening – *burning alive before my eyes*—'

'Uncle!'

The quiet voice of the girl Carmen cut softly across the muted shriek in which the last words were spoken, so quietly and normally that it was only in the contrast that Simon realized that Sardon had not really raised his voice.

The wild fire died slowly out of Sardon's eyes. For a moment his face remained set and frozen, and then, as if he had only been recalled from a fleeting lapse of attention, he seemed to come awake again with a slight start.

'Where was I?' he said calmly. 'Oh yes. I was speaking about the intelligence of ants ... It is even a mistake to assume, because they make no audible sounds, that they have not just as excellent means of communication as ourselves. Whether they share the telepathic gifts of other insects is a disputed point, but it is certain that in their antennae they possess an idiom which is adequate to all ordinary needs. By close study and observation it has even been possible for us to learn some of the elementary gestures. The work of Karl Escherich ...'

He went into details, in the same detached incisive tone in which he had been speaking before his outburst.

Simon Templar's fingers stroked over the cloth, found a crumb of bread and massaged it gradually into a soft round pellet. He stole a casual glance at the girl. Her aloof oval face was pale, but that might have been its natural complexion; her composure was unaltered. Sardon's outburst might never have occurred, and she might never have had to interrupt it. Only the Saint thought that he saw a shadow of fear moving far down in her eyes.

Even after Carmen had left the table, and the room was richening with the comfortable aromas of coffee and liqueur, brandy and cigars, Sardon was still riding his hobby-horse. It went on for nearly an hour, until at one of the rare lulls in the discussion Nordsten said: 'All the same, Doctor, you are very mysterious about what this has to do with your own experiments.'

Sardon's hands rested on the table, white and motionless, the fingers spread out.

'Because I was not ready. Even to my friends I should not like to show anything incomplete. But in the last few weeks I have disposed of my uncertainty. Tonight, if you like, I could show you a little.'

'We should be honoured.'

The flat pressure of Sardon's hands on the table increased as he pushed back his chair and stood up.

'My workshops are at the end of the garden,' he said, and blew out the four candles.

As they rose and followed him from the room, Nordsten touched the Saint's arm and said in a low voice: 'Are you sorry I dragged you out?'

'I don't know yet,' answered the Saint soberly.

The girl Carmen rejoined them as they left the house. Simon found her walking beside him as they strolled through the warm moonlight. He dropped the remains of his cigar and offered his cigarette case; they stopped for a moment while he gave her a light. Neither of them spoke, but her arm slipped through his as they went on.

The blaze of lights which Sardon switched on in his laboratory wiped the dim silvery gloom out of their eyes in a crash of harsh glaring illumination. In contrast with the tasteful furnishings of the house, the cold white walls and bare tiled floor struck the Saint's sensitive vision with the hygienic and inhuman chill which such places always gave him. But Sardon's laboratory was not like any other place of that kind in which he had ever been.

Ranged along the walls were rows of big glass-fronted boxes, in which apparently formless heaps of litter and rubble could be dimly made out. His eye was caught by a movement in one of the boxes, and he stepped up to look at it more closely. Almost in the same moment he stopped, and nearly recoiled from it, as he realized that he was looking at the largest ant that he had ever seen. It was fully six inches long; and, magnified in that proportion, he could see every joint in its shiny armour-plated surface and the curious bifurcated claws at the ends of its legs. It stood there with its antennae waving gently, watching him with its bulging beady eyes . . .

'*Tetramorium cespitum*,' said Dr Sardon, standing beside him. 'One of my early experiments. Its natural size is about three-tenths of an inch, but it did not respond very well to treatment.'

'I should say it had responded heroically,' said the Saint. 'You don't mean you can do better than that?'

Sardon smiled.

'It was one of my early experiments,' he repeated. 'I was then merely trying to improve on the work of Ludwig and Ries of Berne, who were breeding giant insects almost comparable with that one, many years ago, with the aid of red light. Subsequently I discovered another principle of growth which they had overlooked, and I also found that an artificial selective cross-breeding between different species not only improved the potential size but also increased the intelligence. For instance, here is one of my later results – a combination of *Oecophylla smaragdina* and *Prenolepsis imparis.*'

He went to one of the longer and larger boxes at the end of the room. At first Simon could see nothing but a great mound of twigs and leaves piled high in one corner. There were two or three bones, stripped bare and white, lying on the sandy floor of the box . . . Then Sardon tapped on the glass, and Simon saw with a sudden thrill of horror that what had been a dark hole in the mound of leaves was no longer black and empty. There was a head peering out of the shadow – dark bronze-green, iridescent, covered with short sparse bristly hairs . . .

'*Oecophylla* is, of course, one of the more advanced species,' Sardon was saying, in his calm precise manner. 'It is the only known creature other than man to use a tool. The larvae secrete a substance similar to silk, with which the ants weave leaves together to make their nests, holding the larvae in their jaws and using them as shuttles. I don't yet know whether my hybrid has inherited that instinct.'

'It looks as if it would make a charming pet, anyway,' murmured the Saint thoughtfully. 'Sort of improved lap dog, isn't it?'

The faint sly smile stayed fixed on Sardon's thin lips. He took two steps further, to a wide sliding door that took up most of the wall at the end of the laboratory, and looked back at them sidelong.

'Perhaps you would like to see the future ruler of the world,' he said, so very softly that it seemed as if everyone else stopped breathing while he spoke.

Simon heard the girl beside him catch her breath, and Nordsten said quickly: 'Surely we've troubled you enough already—'

'I should like to see it,' said the Saint quietly.

Sardon's tongue slid once over his lips. He put his hand up and moved a couple of levers on the glittering panels of dials and switches beside the door. It was to the Saint that his gaze returned, with that rapt expression of strangely cunning and yet childish happiness.

'You will see it from where you stand. I will ask you to keep perfectly still, so as not to draw attention to yourselves – there is a strain of *Dorylina* in this one. *Dorylina* is one of the most intelligent and highly disciplined species, but it is also the most savage. I do not wish it to become angry——'

His arm stretched out to the handle of the door. He slid it aside in one movement, standing with his back to it, facing them.

The girl's cold hand touched the Saint's wrist. Her fingers slipped down over his hand and locked in with his own, clutching them in a sudden convulsive grip. He heard Ivar Nordsten's suppressed gasp as it caught in his throat, and an icy tingle ran up his spine and broke out in a clammy dew on his forehead.

The rich red light from the chamber beyond the door spilled out like liquid fire, so fierce and vivid that it seemed as if it could only be accompanied by the scorching heat of an open furnace; but it held only a slight appreciable warmth. It beat down from huge crimson arcs ranged along the cornices of the inner room among a maze of shining tubes and twisted wires; there was a great glass ball opposite in which a pale yellow streak of lightning forked and flickered with a faint humming sound. The light struck scarlet highlights from the gleaming bars of a great metal cage like a gigantic chicken coop which filled the centre of the room to within a yard of the walls. And within the cage something monstrous and incredible stood motionless, staring at them.

Simon would see it sometimes, years afterwards, in uneasy

dreams. Something immense and frightful, glistening like burnished copper, balanced on angled legs like bars of plated metal. Only for a few seconds he saw it then, and for most of that time he was held fascinated by its eyes, understanding something that he would never have believed before . . .

And then suddenly the thing moved, swiftly and horribly and without sound; and Sardon slammed the door shut, blotting out the eye-aching sea of red light and leaving only the austere cold whiteness of the laboratory.

'They are not all like lap dogs,' Sardon said in a kind of whisper.

Simon took out a handkerchief and passed it across his brow. The last thing about that weird scene that fixed itself consciously in his memory was the girl's fingers relaxing their tense grip on his hand, and Sardon's eyes, bland and efficient and businesslike again, pinned steadily on them both in a sort of secret sneer . . .

'What do you think of our friend?' Ivar Nordsten asked, as they drove home two hours later.

Simon stretched a long arm for the lighter at the side of the car.

'He is a lunatic – but of course you knew that. I'm only wondering whether he is quite harmless.'

'You ought to sympathize with his contempt for the human race.'

The red glow of the Saint's cigarette end brightened so that for an instant the interior of the car was filled with something like a pale reflection of the unearthly crimson luminance which they had seen in Dr Sardon's forcing room.

'Did you sympathize with his affection for his pets?'

'Those great ants?' Nordsten shivered involuntarily. 'No. That last one – it was the most frightful thing I have ever seen. I suppose it was really alive?'

'It was alive,' said the Saint steadily. 'That's why I'm

wondering whether Dr Sardon is harmless. I don't know what you were looking at, Ivar, but I'll tell you what made my blood run cold. It wasn't the mere size of the thing – though any common or garden ant would be terrifying enough if you enlarged it to those dimensions. It was worse than that. It was the proof that Sardon was right. That ant was looking at me. Not like any other insect or even animal that I've ever seen, but like an insect with a man's brain might look. That was the most frightening thing to me. *It knew!'*

Nordsten stared at him.

'You mean that you believe what he was saying about it being the future ruler of the world?'

'By itself, no,' answered Simon. 'But if it were not by itself—'

He did not finish the sentence; and they were silent for the rest of the drive. Before they went to bed he asked one more question.

'Who else knows about these experiments?'

'No one, I believe. He told me the other day that he was not prepared to say anything about them until he could show complete success. As a matter of fact, I lent him some money to go on with his work, and that is the only reason he took me into his confidence. I was surprised when he showed us his laboratory tonight – even I had never seen it before.'

'So he is convinced now that he can show a complete success,' said the Saint quietly, and was still subdued and preoccupied the next morning.

In the afternoon he refused to swim or play tennis. He sat hunched up in a chair on the veranda, scowling into space and smoking innumerable cigarettes, except when he rose to pace restlessly up and down like a big nervous cat.

'What you are really worried about is the girl,' Nordsten teased.

'She's pretty enough to worry about,' said the Saint shamelessly. 'I think I'll go over and ask her for a cocktail.'

Nordsten smiled.

'If it will make you a human being again, by all means do,' he said. 'If you don't come back to dinner I shall know that she is appreciating your anxiety. In any case, I shall probably be very late myself. I have to attend a committee meeting at the golf club and that always adjourns to the bar and goes on for hours.'

But the brief tropical twilight had already given way to the dark before Simon made good his threat. He took out Ivar Nordsten's spare Rolls-Royce and drove slowly over the highway until he found the turning that led through the deep cypress groves to the doctor's house. He was prepared to feel foolish; and yet as his headlights circled through the iron gates he touched his hip pocket to reassure himself that if the need arose he might still feel wise.

The trees arching over the drive formed a ghostly tunnel down which the Rolls chased its own forerush of light. The smooth hiss of the engine accentuated rather than broke the silence, so that the mind even of a hardened and unimaginative man might cling to the comfort of that faint sound in the same way that the mind of a child might cling to the light of a candle as a comfort against the gathering terrors of the night. The Saint's lip curled cynically at the flight of his own thoughts . . .

And then, as the car turned a bend in the drive, he saw the girl, and trod fiercely on the brakes.

The tyres shrieked on the macadam and the engine stalled as the big car rocked to a standstill. It flashed through the Saint's mind at that instant, when all sound was abruptly wiped out, that the stillness which he had imagined before was too complete for accident. He felt the skin creep over his back, and had to call on an effort of will to force himself to open the door and get out of the car.

She lay face downwards, halfway across the drive, in the pool of illumination shed by the glaring headlights. Simon turned her over and raised her head on his arm. Her eyelids twitched as he did so; a kind of moan broke from her lips, and she fought away from him, in a dreadful wildness of panic, for a brief moment before her eyes opened and she recognized him.

'My dear,' he said, 'what has been happening?'

She had gone limp in his arms, the breath jerking pitifully through her lips, but she had not fainted again. And behind him, in that surround of stifling stillness, he heard quite clearly the rustle of something brushing stealthily over the grass beside the drive. He saw her eyes turning over his shoulder, saw the wide horror in them.

'*Look!*'

He spun around, whipping the gun from his pocket, and for more than a second he was paralysed. For that eternity he saw the thing, deep in the far shadows, dimly illumined by the marginal reflections from the beam of the headlights – something gross and swollen, a dirty grey-white, shaped rather like a great bleached sausage, hideously bloated. Then the darkness swallowed it again, even as his shot smashed the silence into a hundred tiny echoes.

The girl was struggling to her feet. He snatched at her wrist.

'This way.'

He got her into the car and slammed the door. Steel and glass closed around them to give an absurd relief, the weak unreasoning comfort to the naked flesh which men under a bombardment find in cowering behind canvas screens. She slumped against his shoulder, sobbing hysterically.

'Oh, my God. My God!'

'What was it?' he asked.

'It's escaped again. I knew it would. He can't handle it—'

'Has it got loose before?'

'Yes. Once.'

He tapped a cigarette on his thumbnail, stroked his lighter. His face was a beaten mask of bronze and granite in the red glow as he drew the smoke down into the mainsprings of his leaping nerves.

'I never dreamed it had come to that,' he said. 'Even last night, I wouldn't have believed it.'

'He wouldn't have shown you that. Even when he was boasting, he wouldn't have shown you. That was his secret . . . And I've helped him. Oh God,' she said. 'I can't go on!'

He gripped her shoulders.

'Carmen,' he said quietly. 'You must go away from here.'

'He'd kill me.'

'You must go away.'

The headlamps threw back enough light for him to see her face, tear-streaked and desperate.

'He's mad,' she said. 'He must be. Those horrible things . . . I'm afraid. I wanted to go away but he wouldn't let me, I can't go on. Something terrible is going to happen. One day I saw it catch a dog . . . Oh, my God, if you hadn't come when you did—'

'Carmen.' He still held her, speaking slowly and deliberately, putting every gift of sanity that he possessed into the level dominance of his voice. 'You must not talk like this. You're safe now. Take hold of yourself.'

She nodded.

'I know. I'm sorry. I'll be all right. But—'

'Can you drive?'

'Yes.'

He started the engine and turned the car round. Then he pushed the gear lever into neutral and set the hand brake.

'Drive this car,' he said. 'Take it down to the gates and wait for me there. You'll be close to the highway, and there'll be plenty of other cars passing for company. Even if you do see anything, you needn't be frightened. Treat the car like a tank and run it over. Ivar won't mind – he's got plenty more. And if you hear anything, don't worry. Give me half an hour, and if I'm not back go to Ivar's and talk to him.'

Her mouth opened incredulously.

'You're not getting out again?'

'I am. And I'm scared stiff.' The ghost of a smile touched his lips, and then she saw that his face was stern and cold. 'But I must talk to your uncle.'

He gripped her arm for a moment, kissed her lightly and got out. Without a backward glance he walked quickly away from the car up the drive towards the house. A flash-light in his left hand lanced the darkness ahead of him with its powerful beam, and he swung it from left to right as he walked, holding his gun in his right hand. His ears strained into the gloom which his eyes could not penetrate, probing the silence under the soft scuff of his own footsteps for any sound that would give him warning; but he forced himself not to look back. The palms of his hands were moist.

The house loomed up in front of him. He turned off to one side of the building, following the direction in which he remembered that Dr Sardon's laboratory lay. Almost at once he saw the squares of lighted windows through the trees. A dull clang of sound came to him, followed by a sort of furious thumping. He checked himself; and then as he walked on more quickly some of the lighted windows went black. The door of the laboratory opened as the last light went out, and his torch framed Dr Sardon and the doorway in its yellow circle.

Sardon was pale and dishevelled, his clothes awry. One of his sleeves was torn, and there was a scratch on his face from which blood ran. He flinched from the light as if it had burned him.

'Who is that?' he shouted.

'This is Simon Templar,' said the Saint in a commonplace tone. 'I just dropped in to say hullo.'

Sardon turned the switch down again and went back into the laboratory. The Saint followed him.

'You just dropped in, eh? Of course. Good. Why not? Did you run into Carmen, by any chance?'

'I nearly ran over her,' said the Saint evenly.

The doctor's wandering glance snapped to his face. Sardon's hands were shaking, and a tiny muscle at the side of his mouth twitched spasmodically.

'Of course,' he said vacantly. 'Is she all right?'

'She is quite safe.' Simon had put away his gun before the other saw it. He laid a hand gently on the other's shoulder. 'You've had trouble here,' he said.

'She lost her nerve,' Sardon retorted furiously. 'She ran away. It was the worst thing she could do. They understand, these creatures. They are too much for me to control now. They disobey me. My commands must seem so stupid to their wonderful brains. If it had not been that this one is heavy and waiting for her time—'

He checked himself.

'I knew,' said the Saint calmly.

The doctor peered up at him out of the corners of his eyes. 'You knew?' he repeated cunningly.

'Yes. I saw it.'

'Just now?'

Simon nodded.

'You didn't tell us last night,' he said. 'But it's what I was afraid of. I have been thinking about it all day.'

'You've been thinking, have you? That's funny.' Sardon chuckled shrilly. 'Well, you're quite right. I've done it. I've succeeded. I don't have to work any more. They can look after themselves now. That's funny, isn't it?'

'So it is true. I hoped I was wrong.'

Sardon edged closer to him.

'You hoped you were wrong? You fool! But I would expect it of you. You are the egotistical human being who believes in his ridiculous conceit that the whole history of the world from its own birth, all the species and races that have come into being and been discarded, everything – everything has existed only to lead up to his own magnificent presence on the earth. Bah! Do you imagine that your miserable little life can stand in the way of the march of evolution? Your day is over! Finished! In there' – his arm stiffened and pointed – 'in there you can find the matriarch of the new ruling race of the earth. At any moment she will begin to lay her eggs, thousands upon thousands of them, from which her sons and daughters will breed – as big as she is, with her power and her brains.' His voice dropped. 'To me it is only wonderful that I should have been Nature's chosen instrument to give them their rightful place a million years before Time would have opened the door to them.'

The flame in his eyes sank down as his voice sank and his features seemed to relax so that his square clean-cut efficient face became soft and beguiling like the face of an idiot child.

'I know what it feels like to be God,' he breathed.

Simon held both his arms.

'Dr Sardon,' he said, 'You must not go on with this experiment.'

The other's face twisted.

'The experiment is finished,' he snarled. 'Are you still blind? Look – I will show you.'

He was broad-shouldered and powerfully built, and his strength was that of a maniac. He threw off the Saint's hands with a convulsive wrench of his body and ran to the sliding door at the end of the room. He turned with his back to it, grasping the handle, as the Saint started after him.

'You shall meet them yourself,' he said hoarsely. 'They are not in their cage any more. I will let them out here, and you shall see whether you can stand against them. Stay where you are!'

A revolver flashed in his hand and the Saint stopped four paces from him.

'For your own sake, Dr Sardon,' he said, 'stand away from that door.'

The doctor leered at him crookedly. 'You would like to burn my ants,' he whispered.

He turned and fumbled with the spring catch, his revolver swinging carelessly wide from its aim; and the door had started to move when Simon shot him twice through the heart.

Simon was stretched out on the veranda, sipping a Dry Sack and sniping mosquitoes with a cigarette end, when Nordsten came up the steps from his car. The Saint looked up with a smile.

'My dear fellow,' said Nordsten, 'I thought you would be at the fire.'

'Is there a fire?' Simon asked innocently.

'Didn't you know? Sardon's whole laboratory has gone up in flames. I heard about it at the club, and when I left I drove back that way thinking I should meet you. Sardon and his niece were not there, either. It will be a terrible shock for him when he hears of it. The place was absolutely gutted – I've never seen such a blaze. It might have been soaked in gasoline. It was still too hot to go near, but I suppose all his work has been destroyed. Did you miss Carmen?'

The Saint pointed over his shoulder.

'At the present moment she's sleeping in your best guest room,' he said. 'I gave her enough of your sleeping tablets to keep her like that till breakfast time.'

Nordsten looked at him.

'And where is Sardon?' he asked at length.

'He is in his laboratory.'

Nordsten poured himself out a drink and sat down.

'Tell me,' he said.

Simon told him the story. When he had finished, Nordsten was silent for a while. Then he said: 'It's all right, of course. A fire like that must have destroyed all the evidence. It could all have been an accident. But what about the girl?'

'I told her that her uncle had locked the door and refused to let me in. Her evidence will be enough to show that Sardon was not in his right mind.'

'Would you have done it anyhow, Simon?'

The Saint nodded.

'I think so. That's what I was worried about, ever since last night. It came to me at once that if any of these brutes could breed—' He shrugged a little wearily. 'And when I saw that great queen ant, I knew that it had gone too far. I don't know quite how rapidly ants can breed, but I should imagine that they do it by thousands. If the thousands were all the same size as Sardon's specimens, with the same intelligence, who knows what might have been the end of it?'

'But I thought you disliked the human race,' said Nordsten.

Simon got up and strolled across the veranda.

'Taken in the mass,' he said soberly, 'it will probably go on nauseating me. But it isn't my job to alter it. If Sardon was right, Nature will find her own remedy. But the world has millions of years left, and I think evolution can afford to wait.'

His cigarette spun over the rail and vanished into the dark like a firefly as the butler came out to announce dinner; and they went into the dining-room together.

Watch for the sign of the Saint!

If you have enjoyed this Saintly adventure, look out for the other Simon Templar novels by Leslie Charteris – all available in print and ebook from Mulholland Books.

You've turned the last page.

But it doesn't have to end there . . .

If you're looking for more first-class, action-packed, nail-biting suspense, join us at **Facebook.com/MulhollandUncovered** for news, competitions, and behind-the-scenes access to Mulholland Books.

For regular updates about our books and authors as well as what's going on in the world of crime and thrillers, follow us on **Twitter@MulhollandUK**.

There are many more twists to come.

MULHOLLAND:
You never know what's coming around the curve.